The
Novel Habits
of Happiness

The
Novel Habits
of Happiness

ALEXANDER
MCCALL SMITH

Little, Brown

LITTLE, BROWN

First published in Great Britain in 2015 by Little, Brown

1 3 5 7 9 10 8 6 4 2

Copyright © Alexander McCall Smith 2015

The moral right of the author has been asserted.

All characters and events in this publication, other than those
clearly in the public domain, are fictitious and any resemblance
to real persons, living or dead, is purely coincidental

Quotations from the poems of W. H. Auden copyright © the Beneficiaries of the
Estate of W. H. Auden, reproduced by kind permission of the Estate.

A CIP catalogue record for this book
is available from the British Library.

Hardback ISBN 978-1-4087-0663-3
C-format ISBN 978-1-4087-0664-0

Typeset in Bembo by M Rules
Printed and bound in Great Britain by
Clays Ltd, St Ives plc

Papers used by Little, Brown are from well-managed forests
and other responsible sources.

MIX
Paper from
responsible sources
FSC
www.fsc.org   FSC® C104740

Little, Brown
An imprint of
Little, Brown Book Group
100 Victoria Embankment
London EC4Y 0DY

An Hachette UK Company
www.hachette.co.uk

www.littlebrown.co.uk

This book is for Fiona Foster, doctor,
tennis champion (mornings only),
and philosopher (sometimes)

1

'Give it back,' muttered Isabel Dalhousie.

'Won't,' said Charlie.

'What?' asked Jamie.

It was one of those conversations in which two people are talking about different things – unknowingly – and a third tries to make sense of what is said. The setting of this exchange was Edinburgh, in a Victorian house surrounded by rhododendrons and a few leafy trees: an oak, several copper beeches, and a single specimen tree known variously as the dove tree or ghost tree. 'Popular with doves,' said Isabel, adding, 'and, I assume, with ghosts.'

If looked at from above, as from an intrusive, snap-happy satellite, the garden would be seen to be bounded on one side by a tree-lined avenue and on its three other sides by a high stone wall. This wall was a highway for cats and for Brother Fox, the fox who lived somewhere near by and with whom Isabel from time to time communed – to the extent that foxes, in their reserve, will allow anybody to commune with them. The wall was also a parcelling-out, in neat rectangular shapes, of contested suburban territory – mine here, yours there, this shared. Beyond that wall were further gardens; then came roads and buildings of grey or honey-coloured stone, spreading out like skirts until they reached hills on one side and sea on the other. This was the North Sea, cold, blue, lapping at the jagged edge of the country, a reminder of where Scotland lay in the true nature of things; a place that was mostly water and wind and high empty sky; a place where the land itself seemed to be an afterthought, a farewell gesture from Europe.

Isabel was seated in a chair and her young son, Charlie, now almost four years old, was at her feet, under the table, a place that he described as his office and where he did his office work. Jamie, her husband – although she still thought of him as her lover – was standing near the large window overlooking the garden. The whole family was present and had been thinking, from their various perspectives, about lunch.

And thinking of other things too. In Isabel's case, she had been paging through a current affairs magazine in which she had come across an article on the return of cultural treasures. Unsurprisingly, this article touched on the Elgin Marbles: we want them back, said Greece – everybody knew their position on that – while the British Museum, with typical British skill at changing the subject, seemed to be talking about other things altogether. But it was not these much-discussed Marbles that concerned Isabel – rather it was a paragraph about a Maori wood carving that long ago had been taken from a meeting house and had ended up in a museum in Berlin. This carving was of spiritual significance for the Maori and a request had been made for it to be returned to New Zealand. The holding museum said that it was considering the matter, but was still doing so two years after the request had first been made. That was the point at which Isabel, reading about it before she got up to heat the soup for their lunch, said, aloud, 'Give it back.'

She had not addressed anybody in particular, although the advice appeared directed to the museum in Germany. It was one of those comments that we may utter to express strong views and that we do not expect to be overheard or reacted to. But Charlie heard it, and thought that his mother was telling him to give back the roller-ball pen that he had found and with which he was now beginning to draw small lines, tiny tattoos, across his kneecaps. He saw no reason to return the pen as it was *his* knees on which he was drawing; he understood that there was a general prohibition against graffiti, but this was *himself* he was decorating and that, he thought, was his business. It was for this reason that he said, 'Won't.' Not knowing any of this, Jamie had interjected with his 'What?'

Isabel glanced under the table and saw what Charlie was doing. 'Not on your knees, darling,' she said, slipping him a piece of paper. 'We don't draw on our knees, do we? Draw on that. Draw a fox.'

The idea appealed, and the knee tattoos were forgotten. She looked at Jamie. 'I was reading about a carving in a museum that people want returned.'

Jamie nodded. 'Oh yes. But wouldn't it empty all the museums if we started to hand things back?'

'It would diminish them, perhaps – not empty them. Most museums have more things than they can show. The big ones have vast warehouses packed with treasures.'

Jamie peered at a thin rime of dirt on the window glass. An unusual wind had brought dust all the way up from the Sahara and dropped it across Western Europe, even as far as Scotland. He would have to wash the windows soon, as that was his job.

3

Isabel was in charge of the garden, while Jamie did the windows and put the bins out on the street on collection days.

'Oh yes?' he said.

Isabel laid aside her magazine. 'It's interesting,' she said. 'People like the Maori, and the Aboriginal people in Australia too, I suppose, see so many things about them as sacred. The land, the trees, river, carvings . . . And yet we don't have any of that ourselves, do we?'

Jamie peered even more closely at the glass. He had washed that particular window two or three weeks ago; winds from the Sahara had no business coming this far north. *Who bids the mighty ocean deep / Its own appointed limits keep* . . . The words came back to him unexpectedly; he had been a choirboy in his time and choirboys remembered what they were obliged to sing, or some of it. Winds had their appointed limits too, he thought, not just oceans.

'Maybe we had lots of sacred places,' he said. 'And then we just forgot about them.'

Isabel looked thoughtful. 'Stonehenge? Iona? Those odd stone circles that you sometimes more or less trip over?'

'Yes. All of those.' He paused. 'It's not just people like the Maori who have ancestors. What do they call the other New Zealanders – the rest? People like Jenny?'

It happened that Isabel knew. She had a New Zealand cousin who had visited her several times and they had shared a memorable conversation about belonging.

'*Pakeha*,' said Isabel. 'That's the Maori word for . . . for us.'

'*Pakeha* have ancestors too . . .'

Jamie remembered Jenny's visit. 'I wonder what she's up to,' he said.

'She's writing a cookery book,' said Isabel. 'And she still has that television show. *The Creative Kitchen*. She says that it's very popular in Spain, for some reason. She's dubbed into Spanish.'

But it was not Jenny she wanted to talk about; it was what Jamie had said about ancestors. 'I suppose you're right,' she said. 'We all have the same number of ancestors, don't we? We don't go on about them, but we have them, surely. I mean, there's no monopoly on ancestors. One can't be ancestor-rich, so to speak.'

He left the window and came to sit down at the table, opposite Isabel. 'It depends on whether you think they exist. If you think that they're not there any more – because they've died – as ancestors tend to do – then ... well, then you can't really have them in your life, can you?'

'So what counts, then,' said Isabel, 'is whether you have an eschatological dimension to your *Weltanschauung*.'

For the second time in those few minutes, Jamie said, 'What?'

She laughed. 'Sorry, I couldn't resist it. You can get your revenge by saying something utterly opaque about Wagner, if you like. Or, perhaps more likely, somebody like Schoenberg.'

'Escha ...'

'Eschatological,' supplied Isabel. 'And I use it loosely, and just to keep you on your toes. It's more about last things, but I suppose the ancestors come into that.'

'Put it simply,' said Jamie.

'Well, if you think that we survive in some way ...'

'After we've kicked the bucket?'

Isabel hesitated, momentarily brought up sharp by the thought that there was a bucket waiting to be kicked by all of them – including Jamie and Charlie; morbid thought, she told herself – we're young, or sort of young. She decided to laugh, both at his use of the expression and as an act of defiance of mortality. 'To use a philosophical term of art,' she said. 'Yes. If you think we survive death in some way, then you may well be concerned with ancestors. But that depends on whether you

5

think they continue to have any interest in us. That's the important thing, I think.'

'You mean they may say, *That's it, goodbye?*'

'Yes. And if they did, then there's no point in talking about the ancestors. Yet a lot of people don't think that way – they feel there's some connection between their ancestors and themselves. They still feel somehow involved with them.'

'Watching over us?'

She thought so. 'Or still occupying the places where they lived,' she said. 'Hence the spiritual significance of place. Holy mountains – that sort of thing.'

Jamie nodded. 'Some of my friends who play rugby talk about Murrayfield Stadium as sacred turf.'

'Well, it is a special place for them, isn't it?' said Isabel. 'Rugby is such a tribal game. All those men getting physical with one another. Painting their faces with the Saltire. Singing "Flower of Scotland". Bagpipes. Pure tribalism, surely.'

They were both silenced, perhaps by the realisation that anthropological observation applies as much to *us* as to *them*. From under the table there came a faint humming. They both recognised it at the same time as 'Pop Goes the Weasel'.

'He loves that tune,' said Jamie. 'Half a pound of tuppenny rice, Charlie.'

A small voice responded tunefully, 'Half a pound of treacle.'

Jamie continued the nursery rhyme: 'That's the way the money goes.' And Isabel said, 'That means nothing to him. He has no idea of money yet – lucky him.'

'Expensive,' said Charlie.

They looked at one another in astonishment.

'Prodigy,' whispered Jamie.

'Porridge,' came the small voice from below.

Isabel winked at Jamie. 'His ancestors – his Scottish ancestors –

ate an awful lot of porridge. Porridge links us to them.' She paused. 'Porridge binds.'

Jamie remembered something. 'Who's that person you keep quoting – the one who wrote that book? *The Art of Living*?'

'Lin Yutang.'

'Yes, him. You once told me something that he said about patriotism and food. What was it again?'

Isabel smiled at the recollection. She had not read Lin Yutang for some time, but she knew where he was on her bookshelf. That, she felt, meant that he had not been forgotten. 'He said: What is patriotism but love of the food one ate as a child?'

He thought about that. 'Very good. Yes, spot on.'

But she was not so sure; Isabel was a philosopher, and philosophers were distrustful of broad propositions. 'Well . . . '

'No, he's right,' said Jamie. 'You love your country because it's your country, because it's familiar and it's full of things you've always known. That includes childhood food.'

Isabel was prepared to concede that this came into it, but was it enough to explain why people – or some of them, at least – were prepared to sacrifice everything for their country, even their lives? But food was just a shorthand expression for the familiar. Was patriotism, when boiled down, merely a love of one's own familiar things . . . above the familiar things of others? The familiar things of others, of course, counted for less, it seemed: people were usually patriotic in the face of the assertions of others – who also loved what they ate in their own, foreign childhood.

But even that, she suspected, was a reduction too far. What about people who were patriotic because they loved the values their country espoused? She remembered, as she asked the question, a conversation she had had years earlier with an elderly man in the Scottish Arts Club. They had got on to the subject of national characteristics and he had revealed that as a refugee from Central Europe he appreciated the kindness and tolerance he had found in Britain. 'That is why I have become a British patriot,' he had said. People had forgotten that there had been many who thought that way.

She expressed her doubts to Jamie. 'I think the food of childhood is probably just a metaphor for one's people and place. I think that lies at the heart of patriotism. Our *own* people, our *own* place – that's what stirs patriotism.'

Jamie looked thoughtful. 'Maybe. But it sounds so neat and tidy, doesn't it? It sounds so apt.'

'All aphorisms do. They must have a kernel of truth in them – somewhere – but they often don't provide the full picture.' She paused. 'I can imagine somebody like Lin Yutang getting up in the morning and thinking: *What aphorisms shall I come up with today?*'

Jamie laughed. 'Like Oscar Wilde, perhaps? Can't you imagine him getting out of bed in the morning and asking himself what witticisms he should let slip by breakfast.'

'I can,' she said. 'Although I somehow doubt that Wilde got out of bed in the morning. These people tended to get up in the afternoon, I think. Look at Proust – also a rather louche character. He got out of bed in the evening, if at all.'

'All right – afternoon, then.'

'Yes, I can picture it. Oscar Wilde's last words, of course, were very well chosen. I can see him lying there in Paris, contemplating the wallpaper with distaste, and thinking *It's almost time, I'd better come up with something good.* And then saying, "Either that wallpaper goes, or I do." And then he went.' She sighed. 'Except for one thing.'

Jamie grinned. He would have liked Oscar Wilde, he thought – in small doses. But it would have been exhausting to listen to him for too long. That was the trouble with very witty people – they tire the rest of us. Boswell, he had always imagined, must have found it rather wearying to be in Dr Johnson's company day after day on their trip through Scotland. *Oh just shut up, will you, we've got miles to go and you keep coming up with these wise observations . . .*

He frowned. 'One thing?'

'They weren't his actual last words. Apparently he said that a few weeks before he died.'

Jamie shook his head. 'Nice try, though.'

Isabel brought the conversation back to Lin Yutang. She would look for his book that evening, she decided. 'There's something else Lin said that I must look up. He wrote an essay on flowers, I seem to recall, and he lists the conditions that displease flowers. Isn't that a marvellous notion – that flowers should be displeased by certain things?'

'Flowers with attitude,' said Jamie. 'Sure. But what?'

'I don't remember everything on the list – in fact, I can only remember one thing he said flowers definitely don't like.'

'Which is?'

'Monks talking noisily,' said Isabel. 'Apparently that displeases flowers.'

'And oysters,' said Jamie. 'What annoys them?'

Isabel thought for a moment, but only a moment. 'A noisy noise,' she said. 'A noisy noise annoys an oyster. Or so the tongue twister would have us believe.'

She glanced at her watch. She would have been happy to talk for ever about ancestors and rugby and Lin Yutang but she had to put on the leek and potato soup for lunch and then, at two o'clock, she was expected to help in Cat's delicatessen. Her niece, whose delicatessen had recently become increasingly popular, had chosen a busy summer weekend to go off to Paris. She had not explained what took her there – or who, thought Isabel –

and Isabel did not like to pry – or wish to pry, perhaps, as she enjoyed prying a great deal. Cat had arranged cover for Saturday morning, but was short of a hand for Saturday afternoon. Eddie, her long-standing assistant, was generally competent but was subject to panic attacks if there were too many people waiting for service at the counter. He was always reassured by Isabel's presence and never felt his panicky symptoms if she was there.

She rose to her feet, and so did Jamie. He came round to her side of the table, took her hand, and squeezed it.

'What's that for?' she asked.

He looked down at her; he was four inches taller than she was, which Isabel found just right. But everything about Jamie was just right, in her view. His eyes, the nape of his neck, his chin, his laugh, his gentleness. And she liked, too, the way he was filled with music; it was there in his mind, and it came out so effortlessly when he sat at the piano or played his bassoon, or when he sang. It was as if there were wells within him, deep wells of music waiting to be drawn upon.

'It's for you,' he said. 'Just a random thank-you. And because I really . . . well, because I actually rather love you.'

He leaned forward and kissed her upon the lips. He had been eating mint chocolate and she loved mint chocolate at that moment.

'Let's have a special dinner tonight,' he said. 'I'll cook. I'll do something from that Israeli chef. The one who does Near Eastern cuisine. You like his things, don't you?'

'I do. But be careful with the cous cous. Watch the quantity. They love their cous cous and one can only take a certain amount of cous.'

He nodded in mock solemnity. 'And New Zealand white wine? Before they ask us to send it back?'

She laughed. 'Yes. Yes to everything.' And then she added,

'He's called Ottolenghi, that chef. And he deserves a tongue twister of his own. *Lo, Ottolenghi lengthens leeks laterally.* How about that? Or, *Competent chefs count cous cous cautiously?*'

There was a noise from under the table. 'Silly,' said Charlie.

Isabel and Jamie looked at one another. Isabel mouthed a question. 'Is he talking about our conversation?'

They looked under the table at Charlie. He had finished drawing and now he thrust the piece of paper at them. Isabel took the crumpled sheet and examined it.

'You,' said Charlie. 'You and Daddy.'

Two people, stick figures both, were surrounded by what looked like flowers. Behind them was the typical childish, stylised rendition of a house – all windows and doors and chimneys. There was a benevolent sun in the sky, smiling, as the sun in children's art inevitably is, and birds. The taller of the two figures held the hand of the shorter.

Jamie noticed something else. Behind the birds, what looked like an aeroplane crossed the sky. There were lines drawn around it – wavy lines suggestive of movement, of chaos.

'And a plane,' said Jamie. 'Charlie, you've drawn us a plane as well. Clever boy!'

Charlie was standing now. His knees showed the tattoos; his fingers were blackened by ink from the pen. 'Plane crashing,' he said. 'Bang.'

Jamie affected dismay. 'But it was so nice, Charlie. Look – those pretty flowers and the birds and even the sun smiling on it all. So nice.'

Charlie peered at his own drawing. 'Nice before,' he said.

Nice before. Isabel wondered how Jamie was going to handle this. And then she thought, *But what Charlie has said is exactly what Lin Yutang meant.* She would talk to Jamie about that later – over the Ottolenghi dinner and the New Zealand white wine.

11

2

Immediately after lunch Jamie and Charlie set off for the Zoo while Isabel made her way to Cat's delicatessen. She had promised Cat that she would be there at two, and she was going to be a few minutes late. That would not matter too much, though, as the assistant who had been helping through the morning had said that she would be happy to stay until Isabel arrived.

She was vaguely annoyed with Cat. Isabel was happy enough to lend a hand in her niece's delicatessen, and did this often, sometimes with very little notice. If Cat were ill, or if she had to stay in her flat to await the arrival of the dishwasher engineer, Isabel would drop whatever she was doing and cover for her. Cat's dishwasher was temperamental, and obviously needed replacing, but she had a service contract that entitled her to the attentions of an engineer whenever necessary, and without further charge. It was a vastly disadvantageous contract for the company, but they answered her calls without complaint and Cat, it seemed, had no intention of purchasing a new machine.

'It still works,' she said to Isabel. 'And I'm fond of it.'

Isabel had listened to this explanation with a certain degree of puzzlement. 'Frankly,' she said, 'I can't see how one can become fond of something so patently inanimate, like a dishwasher, or even a fridge. They're just machines, after all.'

She saw Cat looking at her with disbelief. 'But of course you can. Look at people with their old cars. They love them to bits.'

There was some truth in that. 'But cars have personality. People give them names.' *I love my green Swedish car*, she thought, *although I've never told it I do . . .*

Cat was staring at her. 'Why are you smiling?'

'Oh, nothing . . . Well, I was thinking about the love of cars. Are there men, do you think, who love their cars more than they love women?'

'Hundreds,' said Cat. 'Thousands.'

Isabel imagined a woman desperately giving her man an ultimatum. *You have to choose between me and the car . . .*

'And football too,' said Cat. 'There are a lot of men who think more about football than they do about relationships.'

Isabel could believe that. But now, walking along Merchiston Crescent, she thought about the latest call from Cat; none of us likes being taken for granted, including those who will rarely turn down a request for help; even St Francis, she imagined, might have felt a bit imposed upon by the birds. *They assume I'm going to feed them every day . . .* Paris: the city of light; Cat walking by the Seine; Cat in the Tuileries . . . But what exactly was she doing there? If I went off to Paris and asked somebody to look after things for me, I would explain why I was going. I would say something like *I'm going off to Paris because there's a Monet exhibition* or whatever. There was always a special exhibition to see in Paris. Isabel would not have said that she was simply going off to Paris and could you please give up your Saturday afternoon to work in my delicatessen. Or would she?

13

She wondered whether Cat took her for granted. Their relationship was an unusual one; although Isabel was her aunt, there was not a very great age gap between them, and in some respects they were more like cousins; cousins were often a decade or so apart, which was almost like being a coeval, if not quite.

But there was another reason why their relationship was unusual, and this was a bit more complex. Cat had notoriously bad taste in men, and over the years had been involved with a succession of patently unsuitable boyfriends. There had been Toby, of course, who had irritated Isabel with his attitudes and his crushed-strawberry trousers. She knew it was unfair to judge somebody by the colour of his trousers, and she had tried not to, but she had ended up doing just that. Crushed-strawberry trousers, in her mind, somehow went with views that were at odds with the way she saw the world. She knew that this was irrational, and unfair, and that she should not hold such indefensible opinions, but she could not help herself. Most of us have preferences that we cannot explain or justify – those who dislike a particular composer's work may not know why they feel that way, but the dislike is real. Some people cannot abide fish, or whisky, or Spanish onions; they may not be able to say why they dislike these things, but that will make no difference to their feelings. It might be cultural: some cultures distrust certain forms of food, or food not prepared in a particular way; or it may be based on some early unpleasant experience – being forced to eat fish as a child; an over-indulgence in whisky at a party; a meal involving Spanish onions *and* a rejection in love – there are so many ways in which we may be turned, in a lasting way, against something or somebody.

Isabel had been pleased when Cat and Toby had split up, although she sought to conceal her satisfaction at the rupture.

But there had been others, post-Toby, who were even worse, and Jamie, who was quite unlike all the others. Jamie and Cat had been involved with one another for a rather brief period. Isabel had approved of him, of course, and had hoped that Cat had come to her romantic senses. But no, she had not, and it was soon all over. Isabel, though, had already established a friendship with Jamie and this had, in due course, and rather to the surprise of both of them, turned into something more. That had caused predictable difficulties with Cat. She might not want a particular man but that did not mean that her aunt could swoop in and pick him up. What niece could fail to resent that?

Isabel had felt her way carefully through the ensuing tricky period and it was only because she was persistent and tactful with Cat that her relationship with her niece survived. But there were further hazards ahead, including the birth of Charlie and her and Jamie's eventual marriage. Again, it was Isabel's tact that had managed to avert an outright split, and now she and Cat got on much better. But she still felt that Cat sometimes asked, and expected, too much. An objective observer would undoubtedly have agreed with that; Cat did ask rather a lot of Isabel, possibly because she knew that Isabel would always respond. There was no selfishness in Isabel – which was half the problem, said Jamie; you have to leave room for yourself, for your own needs. If you were too generous – as he thought Isabel tended to be – you could end up with nothing in the bank.

Of course, to leave this life with an empty current account could just as well be a sign of a life well lived rather than of fecklessness or prodigality. There were people who gave away what they had because they believed this was their duty, or because they were just intrinsically generous, and could even do so to the point of reducing themselves to penury in the process. They were quite different from the very wealthy who, even as they dispensed largesse, were careful to keep a good cushion of funds for themselves.

'Don't worry,' Isabel said to Jamie. 'I'm not planning to give *everything* away.'

'I didn't think you would,' he said. 'People don't do that, do they?'

'Some do,' said Isabel. And she thought of John Maitland Moir, and saw him, for a moment, on his bicycle, in his Orthodox priest's cassock, cycling around Edinburgh. 'John Maitland Moir, for instance. Remember him?'

Jamie thought for a moment. 'That chap on the bicycle? With the grey beard?'

Isabel nodded. 'He was the son of a fairly well-to-do doctor out in Currie. And his mother wasn't short of funds either. So he inherited a lot of money.' She had once been told just how much it was, but had forgotten. 'He gave it all away — all of it. Over the years he just handed it out to people who needed help — tramps, down-and-outs, men who had been in prison and who had nobody else to turn to. He gave them food, coffee, clothing. And at the end, when he died, there was nothing left. Nothing. He died penniless.'

'A good man,' said Jamie.

'Very,' said Isabel. 'Wonderfully eccentric, but completely good. Did you know that he wore a kilt under his cassock? He was a fervent Scottish patriot.'

Jamie wondered how he had ended up as an Orthodox priest. 'Surely it's a bit unlikely — a Scotsman on a bicycle — with a concealed kilt — also being an Orthodox priest.'

It happened that Isabel knew how the conversion had taken place. John had told her himself. 'He found himself in sympathy with Orthodox theology,' she said. 'He went to Mount Athos and studied there. They received him into the faith. And he always held that the Scottish Episcopal Church had been liturgically influenced by Eastern Orthodoxy. It's all very complicated. Something to do with the *epiclesis* – the calling down of the Holy Spirit at a certain point in the service. He thought that very important because . . . '

'How completely pointless,' interjected Jamie.

'Why do you say that?'

Jamie shrugged. 'If there's a god, do you think it makes the slightest bit of difference what form of words you use when you address him? Or her? I suspect they don't like the thought that God could be feminine.'

There was no reason why God should even listen to us, Isabel thought. And there was certainly no reason to assume his good will, much as we might wish for that good will to exist. After all, look at the Greek gods, Isabel reminded herself, who were far from indifferent – to the point of taking pleasure in making our human lives difficult. No, the idea of a benevolent god was very much an exception in the enormous pantheon of gods that people had invented over the course of human history. The most that many people could hope for was that they should not incur the wrath of gods whom they had failed to appease or propitiate; beyond that, gods should be left to get on with their proper business and mortals with theirs.

She looked at Jamie. 'It may well be right to say that God doesn't care. But . . . ' She was not sure what she wanted to say about God. She thought that he might be there – embodied somehow in the perfection of the world, or in the sublime harmonies of a great work of music. Of course, if he was anywhere in music, she felt he was in the grave beauty of the motets of John Tavener, or in the more sublime passages of Bach. The architecture of such music was incompatible, Isabel thought, with a world that was meaningless. Nor did she believe that our reaction to such pieces of music merely resulted from the brain's recognition of pattern and order. That left her sympathetic to those who held religious views, even if at the same time she found it difficult to imagine a god who attended to our prayers. Although she was unenthusiastic about theology, she had long since realised that the real point of prayer was not to flatter those addressed; prayer was a form of meditation, she decided, and it did not detract from its efficacy that nobody was listening. Or so she had reasoned, until she had come across the argument that the prayers of many could amount to a large body of energy directed towards a particular goal, and that such energy could somehow have an impact on the material world. Prayer was directed energy, and we should at least be open-minded on what directed energy might achieve. The roar of a sporting crowd urging on its side could make a great difference to the outcome, she had heard it said. And then there were psychosomatic effects in medicine: if you thought you were going to get better, you often did; and vice versa, of course. *Mind over matter* was how her father had put it – although he was talking about golf.

As she walked along Isabel found herself humming a tune triggered by these thoughts of prayer and imprecation. It was about wishing on stars, and about how kind and benevolent Fate might make your wish come true. She had known the song as a child, and had a dog-eared book in which each line was accompanied by an illustration. She could still see the picture of Fate weaving a cloth of the submitted wishes from those below, and making them come true – just as the song said she would. She had believed that book, and had fervently tried to make one of her wishes develop in just the way they did in the song. Fate is kind, the song assured her; she brings good things

18

to those who dream; Isabel had believed this at the age of eight, and never quite lost that belief. Later, though, she shored this belief up; there was no such person as Fate, but there *might* be something called *karma*, and that, she thought, brought at least some people the things they deserved.

Isabel had never given Cat money, mainly because she had never asked for it and presumably did not need it. Isabel had never been quite sure of her niece's financial position, but she assumed that Cat was comfortable enough. Certainly Cat's father had been in a position to set his daughter up in her delicatessen, and her flat, and he had done both of these. Emotionally, though, he had given her very little, and Isabel had wondered whether this might explain her niece's restless moving from man to man. The amateur psychologist, she imagined, might simply nod and say, *Looking for father*. It would have been a glib explanation of something much more complex, but she thought there was possibly a grain of truth in it. If a woman had a good relationship with her male parent, then she was unlikely to suffer from the insecurity that led to difficulties in maintaining stable relationships with men.

Isabel had reached Bruntsfield Place, and she could now see the delicatessen on the other side of the road. The front of the shop was plate glass, and she could make out a movement within, a patch of white. This would be Eddie, who liked to wear white shirts, the cuffs of which were kept clean by two metal armbands of the sort that nobody wore any more but that did a very practical job. She had never seen him in anything but that white shirt and the thin blue tie that he also liked to wear. He had explained to her once, with some pride, that the tie was washable, which had surprised her. She did not imagine that such things as washable ties existed, but they must do, and Eddie appeared to have one. If the armbands were old-fashioned, as was the washable tie, seeming to belong, as it did, to the nineteen-sixties – that era of breathless, newly discovered convenience – then the rest of Eddie's clothing had the same ring to it: baggy trousers made either of corduroy or of a curious blue twill fabric and striped loose-fitting socks. These were of rough wool and, Isabel decided, home-produced in some remote Scottish town where people still made such things. It struck her as curious that this young man should dress so much at odds with the style of his contemporaries – a style that rarely got beyond jeans and tee-shirts and shapeless, indeterminate jackets.

'He's a young fogey,' Cat had said to Isabel, with a shrug. 'He just is.'

Isabel had been intrigued by this, and wondered why anybody, and in particular a young man in his early twenties, should cultivate an antiquated aesthetic. Why should anybody do that – unless of course the present, or the recent past, was for some reason distasteful, or painful? And she remembered that for Eddie perhaps it had been.

Saturday afternoon could be busy, and on this occasion it was. When Isabel arrived at the delicatessen, there were several people awaiting service at the counter while Sharon, the young woman who helped out a couple of days a week, tried to deal tactfully with an elderly man who was asking her to read out the list of contents printed on various packets.

'If I had my reading glasses with me, I wouldn't have to ask you,' he explained. 'But the print on these things nowadays . . . unless it's me, of course; the print may be the same size and it may be me. One has to be aware of the passage of time.'

'Yes,' said Sharon. 'But what are you concerned about? Have you got an allergy?'

'Maybe,' said the man.

'What to?'

'Well, it may be nuts, but I'm not sure. Some things disagree with me. I think it might be nuts, but I've never had one of those frightful attacks that people with a real nut allergy can get. That can be awful, you know. They carry those pen things that can give them a shot of whatever it is that deals with the nuts, although there was somebody – did you hear about it? – somebody in Morningside Road only a few weeks ago who ate a nut and dropped dead, right there in the street. One nut. It was in the *Evening News.*'

'Yes. Well, this is pasta. There are no nuts in it. Pasta doesn't have nuts.'

The man laughed. 'Oh, I know that. But sometimes the things that go with pasta . . .'

'This is just pasta. Simple pasta. There's nothing in it but pasta, which is wheat, isn't it?'

'And gluten,' said the man. 'There are some people who can't take gluten. I'm not sure whether it disagrees with me – I'm not sure how one would tell. Do you know? Is there a test these days?'

Sharon caught Isabel's eye.

'I'm sorry,' said Isabel, coming to Sharon's aid. 'I'm sorry but we're very busy. Pasta is absolutely fine and this young lady is really going to have to look after other customers.'

She drew Sharon away and smiled blandly at the man's look of wounded annoyance. *That's just the way it is*, she thought, *there is just not enough time to listen to everybody. There never is.*

'He did that last week,' whispered Sharon. 'He goes on and on. It takes him ages to choose.'

'Oh well,' said Isabel. 'Perhaps he's suffering from information overload. There are all those notices on food packages – so much saturated fat, so many calories, so much salt, and so on.

It's rather a lot to read before you eat.' She remembered that she had heard of an Indian restaurant somewhere that required customers to sign a consent form before they served them their hottest curry. *I am aware of the heat of this curry and voluntarily assume the risk of eating it* ... That was a sales gimmick, of course, but we were an unduly risk-averse society, she thought, and we were in danger of becoming obsessed with protecting people from the world and its dangers. Nuts, hot curries, sharp surfaces, death ... *In the unlikely event of the aircraft landing on water* ... No, it could happen; aircraft did land on water, and if they did, they broke up, as if hitting concrete, unless you were terribly lucky and were in the hands of somebody like that amazing captain who landed his plane on the Hudson River with such skill that everybody simply walked off the floating plane as if they were disembarking at an airport.

Eddie spoke to Sharon. 'You should go,' he said. 'Just go. If you hang about, you'll get somebody else and then you'll never get away.'

'Yes,' said Isabel. 'I'm here. Just go.'

She took her place behind the counter and began to serve the next customer. It was two o'clock, and she would be working more or less without a break until six, when she and Eddie would shut up shop. She thought of Paris and saw, for a moment, Cat sitting in a pavement café. There was a man beside her, and Isabel tried to imagine what he would look like, but he was somehow fuzzy, and lacked outline. But he was definitely there, and he was looking at Cat, who was saying something to him, and smiling.

Shortly before four there was a lull in business. It often happened that way on a Saturday afternoon: they would be worked off their feet from lunchtime until mid-afternoon, when people seemed to pause and take breath; then, twenty minutes later, they would remember the things they had to buy for the rest of the weekend. Then they would come in for milk and baguettes, for smoked salmon for their Sunday breakfast, and for the garlic needed for the dish they were planning to cook that evening.

'Sit down,' said Eddie. 'I'll make you a coffee.'

She accepted his offer, and perched on one of the two stools behind the counter. It was a relief to take the weight off her legs and to relieve the sore calf muscle that she had somehow pulled when she went to the Craiglockhart gym earlier that week. Jamie had warned her – 'You should tackle these things gradually. Go straight into it and you pull a muscle. Guaranteed.' She had not told him when she felt the first twinge, but had confessed a bit later, and he had said, 'I'm not going to say I told you so. But I did, didn't I?'

Eddie handed her a paper cup of coffee. He had made it as she liked it – strong and with a dash of cold milk – and he smiled at her as he passed it over. 'Where's Charlie?' he asked.

'He's at the Zoo with Jamie. Charlie likes the meerkats. He spends hours staring at them.'

'They're very popular,' said Eddie. 'People identify with them, I think.'

Isabel nodded absently. Perhaps they did. Other, less engaging animals would have nobody to identify with them: anteaters, warthogs, or those small creatures with sticky fur and worried-looking expressions – nobody identified with *them*.

She looked at Eddie appreciatively. 'Lovely coffee . . . '

'I wonder what she's doing,' said Eddie.

She realised that he meant Cat. 'Drinking coffee perhaps. In a café.'

'With somebody playing the accordion in the background?'

Isabel smiled. 'That's the cliché. Have you seen those films where they set the scene like that? France is always accordion music or the Eiffel Tower. London is Big Ben or Trafalgar Square – perhaps a bowler hat or two bobbing along, although bowlers have completely disappeared.' She paused. Cinema audiences had to know where they were; perhaps it was not unreasonable to play accordion music in the background to remind people that this was Paris. 'Perhaps they need to do it.'

'She's lucky,' said Eddie.

Of course she is, thought Isabel. She's lucky because she's got a reliable, uncomplaining assistant like you, and a relative who will come and help out for nothing, and a father who bought her the delicatessen in the first place; she's lucky because she doesn't have to worry about her weight and she's a got a good skin and she has that nice flat round the corner and ... The enumeration of those things that made Cat lucky simply seemed to increase the discomfort in Isabel's calf muscle, and she stopped.

'He's lucky too,' added Eddie.

She looked at him. There was wistfulness in his voice rather than resentment. 'He?'

'Her new boyfriend,' said Eddie. 'The one she's taken with her. She's paid for the tickets because I heard her making the booking on the phone. She paid for both of them on her credit card.'

'Oh ...'

He continued before she could say anything else. 'I wish somebody would take me to Paris. I've never been.'

'Never?'

He shook his head, and she made her decision. 'I'll stand you, Eddie. Later this year, when things are less busy. September's a good time for Paris. I'll buy you a ticket.'

'And come with me?'

She had not envisaged that. 'No ... Well, that's nice of you, but I have Jamie and Charlie to look after, as you know, so I'll just buy you the ticket – you and a friend, if you like. And I'll pay for a hotel for a couple of days. You could go on Friday and come back on Sunday evening.'

'You wouldn't ... would you? Really?'

She saw that he was beaming with pleasure. It was so easy; money made it so easy. But then, there was Cat to think about and this new boyfriend of hers, and she felt a curious, rather sick sensation in her stomach, the sort of feeling one gets when an entirely familiar but nonetheless dreaded task comes round.

'Have you met him?' she asked, looking down into her coffee cup as she spoke.

Eddie was thinking of Paris, and he replied absently, 'Yes.'

She put the cup down. She had to face it. 'And?'

'He's all right.'

'Just all right?'

'No. Actually rather cool.'

She waited for more, but Eddie was silent. Men, Isabel had always felt, had limited curiosity about other men. Other men were all right, or not all right. 'Who is he, Eddie? What's his name?'

'He's called Mick.'

She would have to prise it out of him. 'And?'

'And what?'

She made a gesture with her hands – a gesture reflecting both frustration and encouragement.

'She's known him for some time,' said Eddie, as if only now realising that more information was required. 'He fixes dish-washers. I suppose he calls himself a dishwasher engineer.'

25

For a few moments Isabel said nothing. Then she asked, 'Is he the man who fixes *her* dishwasher?'

Eddie nodded. 'That's how she met him.'

Isabel looked out of the window. 'And now she's taken him to Paris.'

'That's right,' said Eddie. He broke into a broad smile. 'I bet he didn't think that he'd go to somebody's flat to fix her dishwasher and then end up going to Paris with her! Some dishwasher engineers have all the luck.'

'I doubt if he anticipated that,' said Isabel.

She lowered herself off her stool. Two customers had entered the store. One of them she recognised as a particularly difficult woman who insisted on squeezing and sniffing her purchases before she paid for them. She had even once suggested that she should be allowed to open a jar of pimento-stuffed olives to try a sample before she made up her mind. Isabel had glared at her and shaken her head. Later she had regretted her firmness – justified though it undoubtedly had been – when she found out that the woman had been abandoned by her husband of thirty years, suffered from alopecia – she wore a wig – and had been the victim of a commercial fraud that had almost resulted in her losing her house. Isabel had resolved that she would show no irritation and would in future help this woman in whatever tests she wished to conduct before committing herself.

She returned to work, and was busy without interruption until Eddie finally announced that it was almost six and they should close the door.

'Six o'clock is seven in Paris,' he said. 'I wonder what Cat's doing right now?'

'Getting ready to go out to dinner,' said Isabel, and then thought morosely of Cat with her dishwasher engineer. She had not met him and had no idea what he was like. There was nothing wrong with being a dishwasher engineer – indeed there was nothing wrong with any honest job, and so . . . She stopped to think. There were some jobs that, although perfectly legal, were of a nature that made one wary. Being a bouncer in a bar or a nightclub was quite above board, but surely suggested a pugnacious temperament: bouncers tended to have broken noses and to look threatening; they were certainly not the type with whom one could envisage having much of a discussion about anything. And then there were those financial traders in the City of London, vocal young men who were skilled at mental arithmetic and remembering figures, whose main concern was to be a few seconds ahead of rivals in tapping in their trades on their keyboards. They were hardly the sort of person one would want to spend much time with, although presumably they all had mothers and girlfriends and had their moments of tenderness. Or possibly not . . .

She decided that she would like Mick; she had to. Disliking somebody about whom one knew nothing – other than that he could fix dishwashers – was, quite simply, wrong. Isabel had a distaste for snobbery – an insidious evil, she called it – and she would not fall into the trap of thinking that she would have nothing in common with him; she had no grounds for thinking that except, perhaps, experience, which we must sometimes discount in favour of principle. We know that there are people who let others down, who treat them shabbily, and yet we must not lapse into cynicism and believe this of everyone. Cat chose badly. She chose men on physical grounds, and that was the worst possible basis for a relationship – Isabel was sure of that. And yet, and yet . . . She pictured Jamie. What if he did not look like he did, but was quite differently built? If Jamie were round and myopic and with a moustache in which food particles became easily trapped, would she love him as she did? Would she have given him a second glance? Moral perfectionism suggested one answer – look behind the physical, it urged us – while honesty suggested quite another. What was that line of poetry she had learned somewhere? It came back to her: it was Yeats. Only God, he said to Anne Gregory, could love you for yourself alone and not for your yellow hair. Isabel sighed: sometimes it was difficult being a moral philosopher, particularly in matters of the heart, but also in a whole lot of other respects.

She looked at Eddie, and was about to say to him: 'Do you think God prefers blondes?' But did not, of course; Eddie would have looked at her blankly and would later say to Cat, 'Isabel is getting really peculiar these days, you know. She asked me whether God preferred blondes.' And Cat would probably say, 'She's always been peculiar.'

But that exchange would not take place, and Eddie simply made an innocuous observation about Cat in Paris. 'She'll be having a good time,' he said.

Isabel pulled herself together. 'Yes, and I'm glad,' she said.

Eddie looked at her sideways. 'I thought you were cross with her.'

'I was,' said Isabel, summoning up every ounce of goodwill she could muster. 'But I no longer am.' She almost convinced herself.

Eddie shrugged. 'Cat's just Cat,' he said. 'She's not going to change.' He paused; he had remembered something. 'Oh, by the way, you know that woman? The one married to that journalist you hear on the radio? You know her?'

It was Isabel's friend Sam. 'Yes. Sam?'

Eddie nodded. 'She came in here the other day. She said that she wanted to talk to you about somebody she's met. She just mentioned it.'

Isabel took off her apron and hung it on the back of the door that led into Cat's office.

'She said that it was something rather unusual,' said Eddie. 'But she didn't tell me what it was.'

Isabel wondered what it was. People were always talking to her about unusual things, she thought: I am a recipient of unusual confidences.

'I'll phone her,' said Isabel.

Eddie reached for his bundle of keys. 'Cat will be having a really good meal in Paris, I should think,' he said. 'You know what the French are like.'

'I do,' said Isabel. Charity, she thought; charity requires us to enjoy the prospect of others having good things to eat – an attitude that was the very opposite of *Mahlneid*, meal envy in invented German, which described the covetous feeling we have when we see others in a restaurant enjoying dishes that look much better than our own. If the word *Mahlneid* did not exist, then there could surely be another German compound noun for regret over one's own choice in that, and other contexts; the German language could come up with long words for anything. Now she thought of what Eddie had said about Sam. Something *unusual*. She would phone her friend when she got back to the house and find out just how odd was this thing awaiting her. Was there a German word for the feeling of anticipation experienced in waiting to hear something that a friend was about to tell you, but that you currently had no idea about? Her German was shaky, and as little used as her French, but some of the vocabulary remained – enough to think: *Eindrucksempfindlichkeitkapazität* or, on second thoughts, *Verständigungsvorfreude,* which had the merit, at least, of being in the dictionary.

3

Charlie returned from the Zoo with a meerkat badge, a meerkat soft toy, and a book about the foraging habits of meerkats in the Kalahari.

'You saw the meerkats?' Isabel asked. 'Were they lovely, darling?'

'Lots of meerkats,' said Charlie.

'So I see. And any other animals?'

'They were sleeping,' said Charlie. 'Even the lions.'

'Oh, well,' said Isabel. 'We can get by without lions, I think.' She did not like lions, those always rather restless, discontented creatures, even when filmed in the wild. They were, of course, high-ranking felines, and, much as she liked cats, she had always felt they were intrinsically psychopathic in their approach to life. They were capable of affection, but only intermittently and always on their terms. No cat, she thought, would make a sacrifice for its owner, whereas dogs did – readily and without question – and meant it too.

Stories of friendship between people and lions were dubious, in Isabel's view. Elsa, the famous lioness of *Born Free*, put on a good act of being on the side of the Adamsons but would have eaten them if she had been *really* hungry. And had that happened, the story of *Born Free* might have been somewhat different. The publishers would have had to publish an incomplete manuscript, explaining in the introduction that the book would have been a bit longer had the authors not been consumed by the subject of their story, but asking, nonetheless, for the reader's understanding.

The lions in Edinburgh Zoo were certainly well fed and well looked-after – a pensionable position, with lots of raw meat, that any lion in the wild might gladly accept. Yet there were some places that large animals simply should not be. She recalled a story told her by a friend who had been obliged to attend a conference in Las Vegas and who had stayed in one of the large hotels there. This hotel had, as many of them did, a casino on its ground floor, and the hotel guests were compelled to walk through this casino in order to get to their rooms. 'I was walking,' said her friend, 'through this hell of tinkling, flashing gambling machines and was suddenly confronted with a large glass-walled cage – in which there was a lion. A live lion.'

Isabel had been speechless. She was only half American – through her sainted mother – but that was enough to make her blush with shame for the mere fact that Las Vegas existed. There was so much of which America could be proud: it had made New York and San Francisco, along with a hundred other cities with parks and art galleries and universities, but then it had gone and spawned Las Vegas, a place that carried vulgarity and venality to undreamed-of heights. And yet people loved it, and flocked there in their millions, to marvel at the entirely false, to be married in Elvis chapels, to lose money, and to listen to flashy crooners singing about love.

Perhaps this was a concomitant of freedom: if people were free, then some of them, at least, would be free of the constraints of good taste. Perhaps Las Vegas was just a great big cultural burp, of the sort that you are bound to get in a free society where people can burp if they wish. Perhaps lions in casinos were what you got if you said: *There are no limits – everything is possible*. She imagined, though, the casino lion escaping – delicious thought – and suddenly finding a way out of its durance vile, romping through the crowds of gamblers, scattering the croupiers, sending the pole dancers up their poles to escape, pouncing on the waitresses with their trays of complimentary drinks, drowning the sound of cascading money with its roars of anguish and anger.

'People were tapping on the glass,' her friend continued, 'and the lion paced backwards and forwards. There were the bones of its dinner on the floor. It lived there, it seemed.' She paused, and looked at Isabel with melancholy eyes. 'It lived there.'

This memory of human perversity made her frown, and Jamie noticed it. He was accustomed to Isabel's patterns of thought, and knew that there were unanticipated avenues always opening up. Down one of these she might suddenly wander, even if only for a few seconds, while she wrestled with some question that most of us rarely thought about, or never dreamed existed. *I am married to a philosopher*, he thought. *What else can I expect?*

'Thinking?' he asked.

'Of meerkats,' answered Charlie.

Jamie ruffled the boy's hair. 'Not you – Mummy.'

'Yes,' said Isabel. 'Of lions . . . and what it is to be a lion.'

'I never think of lions,' said Jamie. 'Or hardly ever.'

'I don't exactly make a habit of it,' said Isabel. And turning to Charlie, she reached down and picked him up. 'Time for your bath, my darling. You may bring your meerkat, but don't drop him in the water.'

Jamie was now off duty as far as looking after Charlie was concerned. He went off to practise a piece for a concert the following week, and as she ran Charlie's bath she heard the rumble of the bassoon in the background. Violins sang, brass crowed, while bassoons, she felt, rumbled according to a Richter scale all of their own. Charlie was allowed to have something they called a Saturday Bath, in which the bathtub was filled almost to its brim. This allowed him to duck himself under the water in a game that he called Big Submarines. Isabel watched closely: Big Submarines was a physical game and from time to time he had to be restrained from slopping almost the entire contents of the bath onto the floor. He was like a seal, she thought, or an otter perhaps, as otters were as playful as four-year-old boys, and as slippery. Big Submarines was a bad name for this game, as submarines, especially big ones, were stately, rather considered boats that slid up and down through the water without anything approaching exuberance.

'What are the rules of Big Submarines?' she once asked.

Charlie had looked at her with surprise. 'No rules,' he said.

'Does the biggest submarine win?'

He looked slightly resentful. Adults should not interfere in games; they did not understand. 'The good submarine wins,' he announced.

'Ah,' said Isabel. 'That's good to hear.' A mental image came to her of a good submarine – painted white, perhaps, with a crew that eschewed swearing (at sea) and hard liquor (when ashore), engaged in heroic acts, never used, as most submarines were, to intimidate others. But there were no such submarines – not in the world we knew. There were only dark prowlers bristling with weapons. One nuclear submarine, armed with its Trident missiles, could destroy our planet as we knew it. One submarine, she thought; one. In such a world, what chance did a good submarine have?

On that particular evening, the game of submarines seemed to fizzle out rather quickly. Charlie was tired; she could see that.

'Time for your story,' she said. 'Babar tonight.' And added, 'Again.' Like any child, Charlie liked the same story time and time again. *The Adventures of Babar* had been a favourite for the past few weeks and attempts to move on to something new had been stoutly resisted by Charlie himself.

She dried him and put him into his pyjamas. She noticed that these pyjamas had pictures of ducks on them. There was another pair with anchors, and one with small, friendly rockets travelling through fields of stars and moons. *Adult pyjamas*, she thought, *say nothing*.

'Babar!' demanded Charlie, and snuggled down in his bed, holding his mother's hand. Isabel felt an overwhelming tenderness. My little boy; this little creature I have created; the person I love more than anything or anybody in this world; who means absolutely everything to me; who provides my answers in the way in which no philosophy, however brilliant, can ever do; mine.

They began *Babar*, right from the beginning. Isabel had toyed with censoring the scene in which Babar's mother is shot by a cruel hunter – some parents skip that page – but she had decided not to shield Charlie from the truth, even if the truth was fictional. He had asked her why the hunter had shot Babar's mother, and she had replied that it was because he was cruel, and cruel people did unkind things since they did not think of the feelings of others. And that, she thought, was as far as one might get in any attempt to explain the cruelties of this world to a four-year-old. She wondered whether more sophisticated explanations could get much further: ultimately it was a matter of the absence of human sympathy. One might dig deeper: the aetiology of evil could be complex and tendentious. What made Hitler what he was? A sense of historical injustice? Personal failure? A malignant, psychopathic personality? The desire to harm those he believed had harmed him? Auden had reflected on this in his disowned poem, 'September 1, 1939', where he had alluded to the lesson that 'all school children learn / Those to whom evil is done / Do evil in return . . . ' And he was right, in that respect at least. Evil was repaid with evil – but only by those who were themselves evil; which brought one back to where one started.

'Go on,' said Charlie.

Babar wandered from the forest and found himself, by sleight of improbable geography, in a French city. Now the transformation comes; he meets the old lady who takes him to the department store to buy him clothes. He is introduced into European society and acquires its baggage. He returns to the Kingdom of the Elephants in a green car and with all the accoutrements of French civilisation. When the King's position becomes vacant after he has eaten a poisonous mushroom, Babar is appointed, and Celeste becomes his Queen. They rule Celesteville with integrity and a sound instinct for orderly planning: rows of neat houses are constructed for the elephants; savagery is repelled.

His eyes began to close; it was time to leave Celesteville. Isabel bent forward and kissed Charlie on the brow. He lived in a world of friendly stuffed toys, of talking elephants, and meerkats too. How long would it last? When would this childhood bubble be penetrated by images of conflict, of bionic superheroes, of pyrotechnics and explosions that made the world of older children what it was? At six, at seven, when the purveyors of these things realised there was money to be made from children? *Don't grow up too quickly*, she whispered.

Jamie finished his practice and came into the kitchen.

'Asleep?' he asked, nodding his head in the direction of Charlie's bedroom upstairs.

'Out for the count.'

'I'm not surprised,' said Jamie. 'He ran everywhere in the Zoo. Ran. I had to chase after him constantly.'

'He's a boy,' said Isabel. 'Haven't you noticed how boys seem to run everywhere? Girls don't. They walk or skip, but boys tear about.'

Jamie went to the fridge and extracted a half-full bottle of New Zealand white wine. He poured a glass for Isabel and then one for himself. They touched glasses; they always did that; Edinburgh crystal to Edinburgh crystal.

'I was ...' He did not finish, as the doorbell sounded. He looked at Isabel enquiringly. 'Expecting anybody?'

She shook her head. 'No. The Lifeboats?' A neighbour collected for the lifeboats charity. It was a popular cause – even amongst the land-bound.

Isabel shrugged. 'Could be.'

Jamie went to answer the door. After a minute or so Isabel heard voices in the hall and went to investigate.

It was her friend Sam. 'I was passing by. I'm not going to stay because you'll be getting ready for dinner and I don't want to hold you back.'

Isabel assured her they had plenty of time. 'Dinner isn't always planned in this house. Sometimes it just happens.'

Sam smiled. She had a husband who could not cook, whereas Isabel had Jamie, who cooked rather well – or so Sam had heard. The injustice of it, some said; to look like that *and* to be able to cook.

'Perhaps Jamie could teach Eric one of these days. Nothing too sophisticated, but to be able to make an omelette would be useful.'

Jamie laughed. 'I'm sure that Eric would be a perfectly good cook. Or even *is* a perfectly good cook. Some husbands don't let on, you know; they can cook quite well but it's not in their interests for anybody to know it.'

Isabel offered Sam a glass of wine, and she accepted. 'But just a small one,' said Sam. 'I don't want to *roll* home.'

The three of them sat down at the kitchen table. Sam, who was in her mid-forties, had been a friend of Isabel's for some years, having been introduced to her by a mutual friend. She was an attractive woman who liked to wear ethnic clothing, on this occasion an embroidered Indian blouse and an elaborate brass necklace, also Indian.

'Eddie said you were in the delicatessen the other day,' Isabel remarked. 'He said you were hoping to see me.'

Sam took a sip of her wine. 'Yes, I did – or rather, do. I do want to see you.'

Isabel smiled. 'Well, here I am.'

Sam put down her glass, fingering the stem as she did so. 'You know that you have a reputation for helping people.'

Isabel blushed. 'I don't do any more than most people do.'

Sam held up a hand. 'But you do. I know that you're modest about it.'

There was an awkward silence. Isabel looked at Jamie, who met her gaze briefly, and then looked down at the floor. She knew that he was concerned about her readiness to help people in all sorts of difficulties. 'You can't do everything,' he had said to her. 'You can't take on the troubles of the whole world.' She knew that he was right, but it had always been hard for her to turn down a direct appeal, especially from somebody she knew. Certainly, if Sam were in some sort of difficulty, Isabel would find it almost impossible to say no to her.

'Are you in trouble?' Isabel asked.

Sam laughed. 'No, not me. My life is too uneventful for trouble – or for real trouble. No, not me, but . . . '

'Somebody you know?'

Sam nodded. 'Not trouble as such, but . . . well, troubled. There's a difference.'

Isabel agreed. 'Of course.'

'There's a woman downstairs in my building, in the ground-floor flat,' Sam continued. 'She moved in about six months ago. Her husband's a pipe major in the Army. They no longer live together, and I've only met him briefly, when he's been round to pick up their son. But I've got to know her reasonably well.'

Isabel was busy avoiding Jamie's eye. He looked at her, glanced away, and then looked at her again.

'Her name is Kirsten. The boy's called Harry,' Sam continued. 'He's six. A rather serious-looking little boy. I see her taking him off to South Morningside School every morning if I look out of my window at the right time. The two of them walk off, hand-in-hand.' She paused. 'Your wee Charlie hasn't started yet, has he?'

'At nursery. Two days a week.'

Sam nodded. 'Mine are growing up so fast. Fiona's fourteen now, you know, and Nicholas is twelve, and is shooting up like a bean-pole.'

Isabel thought of Charlie, upstairs with his new stuffed meerkat on his pillow. He had been a baby just a few months ago, it seemed, and she had thought it would never end. *I thought that love would last for ever. I was wrong;* that line of

Auden's that contained a truth about everything, not just love. And we had to act as if things were not going to end, because if we did not then we would do so little in life. People still planted oak trees and created gardens, which they might not do with quite the same enthusiasm, or would not do at all, if they stopped to think of the brevity of life.

'I feel rather sorry for her. I know that being a single parent is pretty common these days, but it can't be much easier than it's ever been. In other words, it's tough.'

'Yes,' said Isabel. 'I can just imagine. It's twice as tough. I don't know if I'd be able to cope.'

Sam thought that Isabel would manage very well. 'You might surprise yourself, you know.' She paused. 'She dropped in the other morning after she had taken him to school. She works part-time, three days a week, I think, as some sort of receptionist – while he's at school.'

Isabel nodded. 'And?'

'And she told me the most extraordinary story. Well, I don't know if everybody would find it extraordinary, but I did. Apparently the boy is convinced that he's had another life. He's adamant about it, and talks about it every day, she said. He says that he had another mother – another family – he's matter-of-fact about it, but she's understandably worried.'

Isabel said that she could imagine it would be unsettling for any parent. 'But it's not all that unusual, is it? I've heard of things like that, haven't you?'

'Vaguely,' said Sam. 'I think I read about something of the sort. But somehow this seems rather different.'

'Why?'

'Because he's very specific. He's come up with a name for the family, as well as a very detailed description of the place he lived. And he's been consistent.'

39

Isabel looked out of the window. She wondered how she would feel if Charlie were suddenly to claim to have been somebody else? She would treat it, she imagined, as a figment of childish imagination: very young children simply did not grasp the difference between truth and falsehood. Charlie had announced a few days earlier that he had seen a squirrel wearing pyjamas. He had sounded so convincing, and had appeared hurt that he had not been believed. 'He was,' he protested. 'He was.'

Sam continued: 'She's spoken to various people about it. She took it up with her doctor, and he said that he could arrange an appointment with the child psychiatry services at the Sick Kids' Hospital. That happened, she said, and they saw him. But at the end of it they explained to her that he seemed an entirely normal young boy. They reminded her that children could create elaborate stories and then forget about them. They said it was harmless.'

'And it probably is,' said Isabel.

'I thought that too,' said Sam. 'But she's really concerned about it. She feels that there's nobody she can discuss it with. Harry's father is very dismissive of the whole thing, as is his teacher.'

'She has you to talk to,' said Isabel. 'That must help.'

'Perhaps, but I think she wants to speak to somebody other than a neighbour. And then she said something that made me think of you.'

Isabel was silent, but she already knew that she would have to help.

Sam was looking at her intently. 'She said that she wanted to put her mind at rest, and the way to do this would be to investigate the story. She says that Harry has half convinced her that what he says is true, and that if she could just look into it and establish that there's no truth in what he says, then she'll feel much easier about it.'

Isabel inclined her head. 'I can understand that, but frankly ...' She was about to say that she was not sure how much help she would be able to give, but Sam interrupted her.

'He's given her a lot of information, you know. The description of the house he says he lived in is very specific.'

'That may be, but how on earth could one do anything with that? If he says it was a house with a path leading to a red front door and so on, how could one possibly do anything with that? How many houses in Scotland match that description? If it's in Scotland, that is – presumably it could be anywhere.'

Sam shrugged. 'He's more specific than that. He describes the view from the front. He says that it looks out on islands. He describes those.'

'There are plenty of islands in the west of Scotland,' said Isabel.

'Yes. But he talks about a lighthouse, and she says he's drawn it. She has a picture of the lighthouse.'

Isabel looked thoughtful. She was imagining herself in the shoes of this woman, with nobody to turn to. She had Jamie; she had her editorship of the *Review*; she had Grace to help her in the house; she had her network of friends and contacts. She recalled what her mother had said to her: *Remember what you have and what other people don't have.* What mothers said often seemed embarrassingly trite, but as we grew older we saw the truth in it, sometimes to our chagrin.

'Of course I'll talk to her,' she said.

Sam smiled. 'I knew that would be your answer,' she said. Then she frowned. 'Do you believe in reincarnation, Isabel?'

Isabel shook her head. 'No. As a general rule I don't believe in things for which there is no satisfactory evidence. And what about you? Do you think it's anything more than wishful thinking?'

Sam was more hesitant. 'Not really. But then half of humanity believes in it, you know. Belief in reincarnation is ... well, it's fairly mainstream.'

'That may be,' said Isabel. 'But then half of humanity is prepared to believe the most extraordinary things.' There were so many examples of this – and not just the obvious ones. The *Scotsman* had recently reported a survey that showed that an astonishing number of people believed they would win the lottery – and made that belief part of their retirement planning. They actually believed it, even when the odds against that happening were explained to them. Then there were those who were convinced they had been abducted by aliens, or who thought that unproven remedies would protect them from all sorts of illness, or who believed in the Loch Ness Monster. They held these beliefs in spite of a complete lack of evidence; vitamin supplements had never been shown to do half the things claimed for them, and if there were some unknown creature in Loch Ness, some secretive survivor of an earlier age, then surely bodies or skeletons of these peculiar animals would have washed up, or somebody would have photographed one. There were photographs, of course, but they were always conveniently blurred, or taken in half-light, and could just as easily be of otters or a jumping salmon, or of something equally prosaic and explicable; it had been pointed out that a duck could, in certain lights, look like a monster. One might as well believe in Santa Claus ...

Isabel stopped herself. A well-known campaigner against religion had recently suggested that we should stop telling our children fairy stories because these encouraged irrational habits of thought. She did not want to end up in that camp, because the imagination was a delicate plant that could be so easily destroyed, and childhood's stories were the mulch that it needed to thrive. Without imagination we find it more difficult to be good, because imagination enables us to understand the pain of others: destroy imagination and you destroyed empathy.

Charlie believed in Santa Claus, and she would not have it otherwise. And he believed in the Tooth Fairy too, and in kelpies, those skittish Scottish horses that lived in the sea. He would find out the truth about all these things soon enough, but for the time being she was content for him to believe in things that did not exist but that we wished were there.

'They may be right, of course. For all we know, that is.' There was a gentle note of reproach in Sam's voice, and Isabel picked this up.

'Yes, they may be.' *For all we know* – it was the essential, if unspoken, qualification to everything we said about anything.

'Not that I think it is,' said Sam.

'No, I don't either. And anyway, can you think of anything more depressing than the thought that we come back time and time again? What an awful thought – to have to do it all over again – as somebody else, of all things.'

'But things might be better,' said Sam. 'You may have a better deal, so to speak, next time round.'

'Or a worse one.' Isabel had always thought that reincarnation provided rather convenient solutions to the problem of evil in moral philosophy. If evil were to be punished, then the moral balance would seem much less out of kilter. The bully would become the bullied; the proud would become the humbled; the exploiters would be the exploited. There was a certain attraction in it, but the problem with attractive solutions was that they were often just wishful thinking. *There are no ships that will come to save us*, she thought.

She thought of Harry, that small boy, living with his mother in their flat in Morningside. She pictured the boy thinking of his father, the pipe major in the Army, and she saw the father, too, in his swathes of tartan, twirling his silver-topped baton while behind him marched the band, pipes skirling, crowds applauding, and yapping dogs running alongside the parade. He would admire his father because to a small boy a pipe major would be something grand and wonderful, and he would wish, no doubt, for his father to be returned to him. *Another life. Invent another life to make this one more bearable. A life with a father.* What could she possibly do for this little boy and his mother, other than to bring back the father, which of course was beyond her?

'You'll at least see her?' enquired Sam anxiously. 'You aren't having second thoughts, are you?'

'No,' said Isabel. 'I'm not having second thoughts.' And she realised that she did have second thoughts – frequently – but they were usually about matters other than decisions to get involved in the complicated problems of others. She knew herself well enough to realise that she always kept those commitments, no matter what.

She looked at Sam. 'I'll do what I can.'

'Which is all anybody should ever ask of anyone else,' said Sam.

Oh no, thought Isabel; people often ask more than that – much more.

4

Sunday was a day of doing nothing very much, but Monday saw Isabel back at her desk. *The Review of Applied Ethics*, which she edited – and now owned – was coming up to its twentieth anniversary and Isabel had planned a special issue to mark the occasion. Most issues of the *Review* dealt with a particular theme – the last issue had been 'The Just War' and before that there had been 'The Rights of Trans-gendered Young People'. That issue had included a controversial and fiery paper by a feminist philosopher who argued that males who became female should never be accepted in women-only groups. 'Having enjoyed the privileges of male-dominated hier-archies, reassigned men cannot enjoy the same moral claims as those who have suffered from those very structures,' the contributor had written, provoking a flood of angry correspondence that had taken Isabel several days to deal with.

The anniversary issue, though, was to follow a different pattern, and was to be an open forum for a number of specially invited philosophers to write on whatever happened to interest them at the time. 'A pot-pourri,' Isabel had called it in the letter she had sent to the prospective contributors. 'Say what you like about whatever you like.' It was a dangerous invitation for any editor to issue, but she had chosen her contributors carefully, writing to those whose work she particularly admired, and it had worked, or almost worked. She had approached her friend Julian Bagnini, who had done more, she felt, to bring philosophy to a wider audience than most, and he had agreed to write on an issue in personal identity. She wrote to Bill Childress in Virginia, who said that he would write on rationing resources in medicine. 'A problem that sadly refuses to go away, no matter how much we spend on health,' he wrote in his reply. 'The scale of the problem simply changes. In circumstances of dire need, there may be a decision to be made about who gets aspirin; in circumstances of plenty the argument may be about transplants or the latest miracle drug.' The issue was beginning to look good, and Isabel had boasted to Jamie about the all-star cast. 'Everybody's going to be in it,' she said. 'I'll make it *this* thick.' She held up a hand to demonstrate the dimensions of the issue, but Jamie simply smiled and said, 'The ethics of using lots of trees – is anybody going to write about that?'

She had retorted, 'Spoil-sport,' but his comment had given her pause to think. She had resisted suggestions that the *Review* should become entirely electronic, but was that position defensible? Surely we can use *some* trees, and surely applied ethics was a suitable use for them. And what would be the bad uses for trees? She made a mental list: junk mail, glossy fashion magazines, newspapers she disagreed with, those paper lanterns that you lit tiny fires under and watched as they floated up into the sky? The last of these, she thought, were just litter, and when they landed in fields and were eaten by cows they gave the cows indigestion, even killed them. No, that was definitely a bad use of paper.

Almost everybody she approached had now accepted the invitation to write an article for the anniversary issue, and that Monday Isabel received the last reply – in an email from a professor at a university in California. He said that he would be delighted to write for the issue and that the subject he had chosen was his mother. Isabel read his message with growing incredulity.

'Your invitation came at a very auspicious time,' wrote the professor. 'I have been thinking a great deal about my mother in recent months and I am shortly coming up to a sabbatical. I have planned to spend it in a house I have up at Napa, north of San Francisco. I like the climate there, which is a bit fresher than our climate down here in southern California. You don't know my mother, of course, but I'm sure you and she would hit it off. She's seen so much in her seventy-eight years – her autobiography would fill several volumes, I think – and she's very wise. I know everybody thinks their mother's wise – or just about everybody – but in my case there are grounds for saying this – and how! What I'd like to do in my paper is to try to capture her particular way of looking at the world and analyse how she gets to where she's at. It's intuition, of course – she has plenty of that – but there's something else there, something I propose to call *maternal certainty*. I'd like to capture the essence of that because I think it adds something to what we know of how people make a moral judgement. And as for a title, I was thinking of calling it 'The Ethical World of my Mother', but would obviously be guided by you on that.'

Isabel stared at the screen, carefully re-reading the message in case she had misunderstood it. Was it intended as a joke? She decided it was not; sincerity was one of the most transparent qualities in any prose and one could always tell if something was written in jest. No, Professor Geoffrey Trembling really did want to write 'The Ethical World of my Mother'; he meant every word of it.

She got up from her desk. Jamie had taken Charlie to nursery school and would be back within a few minutes. Isabel waited for him in the kitchen, the printed email in her hand.

'Read this,' she said when he returned.

He took the sheet of paper. 'Is it for me?'

'No, it's for me. But I want you to read it.'

As he read the email, Jamie broke into a smile. 'This is great stuff,' he muttered. 'This is classic.'

'I'm assuming he's serious,' said Isabel.

Jamie agreed. 'Oh yeah, I think this is what he wants to write.' He paused. 'I think this guy loves his mother.'

Isabel took back the piece of paper, glanced at it, and then put it down on the kitchen table. 'I don't know what to do. I asked him because I'm familiar with his work. He wrote a very well-received book on moral psychology. I reviewed it for those Chicago people, for *Ethics*. I like it.'

'And now he comes up with this?' Jamie shrugged. 'I don't want to be unkind, but I think he might just be an *echt* mother's boy.'

Isabel felt slightly defensive of Professor Trembling. 'You don't know that, do you? He *admires* his mother, which doesn't necessarily make him a mother's boy. Lots of boys admire their mothers, with good reason, but aren't . . . ' She struggled with the criteria for being a mother's boy. Was it a case of simply spending too much time with your mother; did that make you a mother's boy? Or was it something subtler than that? She tried to think of mother's boys she had known, which was not many, although the memory of one came to her now, her second cousin, Billy, who lived in Glasgow with his mother. She had always dominated him, and he seemed to accept the situation, even to enjoy it. He went to university in Glasgow so that he could live at home and after graduation he had gone into his mother's wedding catering business and worked as her assistant. They went on holidays together, on bridge cruises in the Mediterranean, on which the passengers played bridge all day, and for most evenings too. He had brought home a girl-friend once and it was generally believed in the family that his mother had seen her off. Certainly that was the view that Cat had taken. 'That woman,' she had spat out, 'she's wrecking Billy's life. It's awful.'

Isabel had been inclined to agree, although she expressed herself less forcefully than Cat did. She could understand the mother's feelings too. She had been widowed when Billy was six and her son was all she had. Of course she would dread the thought of losing him.

'You have to let go,' she muttered.

'What?' asked Jamie.

'I was thinking of mother's boys. The mothers need to let go.'

'Yes,' said Jamie. 'They do. And so do the sons.'

Isabel thought about this. It was possible that at least some sons wanted to be mother's boys, and their mothers were doing no more than respond to the sons' needs. 'Maybe it's hard for both to let go,' she ventured. 'Can you imagine what it's going to be like letting go of Charlie?'

'We'll do it – when the time comes.'

Isabel looked out of the window. 'Perhaps the process starts earlier than you think. Perhaps it begins when they're more or less Charlie's age. We start letting go when we allow them to take their first unaided steps. And then the next stage is to let them go off to nursery school and listen to other adults, not just us, telling them about the world and about what to do. That's letting go, isn't it?'

Jamie thought for a moment. His heart had given a lurch when they had taken Charlie for his first day at nursery school. They had glanced back through the classroom window and seen him immediately absorbed in some task set him by the teacher. They had expected tears, and clinging perhaps, but there had been none of that. *He's launched*, Jamie had thought. And there would be so many more milestones in the future, each of which involved a form of letting go: the first sleepover at a friend's house, the first unaccompanied trip into town, and then, suddenly, he would go off to do whatever he was going to do with his life and he would no longer be there. That was the day that every parent dreaded.

Jamie looked at Isabel. 'Will you find it hard to let go?'

It took her a while to answer. 'I hope not. I'll put a brave face on it – or I'll try to.'

He was not sure why he said what he said next; the words came out, as important words can sometimes do, unplanned, not thought-through. 'We could have another one. Shall we?'

They had never discussed it, which sometimes happens with issues that lie at the heart of marriage. Isabel had been so thrilled with Charlie, so grateful, that she had not thought about another child, or, if she had thought about it, had suppressed the thought rather quickly.

'You could, couldn't you?'

'Yes,' she said. 'It's late, but not too late.'

'Is that what you want?' he asked.

Her answer was as spontaneous as his. 'No, I mean yes. No, yes is what I meant to say. Yes, Jamie. Yes.' She looked at him. 'If you would, of course.'

'I don't think I've got anything better to do.'

She laughed. 'Oh ...'

He explained himself. 'I mean: I can't think of anything

better to do. Or rather, I can't think of anything I'd like more.'

They were both silent. Isabel felt herself trembling inside; she was aware that something momentous had just happened in her life, but was unsure how she felt about it. She decided that what she felt was elation, but elation was too prosaic a word to describe what had happened to her. She felt that the world had suddenly changed and that the colours about her, the colour of the kitchen walls, the colour of the sky glimpsed through the window, had somehow changed, as music will change key to express a different mood.

She struggled to bring herself back to reality. She did not want to talk about what they had just agreed; the decision was too recent, too fresh, and she did not want to disturb it in case either of them underwent a change of mind. 'But what about Professor Trembling?'

'Tell him no,' said Jamie. 'Tell him that nobody will be interested in his mother. Tell him to get a life.'

She looked at him reproachfully.

He immediately regretted what he had said. 'Sorry,' he said. 'That's unkind. It slipped out.'

'Yes,' she said. She hated the expression *get a life*, which was cruel and dismissive. It was arrogant. She also disliked people saying of others that they should get out a bit more. That had the same tone of condescension to it; the same suggestion that what *I* do is far better than what *you* do. 'And anyway, what exactly does *get a life* mean? He has his life. Are you suggesting that everything about his life is worthless?'

Jamie was contrite. 'I didn't mean that. I wouldn't say that to anybody.' He blushed; he remembered that he had muttered those words only three days earlier, when a particularly fussy conductor in Glasgow had laboured a point, keeping the orchestra for fifteen minutes longer than necessary. The cor anglais player had young children to get back to; several brass players had agreed to go to the pub; a cellist had to visit a sick relative in hospital, and Jamie had his train to catch back to Edinburgh. *Get a life*, Jamie had muttered, and the conductor had overheard, as he looked up sharply in the direction of the woodwind section and the muffled giggles that Jamie's remark had caused.

'I'm not holding you up for no reason at all,' the conductor had said drily. 'If you had played this passage correctly the first time, it would not have been necessary for us to re-examine it.'

One of the clarinettists had half turned towards Jamie. 'Proves your point,' she whispered.

'There is no need for wider discussion,' said the conductor, his reedy voice now slightly raised.

Isabel gazed at Jamie. Of course he did not mean to be disparaging; he was gentle in all his dealings with people, as effortlessly strong men so often are. She had rarely, if ever, heard him raise his voice to anybody and he was incapable, she felt, of any sort of insensitivity.

She was thinking. 'Why don't we see what it's like?'

Jamie shook his head. 'It'll be awful. It'll be extremely embarrassing. He's lost the plot.'

'Do you think so?'

'Yes, I do. What reasonable, down-to-earth person would offer to write something like that?'

Isabel picked up the email. 'I don't think we should dismiss him. I think I'll tell him that the offer was not an unconditional one; that obtaining our approval of the subject was implicit.'

'Oh well,' said Jamie. 'You're the editor, not me.' He, at least, was thinking of their new baby. 'What will we call him? Or her, of course. I think I'd like a girl this time. Would you like that too?'

A shadow passed over her face. 'We can't count on anything. It may not happen.'

'I'll try my best.'

'And I will too.'

He grinned. 'When should we start?' And immediately he answered his own question. 'Now?'

She dropped the piece of paper, which fluttered down to the floor and lay there, upside down. She could afford to be generous to Professor Trembling. We all had our own ways of going through life; we all loved in our own particular way, and an account of the life of one person, a mother, might contain insights into the moral life – which, after all, was what the *Review* was meant to be about. Academic journals did not have to be impersonal or desiccated, even if so many of them were just that. Did it matter one whit whom people loved and admired? It did not, she told herself. She remembered Auden's lines, *When I was a boy I had a pumping engine / Thought it every bit as beautiful as you.* It did not matter. She knew people who loved people they had not even met; that was not unheard of.

I look forward to your paper, Professor Trembling, she thought. *Please send it to me the moment you've finished writing it in your house up at Napa. I await it eagerly. And I hope that you enjoy your time up there and that the weather is kind to you.*

Her response went off, not without some misgiving, but nonetheless giving Professor Trembling due encouragement. That done, she had had the rest of the day to catch up with what she called the 'guilt pile' – difficult correspondence that had been shelved for reply at a later date. Grace was coming in later that morning and would be able to collect Charlie from nursery school, which meant that Isabel had until just after three to devote to work. Grace had just returned from holiday, having spent two weeks with her penfriend in the Netherlands. This woman, to whom Grace had first written when she was a girl of sixteen, had proved exceptionally loyal, and the two had exchanged a monthly letter for decades, sharing holidays with each other every second year. Neither had married, and both had similar working lives: Grace had been housekeeper to Isabel's father and then to Isabel, while Sonja, having started as a chambermaid, had become a deputy housekeeper in the official residence of the Dutch royal family. 'She's very discreet,' said Grace. 'They have to be, of course, but she can still tell me interesting, non-controversial things about those Oranges.' Isabel had been amused by the expression – *those Oranges* – the equivalent of *those Joneses next door*, and yet accurate enough: they were the House of Orange, after all, which made them Oranges in a sense.

She had waited for the interesting facts to be divulged, but Grace had at first said nothing. Isabel prompted her. 'Such as?' quickly adding, 'Of course I don't mean to pry. Oranges are entitled to as much privacy as anybody else.'

'She's called Beatrix,' said Grace, who was ironing one of Jamie's shirts at the time. 'She was the queen over there until a short time ago. Then she handed over. She wasn't toppled, you know; she just said to her son, "That's quite enough – you take over now." And she was entitled to do that, don't you think?'

Isabel felt a momentary irritation. Sometimes Grace imagined that Isabel knew nothing, giving explanations of things that were well within common knowledge. Of course I know that she's called Beatrix, Isabel said to herself. And I know that her mother was called Juliana and that her grandmother was Wilhelmina. I also know that Wilhelmina was one of the first people in the Netherlands to have cosmetic surgery.

54

'Beatrix is Queen Juliana's daughter,' said Isabel testily.

'I know that,' said Grace. 'And the grandmother was Queen Wilhelmina.'

'She had cosmetic surgery,' Isabel continued.

Grace was silent, but Isabel noticed that the iron was passed over Jamie's shirt with more than the usual vigour.

'She had it a short time before her husband died,' said Isabel. 'It gave her a permanent smile.' She paused. 'That was a bit of a problem when the King died and there she was, smiling away.'

Grace lifted the iron off the shirt. 'You mean she was smiling at the King's funeral?'

'So I've read,' said Isabel. 'It goes to show that you should be careful about cosmetic surgery.'

'Couldn't they remove the smile?'

'I'm not sure. I have a vague memory that they did, but I'm not sure. It's one of those things you read and you don't forget, but you forget where you read it and you also forget exactly what you read.'

Grace resumed her ironing. 'Sonja has a very nice photograph of her standing with Queen Beatrix outside their palace. She has a very nice smile.'

'Ah,' said Isabel. 'A natural one, though.'

'She likes coffee,' Grace went on.

'I'm not surprised,' said Isabel. 'The Dutch grew coffee in places like Java. There are still a lot of Dutch names out there, I believe.'

Grace nodded. 'Sonja mentioned Java once,' she said.

Isabel waited for further disclosures, but for a while none came. And she realised, of course, that she should not be interested in royal tittle-tattle, because it tended to be so utterly mundane. And yet it was natural, in a way, to be fascinated by things that are only half revealed. If somebody strives to keep a life private, then it is only natural that we want to find out what it is that is being kept from us. We are naturally inquisitive creatures.

Then Grace let slip another detail. 'She likes to wear orange,' she said. 'Not bright orange, of course, but a rather darker version of it. Sonja says she – that's Queen Beatrix – has some really beautiful shoes that are a sort of deep orange – almost brown, but you can tell that they are orange.'

'Very appropriate,' said Isabel, and left the conversation at that.

Now, having dealt with Professor Trembling and his proposed article on his mother, she made a list of the things that remained to be done that day. Several books had arrived for review, and these would have to be dispatched to their reviewers. Two more, one published by Princeton University Press and the other by Oxford University Press, were perched at the edge of her desk and had yet to be allocated to appropriate reviewers. The thought occurred to her that she could send the Oxford book to somebody in Princeton and the Princeton book to somebody in Oxford. She smiled; of all the systems for dealing with books, that would be the weakest, although she remembered that Alistair Clark, an authority on American history and politics, had shelved the books in his library on a geographical basis: books pertaining to Alaska on the top left-hand shelf, those on the Midwest in the middle, those on Florida on the lowest right-hand shelf, and so on, so that the wall of shelves corresponded with the map of the United States. It was a system that must at least have been easy to remember: an alphabetical system was all very well, but if one were to forget the name of an author who wrote about the history of Texas, then at least one would know on which part of the wall of shelves to look: down on the bottom shelf, towards the middle. A variant, of course, might be a political system of shelving: books by authors of a conservative bent of mind would be placed on the right-hand shelves, and those of a more socialist persuasion on the left. Books by women could be in one section, and those by men in another; books by young authors here, by older authors there; books by those authors who were known to like one another could be placed together, while those by authors who felt animosity towards one another would be kept tactfully apart; the possibilities were endless.

No, the book published by Oxford, *On Good Conduct in a Flawed World*, was by a theologian and would be allocated to her friend Iain Torrance, who could also be asked to review the Princeton book. It touched on issues in which he had an interest and he had until recently been at Princeton himself before returning to Scotland. He would be asked to do the two reviews and she expected him to agree. So that solved that.

She looked at her watch. It was ten o'clock, and she had been in her study for exactly one and a quarter hours. Normally she would remain there for a further three hours; then it would be time for the light lunch that Isabel prepared for herself: a bowl of soup and an open sandwich. There was plenty for her to do during those three hours: proofs to be corrected, the printer's bill to be queried, and her own editorial for the anniversary issue to be written – she already knew what she wanted to say – but now she felt disinclined to spend the morning working. She stood up and walked to her window. She felt restless. *Another baby?* She and Jamie had talked about it so briefly and reached their decision so quickly that an inescapable air of impetuosity hung over it. She did not feel that she had even begun to think through the implications. Her first pregnancy had been relatively uncomplicated, although she had endured, as so many women did, a rather extended period of morning sickness. She could face that, just as she could face the slowness and discomfort she had felt in the last two months before Charlie had arrived; and even the pain of giving birth had been helped by her unusually receptive reaction to the electronic acupuncture device they had given her. She had not expected it to work, but it had, and she had been grateful for it.

None of that worried her. Nor was she worried by the thought of the practical side of having another baby – the constant changes of clothing, the carting about of all the imped-imenta that babies seemed to need, the inevitable sleepless nights. What concerned her was the thought that the family she had become accustomed to – that little group that she and Jamie made up with Charlie – was going to be fundamentally changed. She had not expected to be concerned about that, but she was. She and Jamie had not addressed that in any way, and she thought that they might have done so before embarking on the expansion of their household. As she stood at the window, though, she realised that perhaps there was something else behind her vague disquiet. This was something quite simple: the fear that she was about to do something that could radically change the life she and Jamie had created for themselves. Everything was perfect at the moment – or as close to perfect as might be imagined: she was contented, as was Jamie. But what if he suddenly started to feel oppressed by domesticity, as some men can do? Isabel was aware that some fathers were unsettled by the arrival of a new child; one of her friends had complained that her husband had gone completely off the rails when their child had arrived – had taken to spending long hours in the pub and had even joined a football club. 'Very odd,' her friend had complained. 'To join a football club when you don't even play football is pathetic.' Jamie would never get involved in football, she thought; he would never tackle other players – he would *give* them the ball. That was the way he was; and that was *not* a sign of weakness; rather it was, she felt, a sign of maturity. Weak men need to score goals; strong men can let others score them, if it makes them feel better.

Standing before the window, she put a hand on her stomach. Some people claimed they could sense the moment of conception. That was simply unlikely, attractive though the idea might be. What did they think they felt? A flutter? A sudden internal warmth? It was probably indigestion. And there was implantation to think about too. That took place later than many imagined; one could be shopping in the supermarket, peering into the frozen vegetable cabinets, or looking at the price of a tin of artichokes when suddenly, within one, the results of what had happened days before – in the bedroom rather than in the supermarket – would take place, the tiny journey would be completed, and safe harbour reached; biology was matter-of-fact and was nothing to do with romance. So even now, as she stood in her study, it might be happening . . . No. She thought it unlikely. It would take time; months rather than weeks – if it happened at all.

She looked at her watch again. It would be coffee time at the Enlightenment Institute, or almost, and if she called a taxi right now she could be there in time to join them. The one thing she missed about working in a university was the coffee breaks with colleagues and the conversation that entailed. This was not the elevated conversation that people might imagine academics engaged in, but rather ordinary exchanges about who had said what, the events of the previous weekend, and how expensive the car repair – and everything else – was. That sort of conversation was the natural cement of any group, something that could be called gossip, but was not quite that. We needed it, she thought, because we were lonely without such exchanges. She had no colleagues on the *Review* other than the members of the editorial board, whom she rarely saw, or the printer, who for most of the time was just a voice at the other end of a telephone line. She had met him, though, on at least one occasion; his works were in Fife and he had invited her to go up to Dunfermline to watch the printing of an edition of the *Review*. The printing works had been noisy, and the smell of ink hung in the air, an acrid but not entirely unpleasant miasma. He had been proud of his print-shop, showing her a large German machine that struck her as being the printing equivalent of a combine harvester: text went in at one end and a bound copy of the book or magazine came out at the other. She noticed this pride as they watched the machine churning out copies of the *Review* – it was the same expression that she had seen on Jamie's face when he had brought home his new bassoon. It was a very particular look, she decided: the look of a man who has a new toy – a look that combined wonderment with the simple satisfaction of possession.

'It's so different from the presses I trained on,' the printer said above the clatter of the machinery.

'You used type?'

'Not the actual type you're thinking about – not the metal stuff.' For a moment he looked wistful; printing was no longer the craft it once had been. 'No, but we did have flexible plates that we put on drums. There was a physical side to it that's almost gone now.' His voice lowered, and she barely heard what he had to say next. 'Like the customers too.'

She looked at him.

'Sorry,' he said. 'Not all of them. But so many are having all of this done abroad now. China. We're going to lose all of our skills soon, I fear. We won't be able to print because we won't have any trained printers.'

'Outsourcing?'

He nodded. 'That's what they call it. But it has very bad effects: people are losing the ability to make the things they've always made.'

This reminded her of something. She had read recently that there were virtually no engravers under forty in the country – they simply did not exist. And stone carvers? And watchmakers? And people who could actually repair a car engine rather than just replace the parts?

She sought to reassure him. 'I'm not proposing to take my business anywhere else.' She touched him lightly on the forearm – an oddly intimate gesture in the noisy workplace.

His expression showed his relief. 'I like printing your *Review*.'

'Oh . . . Do you read it?' The question slipped out without her thinking about it.

He looked down at the ground. 'Yes, of course. Well . . . perhaps not all of it, I'm afraid. I don't actually read . . .'

She was embarrassed. *I have put this nice man in a position where he felt he had to claim to read something that he doesn't read.* She reminded herself of what a friend had said about the potential tactlessness of asking others if they had read something: people do not like to confess that they have never read *War and Peace*. 'Do films count?' an anxious friend had once asked her. 'Can I say I've read something if I've seen the film?'

She glanced at the printer. 'It's not everybody's cup of tea,' she said quickly.

This gave him his opportunity. 'On which subject,' he said, 'we have tea waiting for us up in the office.'

Now she glanced at the piles of books and papers on her desk. *There are no chains*, she thought, *except those we create for ourselves.* That, of course, was not entirely true: there were plenty of chains, real or imaginary, that people created for others – or that *desks* created, she thought . . .

5

Isabel had loose links with the Enlightenment Institute. There was a separate department of philosophy at the University of Edinburgh – she had worked there years earlier, and still attended their Friday-afternoon seminars when she could – but recently she had found herself having rather more to do with the small institute tucked away on the edge of the Meadows, the green wedge of park that separated the university area from the acres of stone-built Victorian tenements to the south. Its name, of course, was a nod in the direction of the Scottish Enlightenment of the eighteenth century – the period when Edinburgh had been the intellectual centre of Europe.

She had first become involved with the Institute when she had got to know an Australian philosopher, a visiting fellow whom she had helped in a personal search. The following year Isabel herself had been asked to read a paper at the Institute and had written for this occasion a piece on justice between the generations: 'Do the young *really* have to support the old?' They did, she had argued, although not because the old were old, but because they were people. That had gone down well, even if it had led to a spectacular exchange of divergent views – accompanied by accusations of ageism directed, oddly enough, against one of the older participants by one of the younger ones.

Her connection with the Institute had been strengthened when she heard that Edward and Cheryl Mendelson were to spend the summer there, each working on books that they hoped to finish. They came from New York, where Edward was a professor at Columbia, and from where, as the poet's literary executor, he ran W. H. Auden's affairs. Edward had a book of essays to complete and Cheryl was putting the finishing touches to a study of the history of marriage. It was Isabel's interest in Auden that had first put her in touch with Edward: she had written to him with a query about one of his books and he had responded helpfully. The correspondence had deepened and become quite regular; she very much appreciated his willingness to explain the more obscure poems in the poet's canon.

'What on earth does he mean here?' she asked about these poems. 'Am I missing the point?'

She sometimes was.

'He can be somewhat opaque at times,' sighed Edward. 'But that's part of the charm, I think, and there's always a meaning there. It just might be that the references, shall we say, are not always immediately obvious.'

'He knew so much, didn't he? Theology, science, opera – they're all there in the poems.'

Edward nodded. 'Yes,' he said simply. 'All of that – and much more.'

Edward greeted her as she went up the stairs to the coffee room. 'Cheryl's going to be coming in a bit later,' he said. 'She'll be sorry if she misses you. I hope that you can stay until she comes back.' He hesitated. 'Or perhaps I shouldn't ask you. I know how busy you are.'

'Absolutely everybody's busy,' said Isabel, thinking of the one truly idle friend she had, who always complained of having far too much to do. 'But I'm happy to linger. I'm in denial about the state of my desk.'

'Like so many of us,' said Edward.

She knew that he was being polite; he should have said *you* rather than *us*. 'Not you,' she said. 'I can imagine your desk, and it'll be a paragon of . . . ' She struggled to find the right word. How did one describe the state of being uncluttered? 'Unclutteredness.' She rather liked the idea of a category of people singled out for their tidy desks, unlike those whose desks were piled high with papers. *Desk guilt*, she thought; it could be a useful new term to join all the other available forms of guilt and self-reproach. *Desk guilt, gym guilt, chocolate guilt* . . . It was another case for compound nouns, she thought, although the effort of translating it all into German would be enough to give rise in itself to guilt, or perhaps to *compound noun anxiety*, which would sound so much more credible in German, where the word *Angst* could be tacked on to just about everything. She paused at that: angst was different from guilt, and the distinction should be maintained: one could feel angst about something that one knew one should not feel guilty about: angst had nothing to do – or not necessarily so – with any personal failure.

On the landing at the top of the stairs, Edward glanced in the direction of the coffee room. 'I need to talk to you,' he said, his voice lowered.

'Over coffee?'

Edward shook his head. 'In private. I can go and fetch you a cup of coffee, if you like, but we need to talk in my room.'

Isabel was concerned. 'Is everything all right?'

He assured her it was. 'No, nothing's going wrong as far as we're concerned. Our work is going very well, and we're enjoying ourselves. It's more a question of . . . ' He broke off before continuing, 'Look, I'll join you in my room in a moment – I'll get the coffee. Just wait for me there.'

She knew where his room was – a small study at the end of the sort of meandering corridor that was typical of so many Edinburgh buildings. Cheryl's room was next door, and Isabel had visited them both in their respective offices shortly after they arrived. The door was ajar, and she entered the room and sat down on the armchair near the window. The room overlooked a small, three-sided courtyard; facing east, it was still benefiting from the morning sun. This had a buttery quality to it; it played upon her arms as she waited and she felt its heat, rather like the warm breath of some invisible creature. She looked up at the ceiling, with its elaborate cornice. This followed the Greek key design that had been so popular during Edinburgh's eighteenth-century enthusiasm for all things Greek – when the city's ambition had been to recreate the Parthenon on the Calton Hill and when people began to refer to Edinburgh as the Athens of the North. She smiled at the thought; money had run out after the construction of nothing more than a set of imposing pillars topped by lintels; these remained, a reminder of the perils of civic vanity. In Isabel's view, though, they were just right for the city; a completed Parthenon would have been too much – in bad taste, perhaps, whereas a manifestly uncompleted Parthenon was just right. Failure often had a certain style that success simply did not have.

Edward appeared, bearing two cups of coffee. He handed one to her, and then he crossed the room to take his seat behind the desk. The coffee was piping hot, with small wisps of steam still rising from its surface. Isabel raised the cup to her lips, but put it down without taking a sip. Edward looked apologetic.

'Sorry, it's too hot,' he said. 'Give it a moment.'

Isabel smiled. 'Coffee's getting hotter and hotter, it seems. Global warming, perhaps.'

They laughed.

'You have to be careful,' said Edward. 'In some coffee places you now see warning notices: *Our coffee is served at . . .* and then they give the temperature. I suppose they're worried about being sued.'

'Everybody's worried about that,' said Isabel. 'I was in a shop the other day – just a small place – and there was a large sign on the wall that simply said: *The management is not responsible.* That was all.'

'A general disclaimer,' said Edward.

'Of course one can understand it,' said Isabel. 'We're so obsessed with protecting people from themselves – and protecting ourselves from others while we're about it.' She thought of another example; there were so many once one began to think about it. This time it was Charlie's nursery; they had taken the children to the museum and had sent a letter to the parents telling them that a full risk assessment survey had been carried out, and that this had included psychological risk. She told Edward about this. 'You can just see them – visiting the museum with their clipboards, ticking off each risk one by one. Were there any obviously unsafe electrical installations? Were the stairs the sort of stairs down which children might fall? Were there things that the children might see in the museum that were disturbing and might lead to nightmares?'

Edward laughed as Isabel continued. 'Of course, Scottish history is full of disturbing things. Look at Mary, Queen of Scots – her secretary murdered before her eyes, her husband blown up, or strangled, or whatever it was. Any visitor to a Scottish museum may well come away quite traumatised.'

She stopped herself. Edward had said that there was something he needed to talk to her about – and she had led the conversation into the sixteenth century. It was so easily done, she thought . . .

She tried her coffee again. *The management is not responsible for the coffee.* 'You said there was something?'

Edward nodded. 'I wanted to have a word with you before we went into the common room. There are a couple of visitors this morning. I thought I should let you know.'

'But there always are visitors here, aren't there?'

'Yes, but these are . . . Well, I recall a conversation we had a couple of years ago when I was last here. You know how you can forget vast swathes of experience and then you remember something that somebody said to you on a particular occasion; you remember it in great detail; you remember every word.'

Yes, Isabel thought. She remembered conversations she had had in which nothing notable had been said, but of which every word had been laid down in memory. There had been a conversation with a friend when she was seventeen. They had been for a walk together on Cramond beach and the friend had suddenly said that there were some beaches that were sand and some that were made of crushed shells, and that sometimes it was hard to tell which was which. And then the friend had suddenly changed the subject and said that seaweed was very good for you and that was why the Japanese, who ate a lot of seaweed, she claimed, lived such long lives. 'They go on and on,' she said. It was an odd, inconsequential conversation, but she remembered it word for word.

'Yes,' she said to Edward. 'Sometimes that happens.'

'It was a discussion about having enemies,' said Edward. 'I can't remember how we arrived at that topic, but we did. And then you said to me, "Some people seem to have an awful lot of enemies. They go through life gathering them in the same way as other people acquire friends." And then you said to me that you didn't think you had any enemies – at least not ones you knew about – and then you corrected yourself and said that you did: you had two enemies, although you felt reluctant to call them that because you thought it was wrong to keep a state of enmity alive.'

Isabel made a careless gesture. 'I said all that?'

'Yes, you did – and more.'

She looked amused. 'There's a certain embarrassment in being reminded of what you said. Politicians face it all the time, don't they? They have their words quoted back to them and then they have to work out how what they said can be reinterpreted in an entirely different way.'

'I hope I don't embarrass you,' said Edward. 'But I do remember it all rather well, for some odd reason. I then asked you who your enemies were, and you told me. You said, "There's a Professor Christopher Dove down in London."'

Isabel groaned. 'Oh dear.'

'And then,' Edward continued, 'you said that there was an *éminence grise* behind this Christopher Dove, and he was called Robert Lettuce.'

Isabel made a gesture of defeat. 'Yes, I probably said all that. I feel a bit awkward about it, and they're not *real* enemies in the sense that I don't think much about them, and I doubt if they sit there plotting my downfall, but . . . but I'm wary of them, I suppose. Dove is a slippery piece of work and Lettuce is a great pompous whale. I suppose if I were to continue the marine metaphor, Dove is a shark and Lettuce is a whale, or perhaps a sea lettuce – there is such a thing, you know – it's a sort of seaweed.' She trailed off. 'Why . . . '

'They're in the common room,' said Edward quietly. 'They're here.'

Isabel opened her mouth to say something, but realised that she did not know what to say.

'Yes,' said Edward. 'So I thought I should warn you. It wouldn't do, I think, to go into a room and discover that it was full of one's enemies.'

Isabel struggled with herself. They were not *real* enemies; she liked neither of them, but that did not mean that they were people she would avoid at all cost. 'I'll be able to cope,' she said. 'I appreciate the warning, but I don't mind meeting them again.'

Edward still looked concerned. 'Are you sure?'

She stood up. 'Yes, perfectly sure. Let's take our coffee into the common room.'

'If you wish . . . '

'I think we should.' *We* should; but it was not a matter in which she should involve Edward – the presence of Dove and Lettuce were not an issue for him. 'Or should I say *I* should. I mean . . . ' She stumbled on the words; this was getting complicated. 'That's to say, I can't exactly avoid them, and why should I, after all?'

Edward spoke sympathetically. 'Well then,' he said. 'Let's go.'

As they left the room, she asked him, in a lowered voice, why Dove and Lettuce were there. 'Are they on visiting fellowships?' She assumed that this would be the case, as visiting fellowships were the core of the Institute's work; they were its *raison d'être*.

Edward shrugged. 'I have no idea. Perhaps they are. Or perhaps they know somebody here and have just dropped in. It's a sociable place.' He thought for a moment. 'I didn't see their names on this term's programme. So I think we can assume that this is just a casual visit.'

Isabel felt relieved. 'I know I shouldn't be uncharitable, but I couldn't bear the thought of their being here ... here in Edinburgh for any length of time. I know that's childish. I know. But that's the way I feel.'

They had reached the end of the corridor and their conversation had to end. From the open door of the common room, they heard voices. Somebody said something and there was laughter. Elsewhere in the building a telephone rang.

She took a deep breath. She had no reason to be afraid of either Dove or Lettuce, and she would not allow them to intimidate her. But in her heart she found herself back at school, at the age of fourteen, when there had been a bully a few years her senior who had made her dread going into the refectory at lunchtime because this girl would take a seat near a prospective victim and stare at her. It was done quite subtly; on most occasions nothing was said, the bully relying on the power of the contemptuous glance, the look of amused appraisal. *Look at her hair*, might be the implicit message picked up by others and sniggered over; or *her skin!* There was nothing on which one could put one's finger, but the behaviour was unambiguous. Others laughed, grateful, perhaps, that they were not the target; a few girls tried to resist it, but the bully seemed to have the psychological advantage and triumphed. And then she was knocked off her bicycle by a speeding motorist and was obliged to spend four months in a wheelchair. Suddenly her spell was broken, and she became an object of pity. Somebody wrote on the wall of the toilets: *Serves her right*. No name was given, but they all knew who was being referred to. Isabel thought for a moment that what had happened somehow affirmed that there was some justice somewhere – some force that restored the balance. But then she decided that this was not so; we want there to be such a thing, she told herself, but there isn't. That was one of the earliest instances of the inner philosophical debate that became the background music to her life. She went on to think: but perhaps we *need* to believe in justice; perhaps we *need* to think that people will be served right for what they do, just as we need to believe in free will – even in the face of powerful arguments against it.

Do we ever escape from the fears of childhood, from the little things that worry us or frighten us, from the superstitions and concerns that things will suddenly go wrong and we shall be in trouble? For many, that is what childhood amounts to: *a hive whose honey is fear and worry*. The familiarity of the reference puzzled her as she composed herself for her entry into the common room; our thoughts are not always our own but are framed in the words of others.

She entered the room first, with Edward following her, and for a moment the conversation stopped. She saw the room as one might see a painting, with the models posed in their appointed places, immobile under the painter's gaze. Dove was standing near the window, looking contemplative, a cup and saucer in his hands; Professor Lettuce, seated on a chair near the fireplace, was about to take a bite out of a biscuit, his hand poised before his mouth, but arrested in movement, like a child caught dipping into the biscuit barrel; a young woman in jeans and a loose red top, her hair piled up on her head in an old-fashioned hairstyle that looked like Athene's helmet, was perched on the edge of a couch while a middle-aged man, whom Isabel had seen before on a previous visit, sat next to her, his hands raised as if to emphasise a point he was making.

The conversation faltered. The man on the couch had been saying something but his words trailed off. ' . . . unless anybody could show otherwise, which, of course . . . '

Dove looked round sharply; Professor Lettuce lowered the biscuit.

Isabel seized the advantage that her sudden entrance gave her. She was no longer trembling. This was *her* city; they were in Edinburgh, where *she* lived.

'Well, my goodness,' she said. 'Professor Lettuce and ... and Christopher. What a pleasant surprise.' She tried to sound sincere, but she felt that the irony behind the word *pleasant* had surfaced. Hypocrisy required practice, she thought, and I am short of that. She thought of Charlie: he had been exposed to the Pinocchio story at nursery – a young woman from Italy, working for a few months as an assistant, had told the children about it and he had in turn quizzed Jamie about long noses and lies, all the while clutching his own nose to reassure himself that it had not grown. Had he told lies – already? Very small children did not understand the difference between truth and lies and so when they said things that were untrue these were not real lies; a lie required intent to deceive, and Charlie surely lacked that.

The man on the couch stood up. 'It's Miss Dalhousie, isn't it?'

Isabel looked at him; she remembered now who he was. Edward had explained that there was an acting director, as the last Director of the Institute had left to take up a chair in South Australia. The post was now temporarily held by a man who was about to retire from another department of the University. Isabel had met him, and struggled to remember his name.

'George Herrithew,' he said, sensing her uncertainty. 'We met at that seminar ... the one on ...'

Now she was able to fill in the gap in memory. 'On Schopenhauer.'

'Of course, of course.' He paused, and gestured towards Robert Lettuce. 'You know Professor Lettuce, it seems. And Christopher Dove too.'

Isabel moved towards a vacant chair and sat down. She noticed that Lettuce had shot Dove a glance, an exchange so brief, a message so telegraphed, that it could easily have been missed. Dove had looked away, as if wanting to conceal, or even deny, whatever complicity the glance implied.

'We've met on a number of occasions,' said Isabel. 'Here and in London.' She paused. Lettuce was smiling in a sickly, slightly pained manner, as if he were an Edwardian clergyman being obliged to spend time in the company of somebody vaguely beneath him.

'What brings you to Edinburgh?' she asked.

Again Lettuce looked at Dove, and then lowered his gaze. He did not look at Isabel as he answered. 'A purely social visit,' he said airily. 'We have old friends up here.'

Isabel swallowed. She hated the expression *up here* that people from the South of England sometimes used when talking about Scotland. *Up* had to be up from somewhere – presumably what they regarded as the centre. From her point of view that was *down*, but she did not say *down here* when she was in London.

She tried not to stare at Lettuce's nose. He had a fleshy face and yet the nose succeeded in establishing its salience, rising distinct above the surrounding features, as a mound of rocks will rise above the moraine of a valley. They were not here for a social visit – that was a lie, and his ample nose might rise even further.

'I've said something amusing?'

Lettuce was staring at her, and she realised that her reverie had lasted longer than it should have done and she was smiling.

'No,' she said. 'I was thinking of something else.'

Lettuce pursed his lips. 'Dare I ask what?'

'Who nose,' she said. She could not resist it. Yes, it was

childish to make secret puns, but the irredeemable pomposity of Professor Robert Lettuce seemed to call for it.

Now Dove spoke. 'And the *Review*?' he asked. 'Is it still going strong?'

She turned to face him. Christopher Dove was a tall man who dressed with style and acted with an easy urbanity. He always spoke with a slight sneer in his voice – or so it seemed to Isabel – and he did so now. He was pretending, thought Isabel, that he did not know whether the *Review* was still being published, the implication being that he did not deign to notice it. And yet Isabel remembered that he had a current subscription because she had updated the subscription list only a couple of weeks earlier and had seen his name on it.

She struggled to control herself, and failed. 'But you're a subscriber, Christopher,' she said. 'Is your copy not arriving regularly? I shall start enquiries – the copies are sent off directly from the printer – they offer a service that does all that for the journals they print. I'll check with them tomorrow.'

Dove appeared flustered. 'My secretary,' he muttered. 'I expect that my secretary deals with it and then sends it over to the department.'

Lettuce shot Dove another glance – a different one this time. Isabel interpreted it as saying: *Secretary? You don't have a secretary.* It was a further lie. Two lies in four minutes, and therefore thirty lies an hour, or seven hundred and twenty lies a day – a cascade of lies, or was the collective name for lies a mountain? It was a mountain. In this case, then, it was a Ben Nevis of lies, Ben Nevis being the name of Scotland's highest mountain.

Lettuce cleared his throat. 'I must say I enjoyed your special issue on humanitarian intervention,' he said. 'That strikes me as being a very difficult issue for all of us.' He took a sip of his coffee. 'When do we intervene to stop some dreadful injustice occurring in some foreign country? I find myself very torn on that issue.'

Isabel shrugged. 'When we can get away with it,' she said, and then qualified her answer, 'That is, if your question was purely descriptive rather than normative. If you're asking when we *should* intervene, that's another matter altogether.'

Lettuce looked slightly disapproving. 'That's what I meant. I'm sorry if I didn't make my meaning clear enough.'

'Then I think it's a balancing act,' said Isabel. 'You balance the good you can do in terms of lives saved against the harm you do by destabilising the international order. We can't have people intervening left, right and centre in the affairs of other sovereign states.'

'That's rather interesting,' said George Herrithew. 'I'm a classicist, as you may know, and if you look at the roots of just war theory in ancient philosophy you see that they're rather gung-ho when it comes to justifying war. Aristotle expresses the view that you can wage war to subjugate people whom you think should be governed by you.'

Dove laughed at this – a sneering laugh, thought Isabel. 'Not far off the views of some of our own recent leaders,' he said. 'They may not say that people should be governed by them, but they do say that they should be governed by their system.'

'What about slavery?' asked Edward.

Lettuce looked up at him. 'Would you wage war to free slaves?'

Edward explained politely that this was precisely what the United States – or a large part of the United States – had done. 'We had a civil war over it,' he said.

'A long time ago,' said Lettuce.

'Not so long,' said Edward.

Isabel saw Lettuce's eyes narrow very slightly. 'Of course we fought our own war against that sort of thing,' he said. 'We started in 1939 and fought on until 1945.' He paused. 'For much of that time we were unaided.'

Isabel bristled. Gratitude should not be expressed with a snide qualification. You did not comment on the timing of help, whatever you thought. 'And how grateful we were,' she said. 'For everything.' She directed her gaze at Lettuce. 'The Marshall Plan, for instance.'

A mischievous smile flickered about Lettuce's mouth. 'Of course, I was talking about the Soviet Union,' he said airily. 'Our Russian friends go on about their Great Patriotic War, as they call it, but they omit to mention the non-aggression pact with the late Adolf Hitler, and their somewhat tardy arrival at the party.'

Lettuce reached for another biscuit. 'Oh well,' he said. 'Nobody's perfect. For my part, I can't resist shortbread. One of the things that you Scots invented. The greatest, perhaps.'

'Along with television, economics, and so on,' said Isabel.

Lettuce seemed to pay no attention. He had selected his piece of shortbread and was eyeing it enthusiastically. Isabel was conscious of Edward's looking at his watch. 'Yes,' she said. 'I must dash too.'

Lettuce gave her an unctuous smile. 'So nice to see you, Miss Dalhousie, even if so briefly.'

'Yes,' she said. 'And I hope you enjoy the rest of your visit.'

Dove inclined his head gravely. 'We shall,' he said. 'And perhaps you'll come down to London to give a lecture some time. If we can lure you that far south.'

Lettuce took up the suggestion. 'That would be most enjoyable,' he said. 'I'm on the board of the British Institute of Philosophy, as it happens, and we have a lecture series. I'm sure that I could squeeze you in somehow.'

'I wouldn't want to squeeze anybody out,' said Isabel.

'Oh, that won't be necessary,' said Lettuce. 'We could use one of the smaller rooms for your lecture. I'm sure it would be adequate.'

The implications of this remark only struck Isabel several minutes later as she started to walk back across the Meadows. She stopped in her tracks, standing still for a moment while a wave of indignation passed over her. *That great slug,* she thought. *That great, self-satisfied, condescending slug.* The mere thought improved her mood considerably. But then, as she crossed the road that divided the slowly rising Bruntsfield Links from the flat expanses of the rest of the park, she started to dwell on possible reasons for the presence of Dove and Lettuce in Edinburgh. They had some ulterior purpose; that was obvious enough, but they had not disclosed what that purpose was. That meant that they thought she would not approve, and in that respect they were quite right. Whatever they were planning to do will not suit me, she thought. And with that, her mind drifted away from the unpleasant subject of Dove and Lettuce and their schemes; she had noticed two dogs careering around on the grass. Their joy was unmistakable as they leapt up and barked, chasing each other in the tight circles that dogs delight in describing. The sight immediately lifted her spirits. Dove and Lettuce were minor irritations in the face of all that was positive about being there, at that particular spot, in a city so heart-breakingly beautiful, with those dogs cavorting with sheer delight. That was what counted, she told herself: those unexpected moments of appreciation, unanticipated glimpses of beauty or kindness – any of the things that attached us to this world, that made us forget, even for a moment, its pain and its transience.

6

Sam arranged the meeting that took place that afternoon. Isabel had suggested that they meet at Cat's delicatessen, where there were several tables at which coffee was served and where they could talk without being overheard. Eddie would put a *Reserved* sign on one of them as the delicatessen could be busy at that end of the afternoon.

'I won't stay,' Sam said. 'I'll introduce you, but I won't stay.'

Isabel reassured her friend that she did not mind, but Sam was adamant.

'Kirsten's a shy woman,' she said. 'My presence will only make it hard for her to talk.'

They agreed on a time, and Sam consulted Kirsten about it. This suited the other woman; her son, she said, would be at soccer practice after school today, which would give them over an hour.

Isabel had not seen Cat since her return from Paris that morning, and so she made a point of arriving at the delicatessen ten minutes before the agreed time. But when she arrived she saw that Sam was already there, seated at the table with a woman who was obviously Kirsten. Cat was busy with a customer, and so she merely waved to Isabel across the counter, mouthing the words: *Later on*. She seemed cheerful, and Isabel thought: *Paris*. Also behind the counter, where he was slicing a large Parma ham, was Eddie who caught Isabel's eye and smiled. Isabel returned the smile; Eddie was sensitive to Cat's mood and cheerfulness on her part always lifted his own spirits markedly.

At the table, Sam made the introductions. Isabel shook hands with Kirsten and made a quick appraisal of the other woman. Her first impressions were favourable: Kirsten had the expression of one who is prepared to like those whom she meets – an openness that encouraged warmth. Isabel guessed at her age – a bit younger than she herself was, perhaps early thirties. She noticed the rings on her left index finger: a flash of light from a tiny diamond, and a yellow wedding ring; and her clothing, too – a pair of jeans that was functional rather than fashionable, and a casual fleecy top still kept zipped up.

Eddie, who had finished with the Parma ham, came over to the table and took an order for coffee from Isabel and tea from Kirsten: Sam said that she could not stay, as she had to get to the supermarket. Her excuses given, she turned to Kirsten and asked her whether she minded. 'I just have to get things in for this evening,' she said. 'I have people coming for dinner and there isn't a scrap of food in the house.'

'No,' said Kirsten. 'I don't mind. I often leave things to the last moment.'

Isabel had difficulty placing the accent. It was not Glasgow or Edinburgh, but came from somewhere further north, she thought – somewhere like Inverness.

'Then I'm going to dash,' said Sam, rising to her feet.

Isabel thought this rather abrupt but it did not seem to bother Kirsten.

'She's so busy,' she said as Sam made her way to the door. 'She puts me to shame.'

'You have a young son,' said Isabel. 'I know how much work that entails.'

Kirsten nodded. 'And you do too. Sam told me. A wee boy?'

'Yes. He's with my housekeep—' She stopped herself. She knew that their worlds were different, and she did not want to mention Grace. Yet she could not lie. 'With the woman who helps me in the house.'

Kirsten nodded. 'Harry – that's my son – is at soccer practice. He loves it. He comes back covered in mud and cuts on his knees and so on, but that's what they're like, aren't they?'

Isabel laughed. 'Yes, they are. Boys are highly efficient magnets for dirt. And children in general are walking reservoirs of infection – every cold in circulation seeks them out so they can pass it on at school. Ask any parent about that.' She paused. The ice, such as it was, had been broken and she did not want to prolong the small talk. 'Sam told me about you and Harry,' she continued. 'She told me how worried you were.'

Something in Kirsten's demeanour changed. Now Isabel noticed tension around her eyes and mouth – a guardedness.

'I find it hard to talk about it,' Kirsten muttered. 'I know I shouldn't, and that keeping it all to myself just makes it more difficult, but . . . '

Isabel reached out instinctively, placing her hand on the other woman's. She kept it there for a moment, and then withdrew it. 'But you mustn't feel that way,' she said. 'I'm very happy to listen.'

Kirsten looked up, and their eyes met. 'I'm sorry,' said Kirsten. 'I'll tell you. But it's . . . it's not easy.'

Isabel waited.

'It's because I'm a bit embarrassed,' Kirsten went on. 'It's that too. I've never had any time for this sort of thing. Never. Superstition. Rubbish.'

Isabel encouraged her. 'Many people would agree with you,' she said.

'But not everyone.'

'No, not everyone.'

Kirsten sighed. 'I don't want my wee boy to grow up ... to grow up *mental*.'

Isabel was taken aback. *Mental* was a word used so casually to cover so many things – odd or aggressive behaviour. It was a word that had associations for her of pain, of rage, as well as of the despair that such things brought. 'Oh, I'm sure there's no question of that.'

'You've never met him,' said Kirsten flatly. 'You don't know—' She stopped herself. 'I'm sorry, I didn't mean to be rude.

'Mental,' she said again, and shook her head ruefully. 'That's why ... It's because I was trying to convince myself that he was all right that I wanted to find out whether there might be anything in it. I thought we could show him. That's why I wanted to talk to somebody who might be able to help me to do that. I couldn't do it myself ... '

Isabel stared at her. It had just dawned on her that the role anticipated for her was not just somebody to listen, but somebody to do something. 'So you don't just want to talk about it? You want me to find out for you whether there's any truth in this? Is that it?'

Kirsten seemed unabashed. 'She said you would.'

'Who?'

'Sam said you'd help me. She said that this is what you did. You helped people.' She paused, and then added rather lamely, 'She said that you had a reputation for it.'

Isabel had been toying with her tea. Now she lifted her cup and drained it; it had cooled down enough. Over the rim of the cup she saw Eddie looking in her direction. He appeared anxious; he had rescued her before when she had been trapped by somebody. She shook her head slightly, and he looked away.

Isabel made an effort. She felt slightly irritated that Sam had presumed on their friendship, but that was not Kirsten's fault. She would not reveal her irritation to this woman who so clearly needed her help. At the most, she allowed herself an entirely internal sigh – a sigh that expressed resignation. She knew what Jamie would think, even if he did not say it: *Isabel, please think before you commit yourself to everybody else's problems. Just think.* But Jamie had not been asked to help – she had – and that was the difference.

'All right,' she said. 'Tell me about it.'

Kirsten said: 'I should tell you that I'm mainly by myself. I'm married, and my husband is in the Army – he's a pipe major in one of their bands. It's an odd job – he goes all over the place with the band – military tattoos, ceremonies, all that sort of thing. He's a good man at heart, but he was spending a lot of time away and we somehow drifted apart. It just happened.

'We were living in Army quarters up near Redford Barracks, but my aunt went into a home and her flat down here was empty. We were lucky she had it: Morningside is getting really expensive – everywhere is – and I could never afford to buy a place like that myself. She'd been there for ever – her husband bought it for five hundred pounds years and years ago. Five hundred pounds! For a flat!

'Anyway, me and the boy, we moved in and I got a part-time job when I got him a place in a crèche. I got a job as a

82

receptionist in an optician's business. I like it. I help people choose frames while they are waiting for their appointment. I met people that way.' She paused before adding, with a wry smile, 'You should see some of the frames they choose. You wouldn't believe it.'

'Oh, I think I would,' said Isabel. 'Never underestimate the bad taste of the public.'

Kirsten smiled again. 'So that's me. Then there's Harry.'

She fixed Isabel with a gaze that revealed her pride.

'He's a great wee boy. Everybody likes him, and he's a great one for his soccer. They said at the school that he was the best little player they've had for years. And his work, too – they say that his reading is coming along really well and that he's the most advanced in his class.'

Isabel smiled. 'You must be very proud of him.'

'I am. Yes, I am. Very proud. And that ...' She hesitated.

'Yes?'

'And that's what made it so difficult when he started going on about all this.' Her face clouded with distaste. 'This previous-life stuff. This nonsense about having lived somewhere else first, having had another family.

'You see, it started suddenly. He just said to me one day, "You know I used to live somewhere else." I didn't pay much attention, but he brought it up again. This time he said, "I used to live in a house near the sea. We could see hills from it – hills on an island. And there was a lighthouse. And a burn just behind the house."'

Isabel nodded. A burn was a small Scottish stream; a house in that part of the world might well be close to a burn, for its water supply. 'It sounds as if he had a very clear idea of wherever it was.'

'Yes. And he gave me even more detail. He spoke about

having a brother. And then he spoke about his other mother. That was hard for me to take. *His other mother.* I'm his mother.' She paused before continuing. 'He even had a name for them. He said they were called Campbell.'

Isabel was silent.

Kirsten looked apologetic. 'Sorry to go on. This is probably boring you.'

'No, it certainly isn't. Not at all.'

'I thought that this was just a bit of childish nonsense – you know how they make things up. I thought he would forget about it in a couple of days, but no, it went on. He spoke about it every day – every single day – and he still does.'

'That can't have been easy.'

'It wasn't. I went to speak to people at the school and they put me in touch with some sort of counsellor. I don't know who she was. I didn't like her much, I'm afraid. She said it would pass, but it didn't, and so I went back to see them and this time they told me to go to my doctor. I did that, and he arranged for us to go to the Sick Kids' Hospital to see one of the doctors there.

'We went, and I saw this doctor called MacDonald. She's a child psychiatrist. She was very kind and she spoke to Harry on several occasions, sometimes with me there, sometimes by himself. At the end she called me in and told me that in her opinion there was nothing wrong with him. She said that children have fantasies and these fantasies are usually forgotten about when they get interested in something new. She said that they made up all sorts of things and if we paid too much attention to them, then they sometimes used them as a sort of weapon against us. I think that she meant that they would use them to get their own way because they knew we got all hot and bothered about them.'

Kirsten sat back in her chair. She had been tense while telling the story; now the tension seemed to abate.

Isabel waited for a few moments before speaking. She was wondering how she could possibly add anything to what the psychiatrist had said. 'She's probably right,' she said. 'This Dr MacDonald will know what she's talking about. Perhaps you should do as she says – just ignore it for a while.'

The suggestion made Kirsten lean forward in her chair. The tension returned. 'I can't,' she said, her voice rising. 'Because he's said something else. There's another thing altogether.'

Isabel felt a surge of despondency. This other thing would be dark. Abuse?

Kirsten now lowered her voice to not much above a whisper. 'A couple of weeks ago he started talking about going back. He said that he wanted to go back to this other family and see them. He said that they would be wondering where he was – what had happened to him.

'I asked him how he would do that, and he said that he thought that if he died he would go back. Then he could come back to me a bit later.'

Isabel caught her breath. 'Oh . . . '

Kirsten's voice became uneven; she was now close to tears. 'I said that it would be a long time before he was dead, but he just looked at me and said, "Not if I make myself dead."'

Isabel closed her eyes. 'Oh no.'

'He said it again later that day. I told him that he should never talk like that, but he just clammed up and said nothing. I was pretty upset – obviously – and went to see my GP. He called the social work people and we had a psychiatric social worker come round. She spent almost an hour with Harry and then she said to me that children said things they didn't mean. But she said that I should keep an eye on him, and that I should call her if he started behaving oddly. And that was it. That's all she suggested.'

Isabel waited until she was sure that Kirsten had finished. What Harry had said amounted to a threat of suicide. It was childishly put, of course, but that was what it amounted to. Did children that young actually kill themselves? She was not sure. Teenagers did; one read about it in the newspapers. There had been a recent case, now that she thought about it – a case that involved, as many of these cases did, bullying. Would a child as young as Harry intentionally do something like that? It was an appalling prospect, and an unlikely one, but he had said he could 'make himself dead'. No mother, no adult, could ignore a comment like that.

She leaned forward. It was clear that Kirsten had been given a hearing by various people, but she clearly felt that nobody had *really* listened. 'I can imagine how worried that made you. I can understand how you feel. But I'm not at all sure ... ' She intended to go on to say that it was hard to see how she could help. This was a psychiatric matter, and a delicate one at that; it was not territory for amateurs, even for amateurs who had been explicitly asked for help.

Kirsten interrupted her. 'I've had an idea,' she said. 'Can I tell you about it? If I could find this place he's talking about, or even somewhere like it, we could take him there and show him. It could put a stop to all this, and in particular to this awful talk about going back.'

Isabel thought about this. It was possible, she supposed, but if the place was a figment of his imagination, as she was sure it was, then she doubted whether there was anything that could be done.

She voiced her doubts. 'But this place probably doesn't exist. There won't be any family of Campbells. And then?'

'It would distract him,' said Kirsten quickly. 'If we told him we were looking, then he would think that something was being done. He'd stop talking about going back if there was some sort of plan to take him back there.' She hesitated. 'I can't do it myself. I don't know where to start.' And then, 'I left school at sixteen, Miss Dalhousie . . .'

'Isabel.'

'I left school way back then, Isabel. I'm nothing special. I just don't know where to begin.'

Isabel shook her head. 'I have grave doubts.'

'Please,' said Kirsten. 'Please help me. I couldn't bear it if I lost him. I couldn't.' The words came to her slowly, each chiselled out with pain.

Isabel looked into her eyes. She saw the tears. She said, 'Yes.'

7

When she returned home, Grace greeted her with one of her reproving looks. These came in three grades of seriousness, according to the level of offence given. The look that afternoon was strong enough to register, but only just. Isabel looked at her watch. When Sam had, at short notice, suggested the meeting with Kirsten, Isabel had asked Grace to stay on for a few minutes after collecting Charlie from nursery. Grace had agreed, but had mentioned that she did not want to be too late; she had something on that evening and wanted to be home in good time.

'Fifteen minutes late,' she said. 'I'm sorry. I was tied up with someone at Cat's. It was difficult to get away.'

Grace struggled with herself. She could show her displeasure at Isabel's lateness by being tight-lipped, or she could satisfy her natural curiosity and find out what the delay had been at the delicatessen. Isabel noticed the struggle, and knew exactly what it was about. She understood Grace rather more than Grace imagined; and Grace understood Isabel rather more than Isabel imagined.

'That's all right,' Grace said. 'I know how time flies when you're talking to somebody.' There was the briefest of pauses. 'A friend?'

Isabel suppressed a smile. 'Not really. Somebody I've just met, in fact.'

They were standing in the kitchen. Grace reached to pick up a dishtowel and attend to a spot on the surface of the cooker. 'A friend of Cat's?' she asked, with elaborate casualness.

Isabel decided against a game of cat and mouse. 'Tell me something, Grace: you're the expert in these things, I think. What are your views on reincarnation? I was talking to this person about it, you see, and I wondered what you thought.'

Grace was an enthusiastic member of a spiritualist group and kept Isabel informed of their lectures and séances. The group met at the Edinburgh College of Parapsychology. Reincarnation, Isabel imagined, would be precisely the sort of subject in which Grace might have an interest.

Grace abandoned her polishing of the cooker. 'That,' she said, 'is very important. It's a big subject.'

'But do you believe in it? Personally?'

'I do,' said Grace. 'Though not everybody in the movement is attached to the idea. No: some are of quite the opposite view. I've heard them.'

'But you're satisfied that we ... that we come back.'

Grace turned to look out of the window. Isabel had noticed how, when she wanted to make a particular point, she would turn away from her, as if addressing some imaginary, larger audience.

'Most, no, I'd say all spiritualists,' she said, 'believe that when you die you move into the astral realm. You spend an indeterminate time there – maybe years – and then you may come back as another person. It depends on whether you're ready.'

The doctrine was stated as if it were a rule, rather like a rule of a golf club, or a game: *Members should not spend too long on the green after sinking the ball, in order to allow other members to play through.* Or, *Passing Go you are allowed another shake of the dice.* The difference, though, was how did the proponents of the rule *know*?

That was the trouble with any theory about the world – or about the next world, for that matter: people claimed to know things they could never prove.

'How do you know that?' Isabel asked the question before she had time to think about it, and she was immediately concerned that Grace would regard this as an attempt to undermine her. But Grace did not. She turned to look at Isabel again. 'It's not me who found it out,' she said. 'I didn't invent it, I can assure you. No, this comes from people who have experienced these things.' She now took on the expression of one explaining the elementary, the obvious. 'That is where we get all our knowledge of the higher sphere.'

'I see,' said Isabel.

'In my view,' Grace continued, 'we are allocated the next life on the basis of merit. What you do in this life is taken into account in the allocation of future existences. I'm sure that it's all done very fairly.'

Isabel thought of the bureaucratic implications. And it did sound like a bureaucracy to her – rather like the system of allocating social housing, where points were awarded on various criteria. She wondered whether there could be any appeal; if there were, then the appeal would have to be made well in advance of the actual reincarnation, and presumably in writing. Once that happened, there would be no going back.

Grace suddenly looked reproving. 'You may laugh,' she said. 'I know you think this is all nonsense.'

Isabel shook her head. 'I'm not laughing, Grace. I promise you. I may be sceptical, yes, but that's not the same thing as laughing.'

'Scepticism is all very well,' intoned Grace. 'But where does it get you?'

Isabel was about to answer 'Everywhere', but then she realised that there was some truth in what Grace had said. Scepticism had its place, but we should not lose sight of the possibilities that some beliefs were both necessary and beneficial, a belief in human goodness being a prime example of this. There were plenty of grounds to doubt human goodness, but if one ceased to believe in it then we would lose the comfort of trust. And people needed their scraps of comfort in this world if they were to be able to deal with hardship and disappointment.

'I don't think you have an open mind,' Grace went on, looking pained. 'I'm not being critical, but I really don't think you do.'

Isabel apologised. 'You're right. I haven't been open about this.'

'And the fact of the matter,' Grace said, 'is that a very large number of people believe in reincarnation. Hindus do, for instance, but not just them. So when you think that *you're* right and that everybody will agree with you, you may actually be in a minority. *You* may be the one who's out of step.'

Isabel held up her hands. 'I know, I know.'

'May I ask you something?' Grace went on. 'This person you were discussing reincarnation with – has she lost somebody?'

'Why do you ask?'

'Because it's often when something like that happens that people take an interest in these things. Look at the people who turn up for the first time at one of our meetings – as often as not it's because they've lost somebody very important to them – a husband, a parent, somebody like that. And suddenly they realise that the answers they get from the usual people are empty. Grief counsellors and so on. What do they say? You'll get over it. Cherish the memories. But do you think that helps people? I can give you the answer to that: it does not.'

Isabel listened carefully. 'Yes,' she said. 'I know what you mean. But there's such a thing as false comfort, isn't there? It's like telling people that something isn't going to hurt when you know very well that it will. Or telling them that something will turn out right when you know that it's going to be disastrous. Does false comfort help?'

She had not expected Grace's answer. 'Yes, it probably does. And what's wrong with it?'

'But it means that you aren't going to be prepared for the inevitable.'

Grace was clearly tiring of the philosophical drift of the conversation. 'Oh well,' she shrugged. 'We each have our views. But going back to this person you were talking to: had she – or he – lost somebody?'

'No,' said Isabel. 'It was a woman who has a small boy. He's been talking about having had another life. Children do, apparently.'

'Oh they do ...' Grace trailed off. 'A woman here in Edinburgh?'

'Yes. She lives in Morningside.'

Grace was frowning. 'And the little boy? What's his name.'

'Harry. He's six, I believe.'

Grace gasped. 'I know who that woman is. I've met her. She came to one of our meetings. She spoke about it.'

Isabel was silent. Kirsten had said nothing about that. She had mentioned the counsellors and the psychiatrist, but she had said nothing about the College of Parapsychology, presumably from embarrassment.

Grace continued with her explanation. 'You see, we had a session on reincarnation. It was a lecture given by somebody who came up from London. And then we had a medium who was interested in it – a woman from Glasgow – and people were invited to ask the spirit world about this. Some people wanted to know whether one of their loved ones had come back. They wanted guidance.'

'I see. And this woman? What did she want?'

'She told us about her son, and then she said she wanted to find out whether anyone on the other side knew anything about it. She asked whether they knew the place he was talking about and whether there were any members of the family over there.'

'What family?' asked Isabel.

'The family he lived with. They were called Cameron, or something like that.'

'Campbell.'

'That's it,' exclaimed Grace, as if this were further confirmation of the medium's ability. 'She said they were called Campbell.'

'And what happened? Did anybody come through from spirit?' Isabel had picked up the terminology from Grace and knew how to use it.

'Yes,' said Grace. 'There was a very helpful presence in spirit. It was a man who had drowned in the sea off one of the islands over there. He said he knew those Campbells and that there were members of their family on the spirit side. He said that what the boy claimed was true. He had lived before and he should not be scolded for talking about it.'

In spite of herself, Isabel found herself wanting more. 'Did they say where it was?'

'They just said it was over on the west coast. I think Argyll was mentioned.'

'But Argyll is large. They didn't say anything more?'

'No. Maybe she said something about the island of Mull. Maybe. I can't remember everything that was said – these occasions are quite emotional, you know.'

Argyll ... Mull: that, thought Isabel, was the trouble with the world of spirit: it was very inexact; they hinted darkly, but could never be pinned down. *But which horse, exactly, will win the race this afternoon?* It was the same with astrologers. They never said: you will receive a telephone call at 12.04, or you will meet a man called William next Tuesday at a party given by your friend Jane. It was more a case of: you'll be getting news, or you'll be meeting somebody – vague predictions that would almost always be true, except for those whose lives involved no news or meetings. And anybody could make such vague predictions that would lend themselves to all sorts of interpretations. The quatrains of Nostradamus could be read any way you wanted, as could his Scottish equivalent, the Brahan Seer, who, unlike Nostradamus, took a very local view. He predicted things like the fall of a particular boulder, or a very local death, and did not say much about the Second World War or nuclear power. He did, however, foresee power lines crossing hillsides as well as motor vehicles and trains, although that might have been wishful thinking, Isabel reflected; if one lived in an age in which the main way of getting about was on horseback, then it would be only too understandable if one were to say, 'I wish there were such a thing as the car.' And that wish could easily be couched as a prophecy that there *will be* cars. The idea created the reality: that was a major issue in philosophy, not just in the world of prophets and casters of horoscopes.

Grace had to leave. Her cousin from Stirling was coming

94

into town and they were going shopping. 'She doesn't need anything,' she said. 'But it's an outing.'

'A great deal of shopping is not about need,' remarked Isabel. 'Needs, perhaps, but not need.'

Grace looked at her sideways, but simply said, 'Well, I'm going anyway.'

After saying goodbye to Grace, Isabel went upstairs to check up on Charlie, who was having his afternoon rest. Nursery was exhausting, she had discovered, and he usually came home tired out by all the social interaction and creative play it entailed. The afternoon rest – as sacred as a siesta to an Italian – restored him for the serious play of the late afternoon: the construction sets; the toy fort that, ever since its purchase, had been under unremitting siege from small plastic opponents; the battery-powered digger with the tiny flashing light, of which he was so inordinately proud. All of these would be in full service until Jamie gave him what he called his music lesson – a half hour of banging on drums and picking out on the piano of 'Twinkle, twinkle, little star' and the like.

Now Charlie lay on the top of his bed, still deep in sleep, a copy of *The Adventures of Babar* open on his chest. Isabel gazed at him for a full minute, allowing herself to be enveloped in fondness and pride. *This little boy is my creation.* That was the essential miracle of motherhood: creation. In having a child you created another centre of consciousness, which meant, in fact, another world. It was that simple fact that was so astounding. It was one thing to create some object in the external world: to build a house or make a piece of furniture; or even, perhaps, to write a symphony or a poem; but admirable though such achievements might be, they were nothing compared with the making of a life.

She stepped forward and gently moved the open book off

him. As she did so, her hand touched his chest lightly, and she felt the movement of his breathing. That was another miracle: that tiny pump that was his heart, destined, if he was lucky, to beat without stop for decades, to see him through whatever it was that he was going to go through: joy, sorrow, love, disappointment, anxiety, triumph – all the things that made up our lives.

He stirred, but it was only a stirring in sleep: it would be another fifteen or twenty minutes before they would hear him wake up. There would be the whirring of the digger or the sounds of some awful crisis at the fort: the cries of plastic people being knocked over by a plastic projectile. How perilous was the plastic life, and yet they did not give up: the plastic hearts on both sides were brave.

She went downstairs and switched on the kettle for a cup of tea. Isabel allowed herself two cups of coffee a day, but could drink as much tea as she liked. Now, standing at the kitchen counter waiting for the kettle to boil, she was reminded of the fact that she had not been able to exchange more than a couple of words with Cat when she had been at the delicatessen. Cat had been busy when Isabel arrived and had gone out on some errand when the time came for her to leave. Her niece's cheerfulness pleased her; Cat could be difficult at times, but was engaging company when she was in the right mood. That depended, Isabel had discovered, on what was happening in her far-from-simple love life. Mick was evidently a good choice.

Isabel made up her mind quite quickly. It had been a rather extraordinary day, with its meeting with Christopher Dove and Professor Lettuce, and then the unsettling conversation with Kirsten. Jamie liked impromptu social occasions, just as she did, and if Cat and Mick had nothing better to do . . .

She dialled Cat's mobile number from the phone in the kitchen.

'Can you talk?' Isabel always began that way when she dialled a mobile number. People could be doing all sorts of things when they answered their mobile – one never knew.

Cat sounded breezy. 'Natch.'

Isabel thought: does anyone still say *natch*? Clearly at least one person did. But then Cat also said *fab* from time to time, when everyone else was saying *cool* or even *wicked*, which was good, although good itself had become *bad*.

'I'm sorry I didn't have the chance to speak to you earlier on. I was with somebody, as you saw.'

'No worries.'

'I wanted to—'

She was interrupted by Cat. 'I should have come over and thanked you for Saturday. I hear you were kept pretty busy.'

'Yes, we were,' said Isabel. 'But I was happy to do it. Any time. But what I was phoning about was this: dinner. I know it's no notice, but if you and your friend are free this evening, why not come round? Kitchen supper. I've got a casserole in the freezer.'

There was a brief silence at the other end of the line before Cat said, 'Okay. But one thing: Mick's vegetarian. Is that all right?'

Isabel assured her that would present no problem. She almost said 'No worries' but did not. Instead she said, 'Quiche. I'll do a quiche instead. We all like that.'

'Mick loves quiche.'

'I'm so glad.' *A ridiculous thing to say*, she thought. It was as if loving quiche was an indication of character, or attitude. Perhaps it was: had there not been some discussion about whether real men liked quiche? Was it a sign that one was a *new man* if one ate quiche? Was quiche the bellwether for all sorts of things?

They agreed the time and rang off. Mick, thought Isabel. Mick. Mick? Michaels were more often Mike than Mick. Micky sounded almost juvenile; it was also a good name for a pugilist or a jockey perhaps, because of its jaunty, confident feel. And yet she knew that there was no reason to imagine that a person's name would reflect his character; if we chose our names, then they might say something about us, but our names were the one thing that generally we had no hand in choosing.

No sooner had she thought this than she realised that, as with most conclusions about anything, there were exceptions. There were cases where people did make a choice about the name by which they chose to be known. She knew a number of people who had done just that; who had two given names and who had chosen to abandon the first of these in favour of the second. On her mother's side of the family there had been her much younger cousin Eugenia Dawn Martin, whose parents had intended her to be Eugenia first and foremost, but who opted at the age of fifteen for Dawn. Teasing by other children had ensured that: Eugenia? Nobody's called Eugenia. Jeanie, perhaps, but not Eugenia. Isabel had understood; she liked the name Eugenia, but imagined that Eugenias themselves might have qualms about the old-fashioned sound to it. Some names just had the feel that they had had their day. It was the same with Ruby; that sounded old-fashioned, although it was a warm name, a friendly name, and she hoped that it would become popular again.

She had friends, too, who as adults had changed their name altogether because they felt that the name they had used up to that point did not reflect the way they wanted others to think of them. An unwanted shortening might be abandoned, as had been the case with a boy she had known in childhood as

Chuck. This name had seen him through university and into his profession, but when he had become a partner in a staid firm of Edinburgh lawyers he had suddenly become George. He had sent out a note to his friends and acquaintances: 'I hope you don't mind my telling you,' he wrote, 'that I have chosen to be called George rather than Chuck. My initials, of course, remain the same: CGM.' Most people assumed that the G stood for George, but Isabel knew that it was, in fact, Geoffrey. The *George* came from nowhere, it seemed; it was an act of self-definition – or professional self-preservation, perhaps: would the staid clients whom she imagined the staid firm had want to entrust their affairs to a lawyer called Chuck?

'Would you be happy with a lawyer called Chuck?' she had asked Jamie.

He had been surprised that the question even needed to be asked.

'Of course. Not that I even have a lawyer.'

'But if you had to get one?'

Jamie shrugged. 'Chuck would do fine.' He thought for a moment. 'But I might feel uncomfortable going to a dentist called Dr de Sade.'

Isabel laughed. 'Poor Dr de Sade would have so few patients, and would wonder why. *My practice advertises pain-free dentistry, but somehow we get nowhere . . .* '

She made her tea, and sat down to read the paper. But she could not concentrate on the content. It was a short step from thinking about the choosing of names to thinking about babies. What if she had a girl? No forts, no diggers, and the plastic people would have romances and intrigues rather than battles. There would be dolls, who would have tumultuous inner lives, as dolls owned by little girls seemed to have. They were always waiting for telephone calls from other dolls and planning tea parties. Isabel smiled. She and Jamie would not encourage such stereotypes, although stereotypes were such fun to think about – almost seditiously – and were, one had to admit, so very often completely true. Yes, girls liked dolls and boys liked toy trucks. They just did. It was nothing to do with the toys their parents gave them. You could give boys dolls for every birthday, but that would only break their hearts, and they would acquire toy trucks clandestinely. A life of crime might be launched in that way – unwittingly – by parents who meant well.

She finished her cup of tea and set aside the newspaper, with its uncompleted crossword. She had tried, but was not in the mood to pit her wits against the *Scotsman's* compiler, even if the clue *If slipped a drink by this apparent Scandinavian, don't touch it! (6,4)* had leapt to the eye and resulted in her pencilling in *Mickey Finn*.

That had reminded her, of course, that she would be meeting Mick that evening and that she needed to make an effort to like him. She had to like him; or she had to at least try to like him. Cat had had such terrible boyfriends in the past, but Isabel felt that it was her moral duty to approach each of them with an open mind. To do otherwise, to decide against them in advance, was to judge people whom she had never met, and she knew she should not do that. And quite apart from any moral considerations, the law of probability surely dictated that sooner or later Cat would come up with somebody to whom objection would not be taken. Perhaps it was Mick. Perhaps. She looked at her dishwasher. *I shall not associate him with dishwashers*, she told herself. *I shall not. I shall not.* She knew that these associations did not help; she had made a similar mistake with Cat's Toby – condemned for his crushed-strawberry trousers – and she would avoid doing the same thing with Mick.

'Cat's coming for dinner this evening,' she said to Jamie when he came home at five. 'I hope you don't mind. I organised it on the spur of the moment.'

'Fine,' said Jamie, adding, 'Diversion.'

'And she's bringing her new boyfriend,' Isabel went on. 'He's called Mick.'

Isabel was watching Jamie's expression. She imagined she detected a flicker of distaste.

'Mick,' she said. 'I don't know his other name – all I know is that he's Mick.'

Jamie smiled. 'The name has unfortunate associations for me.'

So that was it. Isabel waited.

'There was a boy called Mick at school,' Jamie said. 'I didn't know him, as he was a couple of years ahead of me. He was a bully. He broke my friend's nose when he hit him. He was much bigger than the rest of us at the time. His nickname was The Fridge.'

Or Dishwasher, thought Isabel.

'I was thinking about names and their associations,' she said. 'A name can be ruined for us just because we've disliked some person who happens to be called that.'

'That Mick did it for me,' said Jamie.

'Try to put it behind you,' said Isabel. 'I'm sure that Cat's Mick will be quite different from The Fridge.'

Jamie said that he thought she was right. Then he said something about his rehearsal and the conductor's radical interpretation of the composer's intentions. Isabel only half listened; orchestral gossip was lost on her, except when it came to the emotional entanglements of musicians. Jamie had said that there was currently a romance in that particular orchestra that had caused both players involved to miss their cue. The whole orchestra had laughed, he said. 'They were staring at one another, lost in thought, and forgot to play.'

'How romantic,' said Isabel.

'But not career-enhancing.'

'No,' she said. 'Romance rarely is.'

'Except sometimes,' added Jamie. 'What about actresses who sleep their way to the top?'

Isabel smiled. 'Unheard of,' she said. 'And it doesn't happen much in engineering, either. Would you care to cross a bridge designed by the contractor's girlfriend?'

'Or boyfriend,' said Jamie.

'I'm happy to be corrected,' said Isabel. 'And in neither case would I trust the bridge.'

Jamie offered to cook. As well as the quiche that Isabel had promised, he prepared a plate of vegetarian canapés – asparagus rolled in filo pastry – to be served with pre-dinner drinks. It was a warm evening, and the Edinburgh air, normally bracing even in high summer, was heavy. While he busied himself in the kitchen, Isabel put Charlie to bed. For the bedtime story there was a further episode of Babar, repeated for the nth time but seemingly every bit as fascinating to Charlie as on the first hearing.

Charlie was sleepy, and Isabel thought that he would drop off before the story's denouement. That suited her, as it would give her time to have a leisurely bath before Cat and Mick arrived at half past seven. She watched Charlie struggle against sleep; that was such a major difference, she thought, between children and adults: how many adults fend off sleep in order to milk the day of its last moments of consciousness? Adults greeted sleep with enthusiasm – looked forward to it, indeed – whereas for children sleep came as a thief, a spoiler of fun.

Then Charlie said something, looking up at her, eyes heavy-lidded with tiredness, but with the urgency with which a young child will seek the answer to a question that has suddenly come to mind. 'Does Babar cook with Delia?' he asked.

Isabel lowered the book. She could not imagine that she had heard him correctly. 'What was that, darling?'

'Does Babar use Delia? In his kitchen? In Celesteville? Like Daddy?'

She struggled with her composure: a child's questions should not be greeted with laughter. Delia was Delia Smith, the English cookery writer whose books Jamie liked to use. Her name had become a shibboleth for entry into a certain sort of kitchen, and men, in particular, relied on her with all the zeal of converts. Delia had taught the British male, including Scotsmen, how to boil an egg: straight into boiling water, one minute there, and then six minutes' standing off the boil. Perfect.

'My darling, of course Babar uses Delia. All the elephants use Delia's recipes. Of course they do, darling.'

The answer seemed to reassure him and his eyes, losing their battle against sleep, closed. Isabel sat still for a moment, listening to the deepening of Charlie's breathing, and then she tucked in the sheet that covered him – it was too hot for his duvet. Against the white of the linen, his pyjamas were bright red; the spaceships had been replaced by cowboys riding lickety-split across the fabric; cowboys, she noticed, waving flags and what looked like bandanas rather than guns. Jamie had laughed at that. 'One can go too far in distorting the truth,' he said. 'Cowboys *did* have guns, you know. Whereas these cowboys are ... galloping because they're late for their therapy appointments?'

She took a final glance at Charlie: a loving look can be as

much a caress as any physical touching. Then she turned out the ceiling light, leaving only his small nightlight glowing in its place on the wall near his bookcase. Charlie shifted slightly in his sleep. She smiled at him and began to make her way downstairs.

Cat had warned Isabel that they might be late.

'Understandable,' Isabel said to Jamie. 'I gave them virtually no notice.'

'I don't want to be too late,' said Jamie. 'I'm teaching first thing tomorrow.'

'Cat never overstays her welcome,' Isabel reassured him. 'She's very responsive to the awkward silence.'

Jamie looked thoughtful. 'What do we know about Mick?'

Isabel was determined to be positive. 'He comes with a perfectly good report from Eddie,' she said. 'He described him as *all right*.'

'Hardly a gushing recommendation.'

Isabel said that it was about as enthusiastic as Eddie would get. The next step up was *ace*, and Isabel had only heard him give that accolade to a popular politician who made extravagant promises. He was ace, said Eddie, because it's about time somebody did something about people not having enough money to lead a decent life. Isabel agreed about that, of course: in a wealthy society there was no excuse for deprivation, but were we wealthy enough to abolish poverty? Could anybody abolish poverty altogether? She tried to explain the difference between funded promises and unfunded promises, but Eddie would have none of it. 'Of course we've got the money,' he said. 'Look at the cars people drive. Look at the Mercedes and Audis and so on. Thousands of them all over the place.'

'Many of them bought on credit,' Isabel pointed out mildly.

Eddie was not for turning. 'No, that guy's ace,' he said.

'His heart is in the right place, perhaps,' said Isabel. 'But there are limits to what any government can do.'

'Same old, same old,' muttered Eddie. 'Talking him down, just because he has the courage to believe.'

She did not answer that because she thought it might take too long, and because idealism was a delicate plant, so easily discouraged.

'He's a *bit* ace,' she conceded. 'Ace, to a certain extent.'

'There you are,' crowed Eddie. 'I knew you'd see reason.'

But now Jamie was asking about Mick. 'What does he do – this Mick character? Did Cat ever tell you?'

'She has said very little about him. In fact, I only learned about him through Eddie. You know how she plays her cards close to her chest.'

'Don't I just,' muttered Jamie. 'But what's his job?'

'He fixes dishwashers.'

Jamie was silent. Then he said, 'I see.'

'I know it sounds surprising,' said Isabel. 'But why should it? Is it because we just don't mix much with dishwasher engineers? You mix with musicians, and I mix with philosophers. Perhaps we need to get out a bit more.'

Jamie looked embarrassed. 'I wasn't being snobbish.'

Isabel grinned. 'No, of course not.'

'It's just that you assume that people who go out together will have something in common. Do you think that somebody like Cat will have that much in common with—'

She cut him short. 'I'm sorry, but that sounds awful.'

He was abashed. 'I promise you – that's not what I meant.'

'I'm sure it wasn't. I suggest that we both keep an entirely open mind. The only question in my mind is this: is this man likely to make Cat happy? That's it, as far as I'm concerned. I just want her to meet somebody who will treat her well. I want her to stick with somebody.'

'But that's precisely what she doesn't do,' countered Jamie. 'Cat doesn't do constancy.'

Isabel sighed. Jamie was right about Cat, perhaps, but why was she like that? Was she an unhappy perfectionist, never satisfied with what she had because she thought there might be something better just round the corner? Or did she suffer from sexual boredom? Was that it? There were so many apparent failings that had, at their heart, a simple sexual explanation. Sex, thought Isabel, makes moral failures of us all. That thought came unbidden, as a completed aphorism. But what a terrible one, she thought, because sex was also such a positive force: indeed, *the* positive force.

Perhaps Cat was a sex addict. In the past, nobody had said much about this, but people seemed to be more prepared to talk about it now. Isabel knew that she could never talk about so intimate an issue with Cat – their relationship was just not close enough to allow of that. Others might know and might reveal the truth – her previous boyfriends, for instance, and this meant that Jamie might know. He had been one of Cat's short-lived boyfriends and presumably he knew what she was like 'in that department' as the biology teacher at school had referred to it.

Yet just as she could not speak to Cat about such a thing, so too could she not discuss it with Jamie; the emotional past of a spouse or lover is normally, and by unspoken understanding, an area of privacy, and rightly so. But she could at least imagine a conversation, in which she might ask, 'Is Cat – how shall I put it? – demanding *in that department*?'

He would answer with delicacy, 'Very.'

And Isabel would exclaim, 'Why, what a saint you must have been!'

'More of a social worker,' Jamie would say.

In reality, had the conversation occurred, Jamie would have blushed and looked away. 'I can't talk about that,' he would have said. 'I'm sorry. I just can't.'

And she would say, 'Of course. You're right. I shouldn't have asked.'

Isabel glanced at her watch. Fifteen minutes. And at that the doorbell sounded. Cat always gave it four short bursts, which she did now, announcing her presence in the same short-short-short-long rhythm with which Beethoven began his Fifth Symphony. It amused Isabel; it always had. That motif was said to be the sound of Fate knocking at the door; in which case Fate, and her friend Mick had arrived.

8

Isabel's first reaction was one of shock, and it was this shock that made her stand quite still, her hand resting on the doorknob, before she composed herself again. The effect lasted only for a few moments, but it was long enough for Cat to pick it up. And Cat's reaction, she noticed, was one of pride – barely detectable, but nonetheless there: a momentary smirk. It was a reaction that said: *You didn't expect this, did you?*

'Here you are,' said Isabel, saying the first thing that came to mind. 'Here you are – on time.'

'Actually, we're a bit late,' said Cat. 'My fault – not Mick's.'

Isabel told her that it did not matter. She had recovered, but her gaze had returned to Mick, who met it, and smiled in a modest, diffident way.

Jamie's double, thought Isabel. *Almost his double.*

Cat had moved on to introductions while they still stood on the doorstep. 'Isabel, this is Mick. Mick, this is my aunt, Isabel.'

Isabel felt a tinge of resentment. *I may be your aunt,* she thought, *but there are not that many years between us. Don't make me feel ancient.*

Mick offered her his hand, and she shook it. His skin was smooth – just as Jamie's was. She looked into his eyes; they had the same look as Jamie's, the same light. And his chin, and his teeth, and the shape of his nose ... Could two people completely unrelated to one another look so similar? Presumably they could. There was a television presenter in Glasgow who looked remarkably like the woman who ran the dry-cleaning depot in Bruntsfield; so much so that Isabel had heard that the dry cleaner constantly – and wearily – had to tell people that she was no relation, not even a remote one, of the woman on television.

Isabel remembered a conversation about physical resemblance with her friend Alistair Moffat, who had written a book on the population genetics of Scotland. Of course people looked like one another, he said; Scotland's gene pool is the size of a footbath. 'Big it ain't. I could probably call you Cousin Isabel if I really looked into it.'

'Meaning?' she had asked.

'Meaning we're all more or less related. Only a few hundred years ago the population of Scotland was very small: you could fit them all in a rugby stadium. So the odds are that people with Scottish blood have a common ancestor or two.' He paused, looking at her as he might at a newly discovered relative. 'It's purely a question of numbers.'

Isabel knew enough to add, 'And genetic markers too.'

'Exactly,' said Alistair. 'They just prove the point that people with the same name can trace their lineage – if they feel so inclined – back to some early holder of that name. Macleods are an example of that.'

Isabel thought of Macleods she knew. There had been a girl at school who was always breaking things. She was never allowed in the science lab unsupervised... Peggy Macleod. And that man in the bakery in Bruntsfield – she knew he was a

Macleod because she had asked him what his tartan tie was and he had replied that it was Macleod; he had spoken with such pride, as if the memory of some feat in some ancient Highland battle still meant something. She might have said to him, as people did when they established remote and tenuous connections between those they met, 'I knew a Peggy Macleod', and, in the way of things in Scotland, he might have said, 'Of course, Peggy Macleod; her mother, I think, was a cousin of my ... '

And so it went on, because, thought Isabel, none of us likes the world to be composed of strangers.

Alastair had more to say about Macleods. 'An awful lot of them have something called the M17 marker on the Y chromosome. That's a Viking gene, by the way. If you want to find out whether you're of Viking descent, look for the M17. Up in Orkney, twenty per cent of men have that; in Norway, it's thirty per cent. Vikings, you see.'

'I'm not sure that I'd like to discover I had Viking roots. All that pillage ... '

Alistair laughed. 'The Vikings were children of their times. They wouldn't have exactly recognised the European Convention on Human Rights.'

'Although perhaps they didn't deserve their fearsome reputation.'

Alistair thought for a moment. 'Maybe not. The problem was that they were so much taller than the people they ... they visited.'

Isabel laughed. 'Visited? I didn't realise their rehabilitation had gone so far.'

'No,' said Alistair. 'It hasn't, and I'm not being entirely serious. The Vikings were like any invaders: badly behaved and unwelcome. But the disparity in size encouraged all sorts of stories about invincible giants making life difficult for much smaller Picts and Scots. But that's not the point I wanted to make: the point is that we're all pretty much connected.'

'A nice thought.'

Alistair nodded. 'Yes, if one's feeling universalist.'

Now Cat said, 'I take it you're going to invite us in.'

Isabel took a step back into the hall. 'Of course. Come in.'

She watched Mick, whose bearing, she noticed, so reminded her of Jamie's. Under the light in the hall his hair, though, seemed to be lighter than Jamie's and she saw, too, that his shoulders were slightly narrower. It was the face that bore the most striking similarities.

'Jamie's in the kitchen,' Isabel said. 'We can go and say hello to him. He'll join us a little later; he still has a few things to do.'

'Jamie cooks,' Cat said, glancing at Mick.

Isabel detected the barb. *Jamie cooks – you don't.* Mick, though, gave no indication of being aware of the criticism.

'I like your house,' he said.

It was the first time he had opened his mouth and there was a further surprise. Only a few words were needed for the appraisal to be made; it was that quick. Mick's voice was measured – and cultivated. Isabel blushed; social expectations were all tied up with stereotypes and prejudices. She did not like to categorise others, and yet so many people did precisely that, expecting people to behave in a particular way, to have a certain look, to use language in a way that revealed who they were and where they came from. And this applied not just at the creaking edges of British society, where the remnants of caste, although weakened and rejected, somehow survived, but in open, egalitarian countries as well. Australia and the United States distanced themselves from all this, but they were not exempt from the canker of class: the Wall Street broker and the Melbourne socialite could be distinguished by speech patterns from the man who tossed hamburgers in the highway diner or the Outback sheep shearer; of course they could, no matter that the official ideology said that those below could join the ranks of those above if they worked hard enough. And of course many did, but that did not obscure the gulf that still existed between those at the bottom and those at the top, and the subtle differences of clothing, speech and attitude that this produced.

People felt uncomfortable even just talking about this, Isabel found, and they preferred to pretend that it was not there. But the differences themselves were not the problem: the real issue, she felt, was that of the significance one attached to these differences. In her view there was no moral difference between people – or at least no moral difference based on ability to use the language or to claw one's way up a social cliff. People should be treated with scrupulous equality whatever their background, and it was never right, she felt, to think the less of somebody who spoke ungrammatically or who did not know which knife to use at table, or how to use it.

That was what we *should* think. And yet, in practice, no matter how committed people were to avoiding prejudice, they all made assessments of others – they summed them up in an instant, or so psychologists claimed. *Thinks only of himself,* or *She's a man-eater,* or *I don't trust you an inch*: such snap judgements, they said, were part and parcel of the way we coped socially. The world was too complex to be looked at afresh every other moment: we needed categories of the familiar, the understandable. Of course that deprived us of a more subtle understanding of the situations in which we found ourselves and could close off possibilities that would only emerge if we approached the world with an open mind.

I have been wrong, thought Isabel. I've judged Mick before I set eyes on him. I had put him down as a *dishwasher-repairing type*, and I've imagined all sorts of qualities that go with that without having a clue as to what he was like, or indeed what other people who repaired dishwashers were like. I have quite simply been wrong.

I like your house. She considered her reply. *Thank you?* Was that how one responded to that sort of compliment; the same reply one gave to somebody who liked one's shoes or necklace or ... or husband? And if one said *thank you*, what exactly was one acknowledging? Perhaps it was a matter of appreciating the compliment that one would have such good taste as to wear such shoes or such a necklace, or choose such a man as a husband. But she had not chosen her house in the same way as she had chosen the things she wore or, for that matter, the husband she had married. She lived in the house because her parents had lived there, and the things we do because our parents did them are not really so much about us as they are about them. So any compliments for such things should be paid to our parents rather than us ...

'I've lived here for ever,' she said. 'It's just ... it's always been here.' It was an odd thing to say – she realised that – and it reminded her of what Mallory had said about why he had attempted Everest: *because it was there.*

They were standing in the hall and as Isabel spoke, Cat looked at her sideways, as if trying to make sense of what she had just heard. 'Sometimes Isabel makes opaque remarks,' she said suddenly. 'She's a philosopher too, you see. You go in for enigmatic statements, don't you?'

'No more than necessary,' said Isabel quickly. 'The razor is applied there, as elsewhere.'

Mick laughed. 'I've always wondered if Ockham himself was clean-shaven.'

Isabel could not help herself from spinning round. 'Oh,' she said. 'You're familiar with ... ' She realised immediately that this sounded rude. One should presume that people know about William of Ockham, she thought, although, in practice, how many people did? .001 per cent of the population?

'Who's he?' asked Cat. 'One of your philosophers? Schopen-what's-his-face and so on?'

The question was not addressed to Isabel, but was directed to Mick. Isabel smiled tolerantly. *Schopen-what's-his-face.* Cat was not stupid, but she sometimes sounded like an ill-informed seventeen-year-old. Mick noticed Isabel's smile and looked, for a moment, almost apologetic. 'Yes,' he said. 'But very different.'

'Ockham's razor,' said Isabel. 'An important logical tool.'

Isabel thought: Cat had said 'one of *your* philosophers ...' She looked at Mick again, and saw Jamie. Now she thought: do I see *myself*? 'You're interested in philosophy?' she asked Mick.

He smiled. 'A bit. I don't know much about it.'

'Well ...' She was not sure what to say.

Cat interrupted. 'Is Charlie asleep?'

Isabel nodded. 'I'm afraid so. But if you wanted to go up and have a peek ...'

'Yes. I'd like Mick to see him.' She turned to Mick. 'He's utterly cute.'

Mick grinned. 'I'm sure he is.'

Isabel was perplexed. Cat had always been slightly distant when it came to Charlie. She was good enough with him when he was in her presence, but she rarely asked after him. It was something to do, Isabel thought, with the fact that Charlie was Jamie's son; perhaps Cat had never fully forgiven her for taking up with Jamie, even if it had been she who had brought their relationship to an end. The ways of the human heart were Byzantine in their complexity, Isabel thought, and one should never underestimate the resentments it could harbour. 'I'll take you up,' she said.

She led the way upstairs. Mick paused before one of the paintings on the stairs and looked at Isabel enquiringly. 'Who did that?' he asked.

It was a study of a woman washing clothes in a tub; through the window behind her were hills and a slice of sky.

'It's by a painter called Adam Bruce Thomson,' said Isabel. 'It belonged to my father. He liked his work.'

'Look at her face,' said Mick, leaning forward. 'Look at the character in it.' He turned to Isabel. 'When was it painted?'

'Nineteen-thirty-something,' said Isabel. 'And it has that feel to it, don't you think?'

'Definitely,' said Mick. 'It's a bit like Bawden or Ravilious, don't you think?'

She had thought that; she had always thought that. 'Yes,' she said. 'Yes, you're right.'

'I love it,' said Cat. 'I really like that woman's face. She's so strong.'

'It's the opposite of a contemporary face,' said Isabel. 'Contemporary faces are so indulged, so pampered. This is a face that's had some work to do.'

Mick clearly agreed. 'A working face.'

'Let's go and see Charlie,' prompted Cat.

They continued upstairs. Isabel thought: Cat has never expressed an interest in any of my paintings before this – never. *I love that face.* It was the first time she had said anything about anything in the house; the first time.

Charlie's door was always left a few inches ajar, for the sense of security it gave him. As they stood before it, Isabel put a finger to her lips in a gesture of silence. Cat nodded; Mick smiled.

'There he is,' whispered Isabel as she quietly pushed the door open.

He was lying on his back, one arm under the duvet, the other above it. His lips were slightly parted – a tiny bow of a mouth, the teeth just visible. His hair was ruffled, a bit spiky even, as if it had been washed and then not properly dried before he went to bed. Beside him, half propped up against the pillow, were a teddy bear and a stuffed fox, the bear's jacket a bright blob of red against the white of the bedclothes.

'See,' whispered Cat. 'See him.'

The remark was addressed to Mick, and Isabel drew back involuntarily, as if she had suddenly found herself eavesdropping on a moment of intimacy between two others.

Then Cat continued: 'Isn't he just . . . delicious?'

Mick nodded. 'He's a great lad,' he whispered back.

Charlie stirred slightly in his sleep and then turned over on his side, pulling the duvet up towards his chin. Isabel gestured that they should leave; he was a light sleeper and she did not want him to be woken.

They crept out, returning the door to its barely open position, and began to make their way downstairs.

'You must be very proud of him,' said Mick.

'Well, we are, I suppose,' said Isabel.

'I've got a young nephew not much older than him,' Mick continued. 'Robbie. You met him, Cat – remember? He's always . . . well, he always seems very dirty.'

Isabel laughed. 'They are. Boys have a special affinity for mud and dust. It sticks to them.'

'And to men,' said Cat.

'I don't think so,' said Isabel. 'Jamie's very clean. He showers every day without fail. You should know . . . ' She cut herself off. She had been intending to say that Cat should know because she had, even for a brief time, lived with Jamie. But it was the wrong thing to say in the circumstances, and she tried now to cover it up. 'We should be careful what we say about men,' she said, in mock conspiratorial tones. 'They might be listening.'

'Don't worry,' said Mick. 'We only hear what we want to hear.'

'Like most people,' said Cat.

Was that true? Isabel answered her own question, privately, with a convinced no. The trouble with generalisations was that they were generalisations, which in itself was a generalisation.

The warmth of the evening meant that they were able to sit outside on the lawn before dinner. Jamie had put out the white-painted garden furniture – the metal table and its four chairs – and had placed on the table alongside the vegetarian canapés a plate of smoked salmon and brown bread triangles. A bottle of prosecco, hastily chilled in the kitchen freezer, stood in a ceramic wine cooler.

They sat down, and Jamie poured the wine. 'I was going to make Bellinis,' he said. 'But I didn't have any peaches. There were a couple of pears in the larder, but I don't think you can use pears for Bellinis.'

'I've already had my fruit for the day,' said Cat.

Isabel looked at her. 'Five pieces? Isn't that the Government recommendation?'

'It's none of their business,' said Jamie.

Isabel disagreed. 'Oh, I think it is. If the Government has to pick up the bill when we get ill, then surely it has the right to tell us how to avoid getting ill in the first place.'

Jamie agreed, reluctantly, and with qualification. 'To an extent, yes. But where does it stop? Wear cycling helmets when you use your bike? Don't drink more than two units of alcohol a day? Don't stay out in the sun in case you get sunburnt? Use dental floss?'

'But you should,' said Cat. 'Of course you should use it. And if anybody doesn't know that, then the Government has every right to tell them. Don't you use dental floss?' She paused, but did not wait for an answer. 'Did I tell you what I saw at the airport?'

'What airport?' asked Jamie.

'At the airport in Cyprus. Last year, when I went there. There was a British family waiting to go home. Typical stodgy-looking parents in straw hats and three kids.' As Cat spoke, Isabel thought: you sound so dismissive – you would never wear a straw hat at an airport, would you?

'The kids were about, oh, eight, nine, something like that,' Cat continued. 'But they were bright red from being in the sun – absolutely bright red. Lobsters. Their parents had obviously let them go out without any sun block and they'd been fried.'

Jamie said, 'There'll always be parents like that. You can't make people intelligent.'

'Yes you can,' said Mick. 'You can educate them.'

'Get them to see how stupid they are?' asked Cat.

Isabel felt the need to save Cat from sounding too intolerant; Cat was, after all, her niece. She raised her glass. 'To the Government,' she said.

Mick looked puzzled. 'The Government?' he asked. 'Seriously?'

Isabel smiled. Were there people who sat about in the garden and toasted their government? *Is this what I've become?* 'Not entirely. I suppose I don't wish them ill, of course. I may not have voted for them, but once they're in, well, they're the Government and they have a thankless task.'

'You get the governments you deserve,' said Jamie. 'Isn't that what people say?'

'Except it isn't true,' offered Isabel. 'Lots of people get governments they really don't deserve. Look at the Kurds.'

'I don't want to talk about the Government,' said Cat. She was staring at her glass. 'Who invented Bellinis?'

'That's more to the point,' muttered Jamie.

Mick knew the answer. 'They were invented in a bar in Venice,' he said. 'Harry's Bar.'

Isabel said, 'Famous, wasn't it? Hemingway?' She realised, though, that Hemingway might mean nothing to them, although Jamie was well read and would know.

But Mick nodded. 'Actually, I've been there.' He looked almost apologetic.

Jamie was watching him. 'And what's it like?'

'It's a bar, even if it's the most famous one in the world – probably. And yes, Hemingway went there a lot, as did just about everybody else. Truman Capote, Noel Coward and so on. There's a story that on one particular day in the thirties there were four kings or queens all having lunch at Harry's at the same time. King Alfonso of Spain, the King of Greece, and a couple of others.'

They were just people, thought Isabel. *Nothing more than that. People.*

'Drinking Bellinis?' asked Jamie.

'Maybe. The owner thought that their pink colour reminded him of a passage in a Bellini painting.'

Isabel watched Mick intently as he gave this explanation, then, when he had finished and her gaze met his, she looked away sharply. There were two things that struck her forcibly: the first of these was that he knew who invented Bellinis: that was not something that could be described as being in common knowledge – not by any means. The second thing was that he had referred to a *passage* in a painting. Who, other than those with a knowledge of art history and criticism, talked about *passages*?

There was a lull in the conversation. There was a limit to

what could be said about Bellinis, and Isabel thought they had probably reached it. She took a further sip of her wine. It was sweet on the tongue; too sweet for her, and the addition of peaches would have made it intolerable. Jamie had a sweet tooth, but she did not. The prosecco made her tongue feel furry; she would have preferred something drier.

'Where do you live, Mick?' she asked. 'Around here?'

He shook his head. 'The other side of town.'

'Ah.' She waited.

'The New Town,' he added.

The New Town was the part of the city built after the spine of buildings running down from the Castle had become overcrowded and too insanitary, even by the standards of the eighteenth century. The term *new* was relative: it was new in Georgian times.

Cat provided further details. 'He lives in Drummond Place.'

'That's a particularly nice part of town,' said Isabel. 'Those gardens ...' She might have added that it was expensive, which it was, but everywhere was expensive these days.

'It was my father's house,' said Mick. 'He died three years ago and I got the house. Or flat, rather. It's not the whole house — there are two flats. Mine and one up at the top.'

'Mick has the basement, the ground floor, and the first floor,' explained Cat. 'It's one of those roomy New Town flats.'

'You're very fortunate,' said Isabel.

'Didn't that painter live somewhere there?' Jamie asked. 'McTaggart?'

'Yes,' said Mick. 'He did. On our side of the square. And there was an order of nuns. They had three houses, including ours.'

Isabel had heard of that. The nuns had left forty or fifty years ago and had moved to the south side of the city. She tried to remember the name of their order ...

120

'The Sisters of the Community of the Holy Souls,' said Mick. 'I came across some papers they'd left behind. I found some invitations they'd typed out for a leaving party. *Reverend Mother would like to invite you, along with other neighbours, to a party to mark our departure for Salisbury Place. RSVP.*'

Jamie grinned. 'Some party,' he said.

'You don't know,' snapped Isabel; nuns could hold parties if they wished.

He looked at her, hurt, and she regretted what she had said. 'Sorry. It's just that I think that nuns probably like parties in the same way as the rest of us.'

He was chastened too. 'Yes, you're right.'

Isabel reached for one of Jamie's buttered triangles of brown bread, placing a small piece of salmon on top of it. 'I hear you're a dishwasher engineer,' she said as she prepared the bread.

Mick looked at her in puzzlement. 'What?'

Cat frowned. 'Dishwashers?' And then, she smiled. 'Oh, that. Mick fixed my dishwasher.'

'Well, not really,' said Mick. 'There was something stuck in the drain at the back. I just pushed that through, and then it went. Well, there was that seal as well, I suppose.'

Isabel swallowed her brown bread. It was Eddie. Eddie had got things wrong. 'I thought you did it professionally,' she said.

Mick laughed. 'No, I wish I could.'

'So what do you do?' Isabel asked.

Cat intervened. 'Mick keeps pretty busy,' she said.

Isabel saw that she was closing down the conversation and judged that she should not persist. She looked at her watch. 'Do you think that dinner's ready now?' she asked.

Jamie picked up the empty prosecco bottle and rose to his feet. 'Yes,' he said. 'Let's go inside.'

*

She lay next to Jamie. They were covered only by a sheet, as the night seemed to have become warmer and there was no need for anything more. The light had just been switched off and her eyes were not yet accustomed to the dark; slowly, though, the shapes in the room sorted themselves out, emerged from the gloom: the large wardrobe they shared; the ornate chest of drawers that had belonged to her mother's family in Mobile and had been brought across the Atlantic, losing several carved wooden adornments in the process; the chair on which Jamie draped his clothes rather than put them in the washing basket. And Jamie himself came into focus, a shape beside her, a head on a pillow, with eyes open as he had not yet gone off to sleep.

She talked to him quietly, in not much more than a whisper. There was no need for quiet, other than an odd, unrequested respect for the night. 'A mystery,' she said. 'We're none the wiser really.'

'Mick?'

'Yes.'

Jamie turned to face her. She reached out and touched his cheek, gently, and then withdrew it. She did that sometimes because she felt that she wanted to see that he was real. He did not seem to mind.

'He seems all right,' said Jamie. 'I quite liked him, but you never know with her, do you? None of them seem to last.'

'No, they don't. But did you see her eyes? Did you see the way she looked at him?'

He was non-committal. 'I suppose I could tell she's a bit smitten.'

'Much more than that,' said Isabel. 'She took him up to see Charlie. I went with them. You were in the kitchen.'

'And?'

122

'I saw how she looked at him when they were in Charlie's room.'

'And?'

Isabel hesitated. Then she decided. 'Broody,' she said. 'Unmistakable.'

Jamie said nothing for a while, and she wondered whether he had dropped off to sleep. Sometimes their conversations in bed ended that way; she would suddenly realise that he had gone to sleep while she was still talking.

'Another thing,' she said. 'Another really extraordinary thing.'

'Yes,' he muttered drowsily.

'Didn't you think he looked just like you?'

Again there was a silence. He might have been awoken by this strange, even unsettling observation, but he did not stir, saying only, in the thick voice of near-sleep, 'Me? I don't think so. But if you say so, maybe. Maybe a bit. But who cares? Who ...'

His voice trailed off. She turned over. She was thinking of the nuns and their party. There might have been a small amount of sherry – not much; no Bellinis, of course, although the nuns would have liked them, she thought: Bellinis and smoked salmon. And then they all left, and went somewhere else where they did whatever it was that nuns did – kept the world out, perhaps; or sallied forth to make it a bit better here and there; lived out their years as best they could. Which is what we all do, she thought, as sleep came to her; we live out our years as best we can, not knowing their number, not really knowing, in the case of most of us, why we do what we do and how we came to be where we are; thinking we know it, but suspecting that we do not really know.

9

Isabel had been in touch with Kirsten, suggesting that she come round for afternoon tea the following day.

'With Harry,' she added. 'Bring him after school.'

'They've just broken up for the summer. He's on holiday.' She paused. 'Are you sure?'

'I'd like to meet him.' And then she asked, 'Can we talk about it? I mean, can I talk to him about ... his previous life?' She felt slightly foolish, but that was what the boy himself had been talking about.

Kirsten had reassured her that Harry was quite open about it. 'He seems quite happy to speak about it. But I don't think you should go into this business of wanting to go back.'

'Of course not.'

'The doctors said that we should ignore that. Or one of them said that; another said that we needed to talk that through.'

'I'll keep off that,' said Isabel.

She asked Jamie to take Charlie to the Blackford Pond while the visit was taking place. Charlie admired older children and would distract Harry with his attention; the long-suffering ducks at Blackford Pond were capable of providing seemingly endless entertainment for the price of a bag of bread crusts.

Kirsten was early, and Isabel was still working in her study when she arrived. She had been editing a particularly opaque article and was beginning to ask herself why she had accepted it for publication. But the letter had been sent, and the author, a post-doctoral fellow at a university in New Zealand, had already been in touch to express his delight at the decision. 'This makes all the difference to me,' he had written. 'It's my first publication, you see, and ... well, I'm just over the moon – I really am. My wife is having a baby, as it happens, and this is the icing on the cake. First baby, first publication!' She would persist, but it was trying, and the sound of the doorbell was a welcome release.

Harry was standing next to his mother on the doorstep, clinging to the fabric of her jeans, a small hand pinched tight for security. He was wearing a striped shirt of a sort that Jamie had bought for Charlie; small red shoes with white laces; stains on the legs of his trousers – mud, she thought; that aversion of eyes with which small children will express their embarrassment. Kirsten had said that he had just turned seven, but he looked slightly younger than that, she thought: five or six – no more.

Kirsten attempted to introduce Isabel, but the boy looked away, and then stared fixedly at the ground.

'You must say hello,' said his mother. 'Come on, Harry. It's rude not to say hello to Isabel.'

Isabel bent down. 'I've got a little boy too,' she whispered. 'He's not here, but he said you can look at his cars. He's got some cars.'

Harry looked up and met her gaze. She was struck by the colour of his eyes: they were grey, or seemed to be grey in this light, and had an unexpected softness to them, like the eyes of some timid, small creature, which is what he was, of course.

She straightened up and led them into the hall.

'I know where some of the cars are,' she said to Harry. 'Would you like to see them?'

'Aye.' The voice was barely audible; the response Scottish.

'Yes? They're in the kitchen. One has a battery, you know, and makes a noise.'

'We'll like that, won't we, Harry?' said Kirsten. 'A car that makes a noise.'

Once in the kitchen, Isabel switched on the kettle and invited Kirsten to sit at the table. A small box of toy cars, jumbled together in democratic confusion, was taken from a cupboard under the sink. Harry watched intently.

'This is the one with the battery,' said Isabel. 'You see, if you put this switch on – here – just like that, the lights go on. And if you press this button here, then the siren sounds. This is a police car, you see.'

Harry took the toy and examined it carefully. 'Police cars have blue lights,' he said.

'So they do,' said Isabel cheerfully. 'But this police car, I think, comes from China, and the Chinese police, it would seem, prefer green lights.'

Harry pressed the button to sound the siren, but there was silence.

'Their siren must be broken,' said Isabel. 'They'll just have to drive carefully.'

While Harry busied himself with the cars, Isabel served Kirsten tea. They talked about local politics: a developer was planning to build on a piece of land currently cherished by dog owners and walkers. Kirsten had signed the petition to oppose this, but was doubtful as to whether the local council was listening. Isabel said that she thought they did listen – some-times – but that one had to shout to get attention.

Harry seemed to have become more relaxed, and Kirsten, exchanging a glance with Isabel, brought him into the conversation.

'You should tell Isabel all about where you lived before,' she said. 'She might like to hear about it.'

'I'd love that,' said Isabel.

Harry had been looking with admiration at a small, battered tow-truck. He spun its wheels contemplatively. 'It was near the sea,' he said.

He had an unusually mature voice, thought Isabel; each word was clearly articulated, and spoken with an almost pedantic deliberation. She encouraged him. 'I'd love to live beside the sea. You're lucky that you did.' She paused. 'Did you swim in it?'

Harry seemed to think for a moment. 'Sometimes. There was a beach with black rocks. The water was cold, though. I sometimes swam with my brother. And the dog. The dog liked to swim.'

'They do, don't they?' said Isabel. 'What was your dog called?'

He did not answer immediately. But then he said, 'I don't know his name.'

Isabel probed. 'You can't remember? Or nobody ever told you?'

He looked up at her. He was a very beautiful child, she thought; and where did the great eyes come from? *From this family or the last one?* No, she told herself; that was ridiculous.

'Nobody used his name. They called him . . . No, they called him nothing.'

'I see. But what sort of dog was he? I like dogs, you know. Do you like them?'

He nodded. 'I like dogs a lot.'

'And they like us, don't they? Or most dogs do. I suppose there are some bad dogs who don't like people all that much, but most dogs are friendly.' She returned to her question. 'But what sort of dog was he? What did he look like?'

'He was black and white. He had black fur and some white fur under his chin. Here.'

A small hand demonstrated where the white fur was. 'He chased rabbits,' he said. 'He didn't eat them – he just chased them.'

'Well, that's good,' said Isabel. 'It would be sad if he ate the rabbits.'

Harry replaced the tow-truck and reached for another toy car – a small black taxi. This had small, functioning doors that he now opened. Tiny moulded passengers were visible inside – a man and a woman, immobile on their seats. This was one of Charlie's favourites.

'You said something about your brother,' said Isabel after a few moments. 'What was his name? Do you remember?'

There was a silence. The door of the little taxi was closed, then opened again.

'He's dead now,' said Harry suddenly.

Isabel caught her breath. 'What was his name, Harry?'

'Nothing.'

'He was called nothing?'

'No. He had a name, but it was nothing. I can't remember.'

Isabel looked at Kirsten, who raised an eyebrow.

'But your brother's dead, you say?'

The taxi was placed on the floor and moved slowly backwards and forwards. 'He went away. He's gone now.'

'And what about the other mummy and daddy? What were their names?'

It seemed as if the boy was going to ignore the question, but then he spoke. 'They're called Campbell. Mr Campbell. Mrs Campbell.'

'Can you tell me about them? What did he do, Mr Campbell, your other daddy? Did he have a job?'

'He worked somewhere else. He didn't have a job there – not in that house.'

'And what was his work?' She pointed at the taxi. 'Maybe he drove a taxi?'

He seemed to think about this. 'He didn't tell me.' Then, after a short pause, 'I think he had an office. Yes, he had an office. A big office.'

Isabel considered this reply and thought: he's making this up – the inconsistencies are just so obvious. First the doubt: He didn't tell me ... and then, almost immediately, the certainty: Yes, he had an office. And then it's revealed as a big office.

She concealed her disbelief. 'And your mummy? The other mummy?'

'She was nice.'

'She was kind to you?'

'Most of the time.'

Suddenly he seemed to lose interest in the cars. 'Can I have some cake?' he asked. He had seen the cake that Isabel had placed on a plate near the sink. It was a sponge cake dusted with icing sugar.

Kirsten reprimanded him. 'You mustn't ask for cake, Harry,' she said. 'It's not polite to ask for cake.'

'Oh, I think it's perfectly all right,' said Isabel. 'Cake is there to be eaten – as a general rule.'

Harry looked at her appreciatively. 'The house was white with blue round the windows,' he announced. 'There was a tree behind it and there were some hills too.' He gave the information as if it were a reward for the promise of cake.

'It must have been very pretty,' said Isabel. 'And the light-house too – what was that like?'

'It was white. No, it was sort of grey. It was very big.' He looked up at the ceiling. 'As high as that. High as a hill.'

'Lighthouses warn ships, don't they? They tell the sailors where the rocks are.'

But he was not interested in that, and now, in a matter-of-fact tone, continued, 'There were some islands. You could see them.'

Isabel hesitated. She did not want to suggest too much to him: children – and people in general for that matter – tended to tell you what they thought you wanted to hear.

'There were lots of islands,' he continued. 'Some were very big, but there was a small one too. There was an island with lots of hills on it. It was behind the other islands.'

Isabel nodded. 'I see.' She saw that he was looking longingly at the cake. 'How silly of me. We forgot to have some cake. Shall we do that now?'

Jamie had offered to cook again that evening, and she had readily agreed. They had had a busy time of it socially, what with the previous night's dinner with Cat and Mick, and with a whole stream of other engagements over the previous few weeks: a fortieth birthday party for a colleague of Jamie's in one of his orchestras, a book launch, a dinner to raise money for a charity that made football fields in deprived areas. Now they were both ready for a quiet night at home, with nobody to entertain or talk to.

'How do people cope?' asked Jamie as he started to chop onions.

Isabel, seated at the kitchen table, looked at the fridge door and then at the clock above the doorway. It was a Swiss railway clock that she had found in a shop in Morningside some years ago and bought on impulse. There was something about a Swiss railway clock that inspired confidence: their railways ran on time, of course, and therefore any clock that purported to guide the Swiss railway system would be reliable; more than that, of course: by owning such a clock one was stating one's wish to have a more ordered life. Isabel had always thought that this was why we bought the things we did – an insight that was as old as the profession of advertising itself.

But a Swiss railway clock can be as reproachful as it can be inspirational. If you had a Swiss railway clock and it declared the time to be only six-fifteen, then it would surely frown on your opening the fridge door and serving yourself a glass of New Zealand white wine at such an early hour. But if it declared the time to be almost seven-thirty – as the clock now did – then even the Board of Management of the Swiss Railways would not disapprove.

She echoed Jamie's question as she rose to her feet and extracted two wine glasses from the cupboard. 'How do people cope?'

'Yes, if they have to do a lot of entertaining because of who they are. Politicians, prime ministers, presidents. These people presumably spend most of their time at official receptions and dinners and so on. It's my idea of Purgatory.'

Isabel crossed over to the fridge. There was an unopened bottle of Marlborough Sound sauvignon blanc that she now broached, pouring a glass for herself and one for Jamie. He abandoned his chopping knife for a moment, wiped the onion tears from his eyes, and raised his glass to her.

'*It is the onion, memory, that makes me cry,*' he said.

She looked at him. 'Who was that again?'

'It's a poem by Craig Raine. I love the idea of memory as an onion – layer after layer that we strip away as we remember things. And those layers of memory make us cry, just as onions do.' He nodded towards the board on which the small pile of chopped onions lay.

She looked into her wine; it was the colour of liquid straw, something between gold and green. 'There are different sorts of tears,' she said. 'I suppose that we generally equate tears with sorrow, or with being miserable; we forget all those other tearful occasions.'

'Reunions. Graduations. Weddings.' He paused, and remembered. 'Did you realise my eyes were full of tears at our wedding?' There was embarrassment in his tone, and she thought: no matter how far men go in abjuring the straitjacket of old-fashioned masculinity, no matter how *new* men may become, they will always be ashamed of their tears.

She wanted to cross the room to embrace him, and the thought came to her that she could do that if she wished, because he was *hers*, and it meant that she could do something physically impulsive – and possessive – without the slightest feeling of awkwardness.

But Jamie had turned to address the onions again and the moment passed. Not that Eros felt rebuffed; he dwelt comfortably in their house, an acknowledged but unseen boarder, present when required, but quite content to wait; a remarkably well-behaved presence by the standards of Greek mythology.

She thought about what Jamie had said. Purgatory? Nobody talked about Purgatory any more, not even the Pope. 'Do Catholics—'

He answered her before she finished the question. 'They still believe in it,' said Jamie. 'One of the brass players in Scottish Opera is a Catholic and I asked him once whether he still believed in Purgatory and Hell and all that stuff.'

She smiled at his use of *all that stuff*. It was tempting for a lay philosopher to dismiss theology as *all that stuff*, and some did, of course.

'And what did he say?'

Jamie reached for a couple of red peppers awaiting the knife. 'He just said, "You bet I do." Then he said, "Are you going to the pub afterwards?" Brass players are not noted for their subtlety.'

'Obedience,' mused Isabel. 'I could never sign up to a set of religious doctrines. I just couldn't. Perhaps I have a Protestant soul. I don't know.'

'I couldn't either,' said Jamie. 'So that, I suppose, means that I couldn't be a member of a political party.'

Isabel disagreed. 'Most political parties have room for differences of opinion,' she said. 'Except, I suppose, for the Communist Party. It was never a good idea to dissent if you were in the CP. In fact, it could be fatal.'

She wanted to get back to Purgatory. 'Of course modern Catholicism, I gather, doesn't think of it as a place. It's meant to be a state – a state of purification from which you're meant to progress.' She took a sip of her wine. She had let it get too chilled, and the cold had shut down some of the taste. 'Maybe it's a pity that Purgatory isn't a place any more, because it could be made to measure, so to speak. Those people you mentioned – the ones who have to do too much entertaining – would have a Purgatory of a constant cocktail party. With nowhere to sit.'

'And tiny canapés,' suggested Jamie. 'And bores by the hundreds – the thousands, even – all wanting to talk about ...'

He looked at her expectantly.

'House prices,' she said.

'Yes!'

The subject of bores, though, was a delicate one. Edinburgh

had one or two notorious bores whom everybody seemed to know, and they came immediately to Isabel's mind. And yet she did not want to say anything about them, even to Jamie, who would not repeat it, because she felt bad about labelling them as bores. The knowledge that somebody else has labelled you in some way can be wounding, no matter how true, and did it make a difference if the remark never got back to the person about whom it was made? She thought not. The harm is done when the words are uttered: that is the act of belittlement, the act of diminishing the other, and it is that act which would cause pain to the victim. *You said that about me?* The wrong was located in the making of the cruel remark, rather than in the pain it might later cause.

But Jamie was thinking of exactly the same thing. 'What was the name of that chap?' he asked. 'The famous bore that people speak about?'

'I don't think we—' Isabel began, to be cut short by Jamie, who said: 'But you must remember. We met him that time when everybody fled.'

Isabel did not like unkindness; not that Jamie was being uncharitable, but she knew how easily unkindness might intrude, even when one did not mean it. 'I'm sure he ...'

'No, remember,' insisted Jamie. 'We heard about him from somebody else, who said that he was trapped by him once and he went on and on about how he used to be ...'

'He must have had his good points.'

It was a valiant attempt by Isabel, but to no avail; Jamie suddenly remembered the name and came out with it. 'Of course,' he said. 'Of course it was ...' And he spoke the name that would be greeted by a sigh when uttered elsewhere.

Isabel looked down into her glass. 'Yes,' she said. 'But at least he doesn't talk about house prices.'

Jamie rolled his eyes. 'House prices. Yes, house prices.'

But there, she thought – there's a fascinating subject – one to marvel at, that could chill and depress those who owned no house and render smug those who did. House prices were the great excluder, the subject that determined membership or otherwise. Talk of house prices, she had always felt, was by its very nature cruel.

She remembered what Kirsten had told her about the flat in Morningside, acquired by her uncle for five hundred pounds all those years ago. Without that, she would have had nowhere to live, presumably, except the Army quarters near Redford Barracks. She thought of Kirsten's life. What did you do if you were a single parent – as she was – once your child had been put to bed? There would be none of the companionship of preparing a meal together, or sitting in the kitchen while one of you made the meal; there would be none of the relaxed chat that seemed to sit so well with the preparation of ingredients or the stirring of pots. The evening hours surely must hang heavily, as you ate your meal by yourself with only the artificial company of the television to look forward to.

And yet that, she thought, painted an unduly bleak picture. People could be perfectly happy living their lives alone, or in the company of a child. Some people preferred it that way, and lived by themselves by choice rather than because they had never found somebody to share their life with. For all she knew, Kirsten had left Harry's father, rather than the other way round. Perhaps the sound of bagpipes had driven her out . . .

'What's so funny?' asked Jamie.

'I was thinking about living with somebody who played the pipes,' she said. 'It could be trying.'

'That woman who came to see you . . .'

Isabel became serious. She had busied herself with Charlie

when he and Jamie returned from Blackford Pond. There had been no time for her to tell him about their meeting. Now, as they sat together in the kitchen, she wondered how Harry's story would sound to him. Jamie was always so rational; so cautious about reaching any conclusions that could not be supported with evidence, distrustful of anything that smacked of mysticism. What would he make of this extraordinary, unlikely tale of a little boy who persisted with detailed claims to a prior existence? 'Yes, Kirsten,' she said. 'And little Harry. He liked Charlie's cars.'

'So I see. I found two in the hall. I trod on one – an old Morris Oxford.'

She gave him an account of her chat with Harry. Jamie continued with the preparation of the meal, but Isabel could tell that he was listening attentively. At the end she said, 'A rather sad story, don't you think? A lonely little boy, probably missing his father, dreaming up a life where things were different. It's what children do, isn't it? It's the same with those imaginary friends they create.'

Jamie nodded. 'I had an imaginary friend when I was a boy.'

Isabel looked at him inquisitively. 'Oh? What was he called?'

'He was called Lolly. I don't know why I chose the name, but that was what it was. Lolly Macgregor.'

Isabel reached for the bottle of wine. She allowed herself two glasses, and if she poured another one now it would have to last through the meal. Jamie shook his head. He would wait.

'Tell me about Lolly Macgregor.'

'Apparently I made him up when I was four or five,' said Jamie. 'He stayed for three years and then I gather I said that he went off to Australia and we never heard from him again. I don't remember that bit, but my mother said I simply announced his departure and that was it.'

136

Isabel had read that children's imaginary friends could come to a sudden – and sticky – end.

'Lolly Macgregor had a wonderful torch,' Jamie went on. 'Its batteries never needed charging. He also had X-ray specs that could see through people's clothes. Lolly could tell what colour their underpants were. This gave him something over them: if Lolly could see your underpants, then you were at an inherent disadvantage.'

'He was a good person to have on your side,' mused Isabel.

'Oh yes, Lolly was a great ally.'

'Which is why children create them,' said Isabel. 'It must be something to do with that. We create friends for ourselves, I suppose, because otherwise the world is just too frightening. We create friends and myths.'

'Beliefs?'

'We need them.'

She thought of the saints of Mediterranean Christianity. There were so many of them, and in a sense they performed much the same role as Lolly Macgregor. It was easy to mock, of course, but she was convinced that a sense of the sacred helped us to value the world. It was Roger Scruton's argument in *The Soul of the World* and she found it persuasive.

'What are you going to do?' asked Jamie.

'Find the place he's talking about.'

For a few moments he said nothing. Then, shaking his head, he said, 'You're going to find somewhere that doesn't exist? Really?'

'We'll see.'

'A house by the sea? A black-and-white dog? That's not much to go on, if you ask me.'

She pointed out that he was forgetting the lighthouse.

'But how many lighthouses are there in Scotland?'

She did not know. 'I've never thought much about light-houses. But I know somebody who can tell me.'

Jamie looked doubtful. He considered this for a few moments. 'You say that he mentioned being able to see islands? Big ones and a small one too? I suppose that narrows it down a bit.'

'He talked about islands, with hills behind them on another island.'

'That could fit an awful lot of places,' said Jamie. 'Jura has hills on it. It's an island.'

'But which Scottish island has most hills? If you think of a hilly island, which one do you think of?'

Jamie shrugged. 'Mull has hills. There's Ben Mhor. I suppose if you looked at Iona from the open sea you would see Ben Mhor sticking up behind it.'

'You could do. But somewhere else comes up in my mind. Skye. Think of the Cuillins.'

Jamie looked thoughtful. 'Yes, possibly. Skye is admittedly mountainous . . .'

'So it could be somewhere up there.'

He looked at her incredulously. 'You aren't seriously going to try to find this place, are you?' He paused. 'You may as well go off and look for Celesteville. You may as well go and search out Babar.'

She laughed. 'That would be fun. I'll add it to my bucket list.'

After their dinner, they took a tray of coffee into the room they now called Jamie's practice room. His bassoon lay assembled on a table, but he went to the piano instead and lifted the keyboard lid. Isabel sat and watched him.

'Well?' he asked. 'What sort of mood are you in?'

She considered his question. She was not sure of her mood.

She felt a bit sad, perhaps – a touch melancholic. Why? She thought that it was something to do with the pointlessness of what she was proposing to do. She was involving herself in the affairs of that small, rather vulnerable family, when there was no obvious outcome to her involvement. In one way of looking at it, she had been asked to help in the destruction of a myth, in the discrediting of a small sliver of happiness dreamed up by a disappointed little boy as a memory of something better than what he had now. It was a task of iconoclasm, and she took no pleasure in it.

Jamie picked up her mood. 'I'm not going to sing about crossing the Minch to Skye,' he said. 'I refuse.'

'I wasn't going to ask you,' she muttered.

'How about this?' he said.

She closed her eyes as he began 'The Wild Mountain Thyme'.

'I shall build my love a bower,
By that clear crystal fountain,
And on it I shall place
All the flowers of the mountain . . .'

She opened her eyes, and joined in the next verse:

'If my true love, he should leave me,
I should surely find another . . .'

Would I? she thought. She was reminded of something she had read in the newspaper that morning. One thousand women had been questioned as to what their plans were, should their existing relationship with their husband or boyfriend fail. Half said that they kept somebody in mind to whom they felt they would turn, this usually being an old friend, perhaps a former lover, who had always been fond of them. Isabel had been surprised by this, but even more surprised by the disclosure that one in five of these women who had this Plan B believed that the man in question would drop everything to come to them. Isabel thought of Cat. If the researchers had asked Cat, they would have discovered that there were some women who had not only one man in reserve, but three or four. Whereas if they asked me, she thought, they would have discovered a complete lack of planning because *I would never need it*. But even as she thought this, she reminded herself that she might be wrong. None of us was immortal; but this was a morbid line of thought, and not one she cared to pursue.

Jamie looked up from the piano. 'You're not in the mood, are you?'

She shook her head. 'I feel like crying.'

'There's a song about that. An Irish song.' He played a few chords and sang the refrain. 'Let's not have a sniffle, let's have a jolly good cry / And always remember, the longer you live, the sooner you jolly well die.'

She smiled, in spite of herself, in spite of the way she felt. She felt that she could cry buckets, for no particular reason, but in spite of that she smiled.

'There,' said Jamie.

She held him in her gaze. *My entirely beautiful one*, she thought. *My lover.* She savoured the words in her mind. *My lover.*

10

The following morning, Isabel found herself alone in the house. Jamie had taken Charlie to nursery and Grace had gone off with a shopping list to the supermarket. Her shopping trips were important for Grace, and although Isabel bought most of the household groceries herself, she left some things for her housekeeper to buy. In fact there was not really enough work for Grace to do, but Isabel kept her on because she had worked for her father and she felt a moral obligation to continue the arrangement. She felt slightly embarrassed about having a housekeeper, even though Jamie had done his best to persuade her that such feelings were misplaced.

'If you didn't employ Grace, then what would happen to her?' he asked. 'She'd just have to look for a similar job with somebody else.'

'Maybe . . .'

'No, not maybe – definitely. And you could be pretty sure that whoever gave her a job wouldn't treat her as well as you do. I'm pretty sure of that.'

Isabel knew that this was probably true, but it did not help relieve her of a nagging sense of guilt. She was undeniably well-off – and that made her feel uncomfortable. Again, Jamie had tried to assuage these doubts. 'You don't use your money selfishly – quite the opposite, in fact. So what's there to worry about?'

'The thought of what other people have to put up with,' said Isabel.

'You can't change that single-handed,' Jamie pointed out. 'And as far as I can work out, you give most of your income away. You've got to eat, you know. You've got to have a roof over your head.'

He was right. Isabel eschewed the trappings of wealth; her car was now over twenty years old; her clothes, although well made, tended to be inexpensive (she had no time for designer labels); and even the New Zealand white wine served in the kitchen was from the cheaper end of the New World shelf at Cat's delicatessen. But money disappeared effortlessly, of course, as it always does. The *Review* had become a drain on her finances, having dipped from making a small profit to running at a loss after a number of academic libraries, their budgets squeezed, had cancelled subscriptions. Now each issue cost her at least five thousand pounds in subsidy, a sum never mentioned to anybody (except Jamie and those members of the editorial board who had bothered to enquire). Printing became no cheaper, although Isabel had been offered – and turned down – the prospect of inferior paper that would have cut the costs appreciably. The less costly paper, however, smelled strange and suffered from what the printer referred to as 'show through'. 'I don't think we need to read both sides of the paper at the same time,' said Isabel drily.

Then there were the causes. Scottish Opera relied on Isabel for an emerging artist scholarship and the Conservatoire in

Glasgow received similar largesse. There were other causes – the Museum, the National Galleries, the University – the list had grown with every year. She did this discreetly: she was one of the donors described as *anonymous benefactors* at the end of many programmes, and only Jamie knew exactly how much went out each month to the various charities. That was why he said, with some astonishment at her discomfort, 'Don't even think about what you've got. You do ten, twenty times more than you need to. Stop brooding over your good fortune. Just stop.'

Grace, in a sense, was one of the causes. She cleaned the house, but that could have been done in the space of one morning a week, rather than five. She helped with Charlie, but that, again, was something that Isabel and Jamie could easily have managed. So the shopping expeditions, which took place once or twice a week, were an important element in making her housekeeper's job seem more important than it really was. And of course there was the call in at La Barantine on the way back; Grace liked to have a leisurely coffee in the small French bakery in Bruntsfield on the way home. They spoke French to their customers, and although her French was ancient – and weak – it was sufficient to see her through the ordering of a coffee, a madeleine cake, and a short conversation about the weather.

That morning, while Grace sat in La Barantine and, like Proust, contemplated her madeleine cake, Isabel sat in her study and looked at the ceiling. She was not sitting idly – her mind was rehearsing the arguments of a paper she had just read for publication in the *Review*. There was something wrong with the paper, but she was not quite sure what it was. For some reason it made her hesitate, but she could not work out why that was. Was it that the author came across as arrogant? Was he showing off? Some philosophers, after all, wrote papers because they wanted to demonstrate to others their own intelligence. This, she felt, was particularly the case with those whose footnotes were in German. That, in her view, was a discourtesy to those readers who did not know German; there was enough said about everything in English to make it possible to have all footnotes in that language, at least for the *Review*'s international readership. She looked again at the paper; it was littered with German footnotes. *Nein*, she muttered, and noted *probably reject* on the top right-hand corner of the paper's title page; hesitated, and then struck out the *probably* and substituted *definitely*, but added, *with regret*. That latter phrase was unnecessary; the author would not see her comment, but it made her feel better.

It was then that the telephone call came from Edward Mendelson. He and Cheryl were taking a walk down to the canal and could they call in?

'Only if you're not busy,' said Edward. 'We don't want to interrupt the flow of thought.'

Isabel welcomed the interruption, and assured him that a visit would be welcome. 'I love distraction,' she said. 'I look forward to it every time I sit down at my desk. I think we all do – secretly, that is.'

They did not arrive until about fifteen minutes later, by which time Isabel had written a polite letter to the author of the rejected article. Her position had softened, and *reject* had been changed, in her mind at least, to *ask for revisions*. Her letter spelled out what needed to be done. 'Our readers,' she said, 'are, for the most part monoglot or virtually monoglot, although I should qualify that by saying that our English-speaking readers rarely have much of a command of another language. The British ones may have a working knowledge of French, but not necessarily of German. Our American readers may have Spanish, but again will not have German. Only the

Germans, I'm afraid to say, can be relied upon to have German, but then they tend almost without exception to have rather good English and so, for academic purposes, they don't *need* their German.' This, strictly speaking, was not true: an important discussion might be conducted in German and in no other language, and German might therefore be needed if one were to participate. But her point, in other respects, stood, and she continued, 'All of this brings me to your extensive footnotes, or *note a piè di pagina*, as the Italians call them . . . ' She struck out the Italian reference; she had been unable to resist it, but there was a difference between things that one could not resist thinking and things that one could restrain oneself from saying. It was petty, and she did not need to make a joke at the expense of this poor man with his German footnotes. *He's burdened enough as it is*, she thought; *all those heavy footnotes in German dragging him down . . .*

Edward and Cheryl stood at the door. They were dressed casually for a walk, with windcheaters tied around their waists, ready for use should the weather turn, and hiking boots.

'You don't have to invite us in,' said Edward. 'If you're working we really don't want to disturb you.'

She reassured them. 'I've just finished a tricky letter. Tea is called for.'

They sat in the garden, as the day was a fine one. A bed of lavender had come into full blossom and scented the air with what Jamie called a 'purple smell'; preoccupied bees, attracted by this, hovered busily. The sky, high and empty, was crossed by two dissipating vapour trails, one heading east, to Scandinavia, and one west to Canada; these had now become two long, thin clouds, stretched out, attenuated by high winds, forming a great St Andrew's cross against the blue behind them.

Isabel served tea in willow-pattern mugs, each showing the

same timeless scene of the fleeing lovers, the bridge they crossed, and the doves they eventually became. They talked about the canal that the Mendelsons' walk would follow; this was no more than five minutes' walk away, and was a favourite spot with Charlie for its ducks and its line of houseboats. These were well lived-in and comfortable looking; a good setting, Isabel had observed, for a long narrow life.

Then the conversation turned to the Institute. Both Edward and Cheryl were enjoying their time there, and each had delivered a paper at a lunchtime seminar.

'And Professor Lettuce?' asked Isabel. 'Any sightings?'

Edward smiled. 'He's there for a few days more, I understand.'

Isabel absorbed this. When she had asked Lettuce what brought him to Edinburgh, he had replied that it was a purely social visit. And then he had said, 'We have old friends who live here.' She had entertained her suspicions, even then, that they had another purpose in coming to Edinburgh.

Lettuce had said 'we', which she assumed meant him and Christopher Dove – the oleaginous Dove, as she called him. But why would Lettuce and Dove come together all the way from London to see friends in Edinburgh? Why would they leave their wives behind? Both of them were married – there was Mrs Lettuce, who was an assistant curator of something or other at the British Museum; Isabel had seen a picture of her in the newsletter of a society of which they both happened to be members. The article revealed her real name, Clementine, although Isabel had heard Lettuce refer to her as Dolly. Then there was Dove's wife, whom Isabel knew nothing about, apart from the fact that she existed and that she was called Sarah. Both were to be pitied ... but no, pity was condescending; both, Isabel thought, were to be *sympathised with*. Clementine Lettuce could not be blamed for her husband's misdeeds; she might, for all one knew, be quite unaware of them. And that name of hers, thought Isabel: a clementine was a small sort of orange, and that meant that her first name was a fruit and her second a vegetable.

No, Isabel reproached herself – a childish thing to think, and she returned to the unanswered question: why would Lettuce and Dove leave Clementine and Sarah behind in London while they travelled to Edinburgh to see these mysterious friends?

The answer, she decided, was that the friends did not exist. It was not that they were, like Jamie's Lolly Macgregor, imaginary friends; these friends were a pure creation, dreamed up in a spontaneous lie to cover the real reason for the presence of Lettuce and Dove in Edinburgh.

Isabel stared up into the sky. 'Why?' she said. 'Why do you think he's here?'

Edward glanced at Cheryl, as if he were seeking her permission to reveal something.

'Go on,' she said. 'Isabel might want to know.'

Oh, I do, thought Isabel.

Edward cleared his throat. 'I was in the Institute the other evening,' he began. 'I normally go back to the flat round about five, when most other people start going home. But on this occasion I was a bit later than usual.'

'Edward was writing a review of a book of Hemingway's letters,' Cheryl explained. 'For the *New York Review of Books.*'

Edward smiled. 'I was engrossed,' he said. 'It's hard to be indifferent to Hemingway.'

'Do you know that Hemingway wore a dress?' asked Cheryl. 'Only as a small boy, but his mother wanted him to be a girl. She put him in a dress.'

Isabel laughed. 'Perhaps that explains the subsequent bull-fighting and big-game fishing.'

147

'Perhaps,' said Edward, smiling. 'Sometimes we feel we need to compensate. But anyway, I was caught up in this review and suddenly saw the time. It was after six and I was meant to be picking up fish from the fish shop in Marchmont. It would be too late, and I wasn't sure what else we had in the flat.'

'We could have eaten out,' said Cheryl. 'And we had some ready-made pasta in the fridge.'

Edward resumed his account. 'I shall spare Isabel the culinary details. The point is that as I walked along the corridor, I heard somebody in the photocopy room. The door was ajar, and the voices were clear and quite loud. I imagine that they thought that nobody was around. I couldn't help but hear what was said. They were making no attempt to keep their voices down.'

'It was Professor Lettuce,' Cheryl supplied. 'Robert Lettuce and Christopher Dove.'

Isabel said nothing.

'I wasn't eavesdropping,' said Edward. 'But I heard Lettuce say very clearly: *I'll do what I can to swing it your way. Of course, these appointments are made by a committee, but I should imagine that as new director they'll want to keep in with me. It may take a while, you know.*'

Isabel's eyes widened. 'And then?'

'And then Christopher Dove said – and I can't remember his exact words, but this was the gist of it – he said, *That's perfectly all right. I need to give them a term's notice down in London before I come up here.* Then he said, *I want a nice office, by the way. I don't want one of those ridiculous little boxes in that new building. I want a bit of light.* And Lettuce said, *Be a good boy and you'll get what you want.*'

Edward stopped, and looked expectantly at Isabel. 'I feel a bit embarrassed telling you this,' he said. 'It's just that the conversation was forced on me, so to speak, and I found it so odd.'

Isabel listened with rapt attention. *Until I get the job here . . .* Now everything made sense. She had heard that the Institute was to appoint a new Director; there had been a snippet about it in the bulletin that the University sent out to its alumni and donors. She had not thought much about that, but now it was obvious to her that Lettuce was in Edinburgh for negotiations over the job; he had probably already been interviewed, had been offered the post, and was spending a few days meeting people in the University before finalising the arrangement.

'I fear that Lettuce,' she began, but did not finish, as Edward anticipated what she was going to say.

' . . . is going to be the new Director.'

Isabel nodded. 'So it would seem. I can't put any other construction on his remarks, can you?'

'I don't think so,' said Edward. 'I'm afraid that Cheryl and I had reached the same conclusion.'

'Not an attractive prospect,' said Cheryl. 'Not that it really affects us – we're just short-term visitors.'

'And we don't really know much about him,' said Edward, 'although . . . '

He did not finish, and Isabel looked at him enquiringly. 'Yes?'

'There was an incident,' said Edward. 'But I really don't know if I should talk about it.'

'But you must,' said Isabel quickly.

Edward glanced at Cheryl, who gave him an encouraging look. 'I know you don't like this sort of thing, but I really think Isabel needs to know.'

'All right,' he said. 'It's just a little thing, but, well, I was rather appalled. It happened in the common room.'

'Many appalling things happen in common rooms,' said Isabel drily. 'And not just in novels – in real life too.'

'I'm afraid so,' agreed Edward. 'One sees nature red in tooth and claw in common rooms. Ambition, intrigue, character assassination, perfidy of every dimension ... It's all there in a common room.'

Isabel smiled at the memory of a conversation she had overheard in Cambridge when a mild college bursar, not present, of course, had been described by a professor of anthropology as being 'every bit as ruthless as Joseph Stalin' when he had introduced a rule that members of the college staff were to be charged for coffee.

Edward now told his story. 'It was the day before yesterday,' he said. 'I was in the common room reading the newspaper when Professor Lettuce came in. He gave me a nod, but didn't strike up a conversation, as he seemed preoccupied with something. Anyway, he crossed the room to the table where the coffee is, and where, as you may know, there's always a tin of biscuits for people to help themselves from.

'Now I knew that there were four biscuits in the tin, because I had helped myself to one a few minutes earlier, when I poured myself a cup of coffee. Lettuce busied himself with his coffee and I heard him unwrapping a biscuit. I didn't pay much attention to what happened over the next few minutes, as I was immersed in an article in the paper. But after a short while, somebody else came in – it was that young Dane – I think I told you about him – the one who's working on Kierkegaard.'

Isabel remembered.

'And he went to the biscuit tin – the Dane, that is – and opened it. Then he said, "Oh dear, the biscuits are all finished; somebody must have eaten more than his fair share." And Lettuce, who was by then sitting down, looked up and said, "Oh yes. I found the tin empty a few minutes ago. Most inconsiderate."'

When Edward finished his story there was a silence. Isabel sat quite still as its significance sank in. It was a small act of dishonesty on Lettuce's part, but somehow it seemed so major.

'He lied to a colleague,' she said softly. 'He greedily ate all the biscuits and then lied about it. How despicable.'

'Not very good behaviour,' said Edward. 'I'd like to think of something in mitigation, but I can't. It was just not very good behaviour.'

'There's no excuse,' said Isabel firmly. 'Biscuits are trivial, but lies are not.'

She suddenly felt bleak. Lettuce would become the new Director of the Institute and would then, it seemed, appoint Christopher Dove as his deputy – or something like that. It would be a take-over.

'I'm glad you told me this,' she said. 'Not that I can do anything about it.'

Edward nodded. 'It's sad when you see the wrong person getting a job, isn't it? And yet we can rarely do anything about it.'

'Perhaps not,' said Isabel. 'But then again . . . ' She paused. 'I suggest we talk about something else. Let me tell you about the canal. There are pike in it, you know, and I once saw a man catch one. He seemed quite frightened by it – I suppose he wanted a . . . a more innocent fish, and instead, he got this great creature with its wide jaws and sharp teeth.'

'Be careful of what you fish for,' said Edward.

Isabel and Cheryl both laughed. 'I love that expression,' said Isabel. '*Be careful what you wish for.* It has such an inhibiting effect. But let me tell you a bit more about the canal. You can walk all the way to Glasgow alongside it, you know. If one had the stamina – or the inclination.'

'We're only planning to walk a couple of miles,' said Cheryl. 'And then we shall turn back.'

151

Isabel acknowledged this information vaguely. Her thoughts had returned to Lettuce. How dare he come to Edinburgh? she thought. How dare he? How dare he eat all the biscuits. How dare he plan to appoint the odious Christopher Dove. He had to be stopped. He had to be stopped in his tracks before it was too late. But then she thought: *it's already too late*, just as it was already too late, she told herself, to do anything about most things – about most of the world's problems: global warming, rising oceans, microbial resistance to antibiotics ... The thought made her put the Lettuce affair in proper perspective: it was a tiny problem in the context of the world's tribulations, and yet, and yet ...

11

'Madeleine cakes,' said Peter Stevenson. 'Isn't that what they call these?'

'Yes,' said Isabel, looking at the small shell-shaped French cake on the plate beside her coffee.

They were sitting in La Barantine in Bruntsfield, at one of the two tables that gave a good view of passers-by on the pavement directly outside. It was at such an hour of the morning that the sunlight, slicing over the high roof-tops, cast a square of buttery light on their table. Before them were two steaming cups of milky coffee, their foamy surfaces decorated with a delicate fern-leaf pattern. Vuillard or Bonnard might have painted this scene, thought Isabel: the tables, their covers, the display case of delicacies – it was all a tiny island of colour and comfort that would not have been out of place in an *intimiste* painting: *Man and woman in a café, morning*, perhaps, or *Madame Dalhousie prend du café avec M. Stevenson.* She liked the titles given to paintings; they could be so pithy and poetic, first lines of incomplete haiku.

Isabel often bumped into Peter at the fish shop, or sometimes in the supermarket where they both shopped, and they would occasionally have a cup of coffee together when they had completed their tasks. On this occasion, though, she had phoned him and asked him to meet her.

'I have to pick your brains,' she said. 'Bring Susie too.'

'She's at her bookshop.'

'Then just you.'

'About?'

'Lighthouses.'

He had laughed. 'I think you may be confusing me with the other Stevensons,' he said. 'But, as it happens, I know a bit about lighthouses. Not a lot – a bit. You probably need to talk to the real experts.'

'One doesn't need to know too much about lighthouses,' said Isabel. 'Although I assume there are those who know a great deal about them . . . ' She wondered what they would be like – these lighthouse experts; not the life and soul of the party, she imagined; they would be people who liked the idea of isolation and getting away from their fellow men.

And now, sitting with Peter in the café, she told him about Kirsten and Harry. Peter was a good listener, and waited until she had finished the story before he said anything.

'So,' she said as she came to an end. 'There you have it. Kirsten is anxious and the boy . . . well, he's fairly matter of fact about it all. He doesn't seem to think that it's at all unusual. Children are like that, I suppose – they accept things we would find very strange.'

Peter took a bite of his madeleine. 'I love these cakes,' he said.

Isabel slipped hers, untouched, from her plate to his, and he smiled at the gift.

'I wondered about this lighthouse he talked about,' she said.

Peter wiped a crumb from his lips. 'Let's get to that in a moment. What interests me is what you make of him – of Harry?'

'In what sense?'

'Well, is he ... how might one put it? Does he seem balanced? No, that sounds odd. Does he strike you as being a normal little boy?'

She answered without hesitation. 'Yes – as far as I know. I didn't have much time with him when they came round. But he seemed to be absolutely normal. He was very interested in Charlie's collection of toy cars. He was very straightforward.'

'And her? The mother?'

Isabel shrugged. 'Nothing unusual – apart from her obvious anxiety over all this. Reasonably well-educated, I think. Certainly, she expressed herself well.'

'Not a neurotic mother then?'

'Not at all. Solid, I would have thought, but not one to look for anything exceptional in her child.'

Peter stared out of the window. 'And was he telling the truth, do you think?' He paused. 'Or rather, do you think he himself believed what he was saying? That can be different from telling the truth.'

'I know what you mean. Something said in good faith may be false; that doesn't make it a lie. I don't think Harry was telling lies. No, I don't think he was.'

'Although that line gets a bit blurred in children, doesn't it?'

She nodded. 'You're right.'

Peter was silent for a while. Then he said, 'You don't believe any of this reincarnation business, do you?'

She was about to say 'No, of course not', but she stopped herself. There was *some* evidence, she thought, but it was impossible to say whether it had any weight. People came up with what they claimed was evidence for all sorts of unlikely things – for UFOs, for the Bermuda Triangle, for telepathy, even for the Loch Ness Monster. But close examination of this purported evidence tended to reveal its shaky foundations, particularly when it came to the Loch Ness Monster, which had somehow avoided affording an opportunity for anything but the grainiest and most ambiguous of photographs. No, there was never any satisfactory proof of any of these unusual phenomena, and yet the absence of proof was not grounds for denying the existence of something. We might believe that things did not exist because we had no evidence for their existence, but they still existed – in spite of our ignorance.

Peter smiled. 'You seem a bit unsure?'

She attempted to explain herself. 'I have no reason to believe in it,' she said. 'But that's not the same as saying I deny the possibility it's true. I've done a bit of reading about it, you see, especially since I first heard of this boy. Most people who reject these things out of hand have never bothered to look at all closely. So what I'd say is this: reincarnation is a *possibility*. I don't think it likely or probable, but it *could* exist, for all we know.'

She knew that she sounded vague, but then doubt never was all that convincing. She looked at him almost apologetically, as one does when one says something that one does not expect to be believed.

Peter said, 'I've never seen any evidence.'

She remembered something. 'Funny ...' It had only just occurred to her. 'It's a bit of a coincidence.'

'What?'

'Your name. Stevenson.'

He looked at her blankly. 'I don't see what you're driving at.' And then: 'Oh, lighthouses? Of course.'

'No, not that. Reincarnation. Past lives. One of the books I read – no, I think two of them – were by a Professor Stevenson. I'd forgotten that.'

'Nothing to do with me.'

'No, I wasn't suggesting that. It's just that one of the people who looked into this seriously was a Professor Stevenson. I forget what his first name was ... No, it was Ian. Ian Stevenson. I found out a bit about him.'

Peter was interested. 'Well, I hope I have an open mind. Tell me.'

'He was a psychiatrist – Canadian, I think, but he spent most of his working life in the States. He was a professor at the University of Virginia. As I recall, he became interested in re-incarnation because he felt that certain psychiatric conditions could not be explained in conventional medical terms – or their origins couldn't – and that issues might have been inherited from a previous existence.'

Peter looked sceptical. 'A bit of a surmise, I'd have thought.'

'Possibly. But what he did then was to look very carefully at people's claims to have lived before. He travelled all over the world interviewing all sorts of people. Some of them were children – I suppose, children like Harry – who were convinced that they had had a past life. He considered them through a psychiatrist's eyes, so to speak. Took case histories and so on.'

'And?'

'And he ended up concluding that there was enough evidence to suggest reincarnation as the most likely explanation. To *suggest* it.'

Peter then asked if to suggest something was different from proving it. 'It sounds more tentative,' he said.

'Yes. I suppose it implies that the jury's still out.'

He sat back in his chair. 'And that's your view too? Do you think that the jury's still out?'

She had no hesitation on that. 'Of course. I think, too, it's highly unlikely.' But did she? She felt uncertain, even as she spoke. 'Well, no, what I think is this – I think . . . '

He laughed. 'You think you think . . . '

'No, what I know I think . . . What I think is this: it's highly unlikely that people have lived past lives. I suspect – and this is just what I believe is the likely explanation – that all these cases can be explained in terms of imagination. Or where imagination is not at play, they can be explained in some other way. They may be instances of sheer coincidence, for instance, or they may be based on memories based on information laid down in the mind and then forgotten.' She saw he was nodding, and she continued: 'There are so many things we take in subconsciously and are unaware we ever saw. There is plenty of lumber like that in our minds.'

Peter liked the word *lumber*. 'The lumber of the mind,' he said. 'Very nice.'

'Well, it's true, isn't it? Our minds *are* full of lumber.'

He dwelt on it. 'It's a great word: *lumber*. It's what you find in lumber rooms. Things that are stored.'

'Yes,' she said. 'And useless things in general – things we're lumbered with. Stuff in the attic that we'll never use.'

She took a sip of her coffee, which had become cold. That was the trouble with conversation in a café: it cooled the coffee. Peter noticed, and signalled to the young woman behind the counter to bring them fresh cups. 'Back to your professor,' he said. 'Perhaps I should look at one of his books.'

'I can lend you one. I bought a copy of the book he wrote on unlearned language. I could pass it on. It's extremely interesting, even if one ends up saying: well, maybe . . . or well, not really.'

'Unlearned language?'

'There's a technical term for it,' she said. 'Xenoglossy. It's the ability to speak a language you've never learned. Some people appear to do so under hypnosis; they're put into a trance and they start talking as another personality. It's regression.'

Peter gave her a sideways look. 'Isabel,' he said. 'Don't get caught up in all that business – it's an awful waste of time. You'll end up like that housekeeper of yours. Does she still go off to those séances?'

'She does. And I assure you I have no intention of getting involved in that sort of thing.' She sighed. 'All I'm doing is trying to help this woman who, whatever one may think, is genuinely troubled. Now, I think it's possible to do this without being so sceptical that one simply dismisses the entire phenomenon out of hand.'

Peter appeared chastened. 'I'm sorry,' he said. 'You're quite right. It's just that I don't usually find myself sitting down and talking about people who speak languages they've never learned. It just seems so odd.' He paused. Their fresh coffee had been brought to the table, along with another madeleine cake each. Isabel again gave him hers.

'Four madeleines in one morning,' said Peter.

'They're very small.'

'Perhaps I'll start talking French.'

She said, 'But you've learned it. I wouldn't be fooled.'

He pointed to her coffee. 'Don't let it get cold this time. But tell me, anyway, what did he decide about these people and their unlearned language?'

'He decided that it was inexplicable in conventional terms. There are two main cases he writes about in the book: a woman called Gretchen in the United States and a woman in India. Gretchen appeared when the wife of a Methodist minister was put into a hypnotic trance. She spoke German, although the minister's wife had never had any exposure to German. He went into that aspect of it very carefully. She had been brought up in a place where there were just no German speakers. And she had very specific things to say about a place in Germany and about events that happened there – in German, although apparently her grammar was not particularly good.'

Peter shivered. 'Sorry,' he said. 'I find this just a bit spooky.'

She agreed. 'Yes, it is. So let's talk about lighthouses.'

'I wondered when they'd come up.'

She explained to him about Harry's description of a lighthouse. 'I thought I'd ask you about it. I knew that you had an interest in the subject, although you aren't a direct descendant of the lighthouse Stevensons, are you?' The lighthouse Stevensons were the family of Scottish engineers who over several generations had built most of the country's lighthouses.

'Not really,' he said. 'There's a distant connection, but it's pretty tenuous. Still, I've read that book about them. I found it rather interesting. And I've visited quite a few of the lighthouses over in the west. I rather like them, actually. They're in beautiful spots, of course.'

She gave him the description, as given to her by Harry, and Peter thought for a moment. 'It sounds like Ardnamurchan,' he said. 'Have you been up there?'

She had. She and Jamie had spent a few days in Argyll when she was pregnant with Charlie and they had visited the Ardnamurchan peninsula. She remembered the lighthouse, which was a large one and in a dramatic position on the most westerly point of the Scottish mainland.

'If you're looking for a view of a big island behind a small island,' Peter said, 'then that fits, don't you think? If you look up the coast from Ardnamurchan Point you see Skye in the distance. But there are the Small Isles in front of it – between you and Skye. Muck's the smallest of them, but there's Eigg and

Rum just behind it. You probably don't see Canna – well, you might; I suppose it depends on the angle. Anyway, that sounds a bit like it to me.'

She asked him whether he could think of any other possibilities. 'There might be, but this is the one that springs to mind.' He hesitated. 'Unless, of course, you're thinking of the lighthouse on the Cairns of Coll. That's a Stevenson lighthouse, I think, but nowhere near as big as the one on Ardnamurchan Point. You'd see Skye and the Small Isles from there, but the Cairns of Coll are just a small group of islands and they haven't been inhabited since some time back – the nineteenth century, maybe earlier. So they wouldn't really fit the bill, would they?'

Isabel said that she thought it all pointed to Ardnamurchan.

'Well,' he said, 'at least that narrows it down. Are you going to try to find this house? Is that what you're planning?'

'I haven't planned very much. But I suppose that's what Kirsten – the mother – would like me to do.'

'Even if it's a wild-goose chase?'

'Even if it's that. I think I'll try.'

Peter sipped at his coffee. 'I could help you, I think.'

'You mean you'd go up to Ardnamurchan?'

He shook his head. 'No, I can't get away at present, I'm afraid – much as I'd like to take Susie up there for a couple of days. No, what I meant is that I know somebody there who knows everything there is to know about the history of the place and who's who. He's one of those people who's steeped in local knowledge. He could be helpful.'

'He would be,' agreed Isabel. 'Could you get in touch with him?'

'I'll phone him,' said Peter. 'He's called Neil Starling. It's a rather nice name, isn't it? All those bird names are rather appealing, I think. He and I were at university together. He took over his father's accountancy business in Edinburgh and then he inherited a house up there from an uncle. He gave up the business in Edinburgh and he and his wife upped sticks for Ardnamurchan. She hadn't been particularly well and I think it just suited them. He loved it, and became fascinated with the history of the place. He learned Gaelic as well and started a Gaelic choir with some local people. I think they were quite good.'

She thanked him. Peter never let her down when she sought information – about virtually anything.

He pointed at her coffee. 'You haven't drunk a drop of it. It's going to be cold.'

She picked up her cup. 'No, it's fine.'

She looked at the last-remaining madeleine cake. 'Can you take back gifts?' she asked.

'Is that a general moral question you're asking me?'

She smiled. 'No, it's specifically to do with the second madeleine cake I gave you. I'd like to eat it, you see. I've changed my mind.'

He moved the cake back to her plate. 'Of course. That will mean I've only had three. I shall feel less guilty.'

She picked up the tiny cake and tasted it. 'Very nice.' And at that moment she saw somebody she knew walking past the window of the café. Peter followed her gaze.

'That's John Scott Moncrieff, isn't it?'

'Yes,' said Isabel.

She looked at the half-consumed madeleine cake. 'A pure coincidence,' she muttered.

Peter looked puzzled. 'I don't get it,' he said. 'What's pure coincidence?'

'John's some connection – a great-nephew or something like that – of C. K. Scott Moncrieff who was . . .'

'Proust's translator.'

'Exactly. His version of *A la Recherche* has never been equalled.' Isabel gestured towards her plate and what remained of the cake. 'And who ate madeleines? The young Marcel. Remember how he dipped his madeleine into tea and felt all those feelings and memories wash over him. All evoked by the taste of the madeleine. It was the most famous Proustian moment of all.'

'Of course.'

'And here I am eating a madeleine and Proust's translator's great-nephew or whatever he is walks right past.'

Peter took a final sip of his coffee. 'It proves nothing,' he said. 'And I mean that semi-seriously.'

Isabel laughed. 'Oh well,' she said. 'One shouldn't let a Proustian moment stand between one and the rest of a madeleine.'

She put the rest of the cake into her mouth and closed her eyes. She saw a lighthouse, high on a promontory, and the sea beyond, with a fishing boat. The boat was moving slowly, describing a white line of wake over which gulls dipped and mewed. Beyond the fishing boat she saw an island, and an island behind that, a distant mountainous coast of attenuated blue, washed so faint as to merge with the sky.

12

Over the following two days Isabel busied herself with preparing the next issue of the *Review* for the printer. She had taken to doing the page layout herself, using a computer programme she had bought at vast expense and that effortlessly – or so it seemed to the user – sized text, chopped it up into page-length segments, and produced what looked like a professionally laid-out page at the end. The effortlessness, she knew, was illusory; behind each simple keyboard stroke was a vast hinterland of human effort. Somewhere, in some distant office, anonymous computer programmers had passed large parts of their lives glued to screens, writing the code that did the work, churning out forests of numbers to produce the tidy miracle at the end. Now, their work enabled her to cut and paste, to line up footnotes neatly at the end of each article, and to vary fonts and the type size of whole screeds with all the ease of a god deciding the fate of hapless mortals.

Halfway through the afternoon of the second day of editing, she had the entire issue more or less ready for the printer. His staff would run a more professional eye over Isabel's efforts and with a few tweaks the whole thing would be ready for printing. With the issue printed, for a few days Isabel would avoid her study altogether before the whole business would begin again. 'My daily grind,' Isabel remarked, but knew, of course, that her lot was infinitely easier than that of most. A true daily grind involved a journey to an office or a factory, often on crowded transport, and the performance of tasks that were boring or repetitive: watching machinery, moving pieces of paper from one place to another, carrying and stacking, cleaning up. She thought of the people who manned those booths at tolls or at car park exits. What of the air they breathed, laced with traffic fumes? What of the sheer monotony of taking the money and handing back the change, hour after hour, through the day? There were jobs that were even worse than that, right down to the most demeaning ways of scratching a living. There were people who picked over heaps of rotting detritus – she had been struck by a picture she had seen of a family scavenging for tins and bottles in a South American shanty town; that was their life, their only life. And in the background of the photograph were the gleaming towers of the city centre; a world of affluence and plenty.

No, the *real* working world was very different from hers. Of course, somebody had to do what she did: if there were to be reviews of applied ethics, then it would obviously fall to somebody to edit them, and perhaps that person should not feel too guilty about her good fortune. Similarly, there were people who earned their living tasting wine, or inventing new chocolates, or designing cathedrals. Isabel thought of people she knew who had daily grinds like that: her friend Will Lyons wrote about wine for the *Wall Street Journal* and was obliged to visit wine estates in Bordeaux as part of his job. And another friend, Charlie Maclean, drank whisky professionally in order to write tasting notes for Scotch whisky distillers. Neither complained about the calling in which they found themselves. Neither would be tempted to go on strike, she thought. And of course there was Evelyn Waugh's Captain Grimes in *Decline and Fall*, who had been offered the job of his dreams by a brewery: 'We employ a certain number of travellers to go round to various inns and hotels to sample the beer and see that it has not been diluted . . .'

With the *Review* safely tucked up in its electronic bed, Isabel rose from her desk and crossed the room to the window. It was just before three, and in ten minutes Charlie would be ready to be collected from his nursery school. She was not to do that, though, as this was a Friday, and Friday afternoon, by unspoken agreement, was Jamie's afternoon with his young son. It was an afternoon of unabashed treats, beginning with a visit to the Italian ice-cream bar in Bruntsfield Place, where Charlie would be indulged in a three-flavour cone, most of which would end up on his face, his hands, and his clothes. Jamie seemed indifferent to this liberal distribution of ice cream, and did not appear to mind when Charlie, a tactile child, transferred a fair proportion of the sticky mess from himself to his father. Then, smelling of peppermint or raspberry or whatever flavour had been chosen, they would go off to the park near the canal, or, more frequently, to the Zoo, where there were penguins and meerkats to be observed. By the time they returned, Charlie would be ready to drop, being almost too tired for his bath, but needing it, nonetheless, for the removal of the now almost-ingrained layer of ice cream. Even if he stayed awake for the bath, he rarely managed to keep his eyes open for the story, and on a Friday he was often half asleep before the first page of the book was finished.

Isabel left her study. She stood for a moment in the hall,

undecided as to how she would spend the rest of the afternoon; the prospect of free time for a busy person, for a mother in particular, can be intoxicating. There were exhibitions she wanted to see, and one of these, an exhibition of Dutch paintings at the National Gallery on the Mound, was due to close soon. On the other hand, Valvona and Crolla, the Italian delicatessen on the other side of Princes Street, beckoned seductively; art or the needs of the kitchen? Art, she thought; art, of course.

She caught a bus to Princes Street, alighting just before the Mound. Looking down into the gardens below the street, she saw, through the thick summer foliage of the trees, the Glasgow train accelerating through the greenery. The train's whistle sounded – a curious, rather plaintive sawing between two notes – and then it was gone; in the bandstand an accordion band played bravely on, although for the smallest of crowds. She smiled; an accordion band might seem out of place in this setting – a folksy, undemanding sound from a Scottish hinterland of village halls and remote Highland bars, but it was a reminder that for all the cosmopolitanism and grandeur of Edinburgh in the month before the International Festival, this was still Scotland. And that particular Scotland was a windswept country of fish suppers and whisky and unfulfilled dreams; a country in which folk music of the sort being played by the accordion band was still in the people's blood, half forgotten, perhaps; overlaid by the bland, promiscuous culture of the age, but still there somewhere, an ancient artistic DNA that went back to the heartbeat of a very different Scotland. 'Mhairi's Wedding': the familiar tune, played at countless dances, reached Isabel from the gardens below, and she stopped for a moment and listened before continuing her walk towards the Gallery.

She did not want that Scotland to disappear, that Scotland of ceilidh bands and kilts; it was hers, shared with so many others, a small fragment, an offshoot of the feeling that bound people together, that meant that people were not strangers to one another. Every country needed that: the French needed their picnics by the river, their pâté, their games of *boules* on dusty squares; the Germans their brass bands and beer, their *Lieder;* the Americans their flag and its rituals, their proms and cheerleaders; little things, yes, and embarrassing too; sneered at; clichéd in their repetition and their superficiality, but part of an identity that saved us from feeling utterly lonely and detached, mere passengers on a circular rock spinning through space.

She entered the Royal Scottish Academy on Princes Street. Above the entrance, a large banner proclaiming the exhibition rippled in the breeze: *The Dutch Golden Age: Masterful Interiors.* Below the inscription was a reproduction of a Vermeer: *Mistress and Maid.* Isabel had seen the painting in the Frick in New York, who had lent it for the show. She liked it rather more than she liked Scotland's own Vermeer, *Christ in the House of Martha and Mary*, a rather sombre picture, she thought, even if brighter in colour than many of the artist's works. *Mistress and Maid* was far better because it had that strange quality that so many Vermeers had; that quality that put you there in the room with the subjects. What was it that David Hockney had suggested about Vermeer? She remembered it as she went into the exhibition: he had said that he had used a camera obscura device to paint his pictures. It had seemed such an unlikely theory, and yet Hockney's explanation made it seem so feasible. It was all to do with angles and perspective; and when you came to look at a Vermeer, there was a definite photographic feel to the artist's work.

Or was it the light? Was that what made a Vermeer so arresting? There was an afternoon quality to it; a stillness, a warmth, that seemed to *support* the people and things in the painting; that gave them body. That was why you felt you could reach out and touch them; might intercept the note being passed between mistress and maid; might feel the nacreous earring sported by the girl.

She walked into the first hall. A child playing in a courtyard, a small dog at her side, and through the courtyard door a view of a passageway and a lane beyond. *The Dutch masters liked to give us a view from one room into another,* said the exhibition guidebook. *There are few interiors that do not reveal other interiors, or even the outside world.* Yes, thought Isabel; that was everywhere in these paintings. That, and things – physical things, possessions, evidence of the habits of the household, evidence of wealth: elaborate dishes, food, the accoutrements of bourgeois life.

The show was not crowded, and what few visitors it had attracted seemed to be drawn to the Vermeers – the *Pearl Earring Effect*, she thought. A group of Japanese students stood around one of these, listening attentively to a lecture from their guide. One of the students produced a camera and took a surreptitious photograph of a girl standing next to him; she dug him in the ribs, playfully, flattered, perhaps, to be of as much interest to him as Vermeer.

On the other side of the room, Isabel stood before a painting by Pieter de Hooch: *A Woman Drinking with Two Men*. The men were seated, the woman stood beside them; a maid hovered in the background. To their side, a great window allowed copious light to fall upon the party; again the light . . .

Suddenly she became aware that somebody else, a couple, had entered the room. Up until that moment it was just her, the Japanese students, and two elderly ladies making their way round the room with earphones and a recorded commentary.

The earphones had required the removal of hearing aids, and this was causing difficulty, as they both tapped at the equipment in an attempt to improve audibility.

She saw the new arrivals out of the corner of her eye and did not pay any attention – to begin with. But then she realised that one, at least, was familiar. The realisation came as a shock: it was Lettuce.

She turned back to face the de Hooch. She did not want to meet Lettuce. That was a rare feeling for her; she would usually never avoid anybody, but Lettuce was somehow different. Was it just dislike, or was it something different – a wariness born of the knowledge that he did not like her and would be perfectly happy to harm her interests – such as they were? She was not sure.

She sneaked another glance. Lettuce's companion was probably Clementine, who must have accompanied him to Edinburgh after all. Poor woman ... There is a particular sort of pity, Isabel thought, that we feel for those married to people whom we do not like. How awful to have to share a bed with Lettuce; not a vegetable bed, she thought, and, in spite of everything, smiled. There were so many otherwise nice men, of course, with whom it would be inconceivable to share a bed; in fact *any* man, Isabel decided, could be a bit of an effort – except one's own man.

And what if you discovered that your husband or your partner was, like Lettuce, scheming and ambitious, or something even worse? The alternatives in such a case were stark, she imagined: you stuck to your man and said, 'Oh well, he may be scheming and ambitious but he ... ' And then you recited his finer qualities. Or you denied it. People had it wrong; he was not like that at all.

She suspected it was the second of these that was more

common. So Clementine Lettuce was probably proud of Lettuce. She would be ignorant of the machinations that Isabel had witnessed, including Dove's attempt – aided and abetted by Lettuce, Isabel thought – to get rid of her from the *Review* – a piece of perfidious plotting that had been so beautifully trumped by Isabel's outright purchase of the company that published it. There were other matters to be chalked up against him, not least this new plot that he was apparently hatching to appoint Christopher Dove – who was considerably worse than he was – to a post in Edinburgh; again she would be unaware of all that, no doubt. So Clementine was probably innocent in the matter of Lettuce intrigues, and Isabel told herself, *I must try to like her; I must try to like her.*

Still seemingly engrossed in de Hooch, but looking, every now and then, at the Lettuces on the other side of the room, she saw that they were making some sort of arrangement. Lettuce looked at his watch, tapped its face in emphasis, and pointed over his shoulder in the direction of Princes Street. His wife listened, then nodded, and reached into her handbag to get something to pass to him. A shopping list, thought Isabel. Lettuce is being sent off to do some shopping. Even philosophers shop, she said to herself; even people like Professor Robert Lettuce.

Lettuce left and Isabel moved away from the de Hooch to look at the painting beside it. This had the look of a Rembrandt, but was not; she did not recognise the name of the artist, but he had achieved something of Rembrandt's effect in his picture of a young boy with his dog – a vague, rather smudged image but one that captured the loneliness of the boy and his relationship with his dog. The dog, a nondescript terrier, was at the boy's feet, gazing up at his young master, but the boy was looking directly out of the picture, straight at the viewer.

Behind him, on a table, stood an hourglass, a symbol, of course, of the passage of time. Childhood was fleeting; life was painfully brief. Art reminded us of that – in case we needed reminding.

She found herself thinking of the boy. This had been a real boy, presumably the son of the family that had commissioned the painting. The boy was dressed in good clothes, which revealed the family's wealth, and he was not undernourished. But he was dead, thought Isabel, and had been dead for centuries. What had life brought him? A career as a merchant – following his father, presumably? Happiness, illness? An end from some trivial infection that would today be cured in hours by a powerful antibiotic? People died of the merest scratch in those days, she reminded herself. His little terrier could have nipped him and that would have been that; no wonder people paid such attention to the hourglass.

For a few moments she was immersed in the world of the Dutch boy and forgot about Clementine Lettuce. But then she became aware that the other woman had wandered across to her side of the room and was standing by an adjacent painting. Isabel turned her head just as Clementine did so, and they found themselves looking directly at one another.

It was one of those sudden moments of contact with a stranger when we find ourselves looking into the eyes of someone we do not know but feel that we must acknowledge. Isabel felt this. *I have to*, she thought.

She smiled at Clementine. 'Mrs Lettuce?'

Clementine gave a start. 'Oh ...' She recovered quickly. 'I'm sorry, I didn't ... No, I'm so sorry, I just can't place you.'

'I'm Isabel Dalhousie. I know your husband slightly. I saw you with him a few minutes ago. He didn't see me, I think.'

The anxiety left Clementine's face. 'Of course! Robert has mentioned you. I knew that you lived in Edinburgh.'

'Well, yes, I do. In fact, I saw your husband a few days ago, in the Institute.'

Clementine nodded. 'I believe he mentioned that.'

'With Professor Dove,' continued Isabel.

'Christopher. Yes. He's here too. We're staying in the same hotel. Christopher's over in Fife today. He knows somebody at St Andrews. Robert was going to go with him, but he decided to stay in Edinburgh.'

As Clementine spoke, Isabel found herself warming to her. She had an open expression and a soft, rather gentle face. She's innocent, Isabel decided. She may be married to Lettuce, but she's innocent of his crimes. Now, on impulse, she said something that she had not intended to say.

'I hear that you're moving to Edinburgh. Will that be soon?'

Clementine hesitated, but only briefly. It was as if she was weighing up whether to make a disclosure. 'It's not widely known yet,' she said. 'But yes, we are.'

Isabel wanted to smile at the words *it's not widely known*. People were odd about confidentiality; irrelevant, unimportant matters were deemed, for some reason, to be state secrets. What did it matter if people knew that the Lettuces were coming to Edinburgh? Perhaps if he had not yet given his notice in London, it might be something to be kept confidential, but otherwise, surely not.

She was aware that she had led Clementine into this admission, and she felt a pang of guilt. But the next moment she thought: but I *had* heard that. What I said was quite true.

'Have you found somewhere to live?' she asked.

'We're looking. We saw somewhere rather nice yesterday and we're getting further particulars from the agents.'

Isabel felt a momentary sense of doom. There was a house on the market round the corner from her own – a matter of a few hundred yards away. What if the Lettuces had seen that and would end up being her neighbours in Merchiston? What if she had to run the risk of encountering Lettuce every time she walked along Merchiston Crescent to Cat's delicatessen? And – excruciating thought – what if Lettuce were to come into the delicatessen and she had to serve him?

'Whereabouts?' Isabel asked. The anxiety she felt made her voice crack.

'In the West End,' said Clementine. 'Near that Cathedral – the Church of England one. Drumsheugh Place. Maybe you could tell me something about the area.'

Isabel winced. She could not help it. 'Episcopalian,' she said. 'The Episcopal Church of Scotland is a member of the Anglican communion, but is *not* the Church of England.' She put more emphasis into the *not* than she had intended, and it had its effect.

'Oh, I'm so sorry. Of course. I have to remind myself that people are sensitive up here.'

Up here. Isabel bit her tongue. It was unhelpful to blame people for their ethnocentrism. Everybody believed that they were the centre of the universe and at times forgot that there were other cultures. It was a familiar complaint in Scotland, where the English assumption that the United Kingdom was the same thing as England particularly rankled. But it was not ill-meant, Isabel reminded herself, and it was pointless working oneself up into a state of nationalistic frenzy over such things.

The Japanese students had moved away from the painting they had been studying and had dispersed in small groups around the room. Two young women, not much older than eighteen or nineteen, were now peering past Isabel at the painting of the boy.

'Would you care for a cup of coffee?' Isabel asked Clementine. 'Or tea, of course. There's a rather nice tearoom on the level below. It looks out over the gardens.' She paused. 'You asked me if I could tell you about the area – that bit of the West End.'

Clementine accepted, and they made their way towards the stairs that led to the tearoom. There they found another group of students, Italian this time, but not so many as to make them wait long for their tea.

'This part of town can get a bit crowded in the summer,' Isabel remarked. 'But when you live here, you tend to avoid the places that get too busy.'

'Oh, it's the same with us in London. We'd never dream of going somewhere like Oxford Street. Robert would expire, I think.'

In her mind's eye, Isabel saw Lettuce lying on the Oxford Street pavement, gasping like a stranded fish, while crowds of indifferent shoppers made their way about him, careful to avoid treading on him but not doing anything to help. *The Expiry of Professor Lettuce.* It could so easily be the title of a painting.

She immediately censured herself. One should not think such things; and yet, of course, one did. *Unwelcome thoughts* was the term psychiatrists gave to such imaginings; most people, if they were honest, thought these things, at least occasionally, but not everybody sought to control them. That, Isabel felt, was one of the great moral challenges: how to think charitably when it was sometimes so entertaining to do otherwise. Sexual fantasies fell into this category: Isabel had read that many people – particularly men – entertained sexual fantasies every day of their lives, and on average slightly over once an hour. She had wondered about this. Did men really think about sex that often? She had asked Jamie, whose eyes had widened at the question before he gave the Delphic answer, 'It all depends, I suppose, on whether they have anything to think about.'

Isabel took a deep breath. 'But do you?' she asked.

Jamie stared at her and then winked. 'What do you think?' he said.

She said nothing. She had crossed a barrier, and must retreat. But she looked at him and thought: *every hour?*

There were other fantasies, of course, and if she were to confess to being a fantasist, then these were more her province; she had a tendency to picture things like the last moments of Lettuce in Oxford Street, or Cat's former boyfriend, Toby, who had irritated her so much, being caught up in an avalanche on the ski slopes and ending up with his legs sticking up out of the snow, legs encased in those crushed-strawberry corduroy trousers he invariably wore. Only his legs would show above the snow, but these would be enough, of course, to guide the rescuers. They would dig him out and dust him off – he would be miraculously unhurt – chastened, yes, but not hurt – and they would scold him: *You really shouldn't show off so much, you know; keep on piste . . .* And suddenly Toby became Christopher Dove, and it was the arrogant Dove who was pursued by the roaring avalanche, only to be saved at the last moment by Isabel herself, swooping down from a higher snowfield, guiding him down to safety. And Dove would say, 'I don't know how to thank you . . . ' She would say, 'Don't think twice about it – you'd do the same for me' – which of course he would not; there were times when one said *You would do the same for me* in the full knowledge that the person to whom you said it would not; that was the reason for saying it.

She tried to control these thoughts because she recognised their pettiness and knew they were all about revenge. Revenge was wrong in principle; that at least needed no further discussion: a dish eaten hot or cold, it was always wrong. Imagining humiliation for others was not something of which one could be proud; it was what inadequate people did to build themselves up, and she would not allow herself to become inadequate. Mind you, she thought, some of these fantasies are *funny*, and she was only human. She was a philosopher, and she was well aware of the stern requirements of duties to self, but she was also human, and being human involved a certain amount of weakness, and silliness too; not too much of either, of course, but some. It had once occurred to her that perhaps somebody could market a notebook with *My Failings* printed on the front cover. You could give it to your friends for their birthdays, and encourage them to use it. 'You won't need many pages of this, my dear, but still . . . '

In the Gallery tearoom Isabel and Clementine found a table by the window.

'That really is a most peculiar edifice,' said Clementine, as she settled in to her chair.

Isabel followed her gaze to the Scott Monument. 'Yes,' she said. 'A lot of people think of it as a sort of Gothic spacecraft, poised to blast off. And yet I'm rather fond of it, in an odd sort of way.'

Clementine inclined her head. 'This is a very unusual city,' she said.

'Oh, in what sense?'

'It's hard to put one's finger on it. People talk to one another, I suppose. That makes it a bit different from some places.'

'You should go to Glasgow,' said Isabel. 'If you want people to talk to you. They do that a lot. All the time, in fact.'

Clementine smiled. 'No, I'm serious. I don't think that you

would have talked to me, had we been in London. You would have been too busy. You would have been too reticent.'

Isabel poured their tea. Proper china. Proper cups. 'I believe you work in the British Museum,' she said. 'Are you going to be giving that up? Now that you're moving to Edinburgh?'

'The Museum? Yes, I'm an assistant keeper there. I'm one of the people who works on the cuneiform collection. We have the largest collection of cuneiform tablets in the world, you know. Clay tablets. About one hundred and thirty thousand of them.'

Isabel showed her surprise. Somehow she had not imagined that this is what Clementine Lettuce would do. 'You mean, you read cuneiform? You decipher it?'

Clementine Lettuce smiled weakly. 'Yes, people are sometimes taken aback a bit. They don't expect people to be able to read these things.'

'There can't be many of you who do.'

There were, Clementine said, not more than a few hundred people in the world who could make any sense of the scripts. There was, she thought, one person in Edinburgh who could. There were none in Glasgow.

Suddenly Clementine reached into the pocket of her jacket and took out a small notebook. From this she tore a page, and wrote on it, in ink, a collection of odd, angular strokes. She handed this to Isabel. 'Your name,' she said. 'Isabel Dalhousie in the Hittite language. I've done it phonetically, of course.'

Isabel examined the inscription. 'So that's me.'

'Yes. I'm sorry it looks so spiky, but none of us, I assure you, looks glamorous in Hittite.'

Isabel tucked the piece of paper into a pocket. She would show it to Jamie: *my Hittite self – see?*

'So Edinburgh will mean you're going to give up the job?'

Clementine put her notebook away. 'Yes.'

'With regret?'

'Of course.' She paused. 'I've spent years of my life on cuneiform. Years. But . . . ' She shrugged.

Isabel waited for her to continue; she sensed that something important was coming.

'The truth of the matter is that this move is important for Robert. If it were just me, then I'd stay in London – I'd stay in my job in the Museum. But it isn't just me.'

Isabel was silent. She liked Clementine Lettuce. She liked the way she looked; she liked the way she spoke. She felt this way although she had been predisposed to dislike her intensely; that was strange – and unexpected.

'You see,' Clementine went on, 'the last few years have been very tough for Robert. And for me, I suppose, but particularly for him. He needs a fresh start, and that really means getting away from our house in London. Getting away from so many associations there.'

'I thought he was happy in London,' said Isabel. 'I thought he enjoyed the Society of Philosophy. Isn't he on the Council? And his chair there; I thought he'd enjoy that.'

'Oh, professionally everything has been fine for him. It's not that, though – it's what happened to us. We lost our daughter you see, our only child – our daughter, Antonia.'

Isabel looked down at the table. 'I'm so sorry . . . '

'Thank you.'

'Please don't feel that you have to . . . '

Clementine held up a hand. 'No, it's important to be able to talk about it. I often say that to Robert. It causes him immense pain – I can see it in his face – but I always encourage him to talk about her.'

Isabel spoke quietly. 'What age was . . . was Antonia?'

'She was eighteen.'

Isabel said nothing.

'She went off to look at a university – it was Durham, actually. She wanted to apply for a place there and they had an open day. She went with some school friends and there was a road accident. Somebody was driving a bit too fast. It doesn't matter who that was. I don't bear them any ill feeling because they couldn't have known what would happen. Robert found that harder, but he came round to my view eventually.'

'I see.'

'But his heart was broken.' She paused. 'Have you ever known anybody with a broken heart?'

Isabel was not prepared for the question. Had she? She was not sure.

'It's the saddest thing there is. Something goes out inside them. It just goes out.'

'I'm sorry to hear this.'

'Thank you. But that's why Robert needed to apply for this job. Edinburgh or Oxford are the two places he says he would be prepared to move to. There's nothing coming up in Oxford, and anyway, I think that there are people there who don't like him, so he won't stand a chance. So it's going to be Edinburgh, I hope.'

The words were not intended as a reproach, but that was what they were – in Isabel's mind at least. *There are people there who don't like Robert.* And in Edinburgh? There were people there who did not like him either. She imagined the anti-Lettuce faction in Oxford – a group of fussy, argumentative dons, united at least in this one thing: their dislike of Lettuce; meeting in secret to discuss the latest doings of their *bête noire*. Adolf Sax, the inventor of the saxophone, similarly had a society of his enemies – he attracted fervid jealousy from people who wished *they* had invented the saxophone; this society had formal meetings in Paris, in, quite appropriately, *la rue des Serpents*. She smiled at the thought.

But the smile quickly faded. She had been without charity, and she now saw Lettuce in a different light. He was a sorrowing father, to whom the most awful thing conceivable had happened. And here was this woman giving up her career for his sake. She obviously loved him. He loved her. They had both loved their daughter. And Lettuce was presumably doing the best he could in an imperfect world. He was vain and he was pompous. But he was human, and his heart had been broken.

'I'm so very sorry,' said Isabel, and reached out to put her hand on Clementine's arm. She saw the first sign of tears in the other woman's eyes. They were quickly wiped away.

'It's very kind of you,' said Clementine. 'It's very kind of you to talk to me. I don't know a soul in Edinburgh.'

'I'm sure you'll make friends here quickly,' said Isabel, and she added, without thinking, 'I'll help you meet people.'

'You're very kind.'

'And Robert too.'

Clementine frowned. 'Robert's not always easy,' she said. 'Sometimes it's more difficult for him. He had a very unhappy childhood, you know. His father was with Shell, you see, and so his parents lived abroad much of the time. Robert went to one of those dreadful boarding schools. It was down on the South Coast. I think some very unpleasant things happened there.' She looked hard at Isabel. 'So many lives were distorted by such cruelty. I know so many men who had to put up with that, so many . . . '

Isabel closed her eyes momentarily. Those schools, and the attitudes that allowed them, were a largely spent force now, but their shadow was a long one. Now she asked the first thing that came into her head. 'And Christopher Dove? What does he think of the move?'

Clementine did not answer immediately. She glanced out of the window and seemed to be studying something. Isabel looked out too. The gardens were busy; a woman with a group of children – six or seven – walked past, and Isabel thought: *They can't all be hers – not these days.* Then Clementine turned her head. 'At times it's difficult to read Christopher. Do you know him well?'

At first, Isabel was unsure how to answer. She knew Dove's faults well enough, she believed, but she could not say that she knew him well. 'Professionally. We've had some dealings. I edit a journal, you know, and he ...'

'Oh, I know you do,' interjected Clementine. 'Robert's spoken about that. He says you're very good at it.'

Isabel tried to hide her surprise. 'That's good of him. I do my best. It's a bit of a burden at times.'

Clementine returned to Christopher. 'Robert's close to Christopher, but sometimes, well, frankly, I don't quite get what he sees in him. Friendships between men can be rather opaque, I find. Men are not particularly given to thinking about their friendships. They just take them for granted. So-and-so is my friend – that's all there is to it. That sort of thing.'

'I know what you mean,' said Isabel.

'Still,' mused Clementine, 'I think that it will be good to have Robert here in Edinburgh and Christopher down in London. I think it will be good for Robert to get out of Christopher's orbit, so to speak. Sometimes I think that Christopher manipulates Robert – or tries to.'

Isabel caught her breath. 'So Christopher wouldn't think of coming here too?' She paused, watching the effect of her words. 'If something suitable came up, of course.'

The suggestion seemed to appal Clementine. 'Oh, I hope not.' She stopped to reflect. 'Of course, I shouldn't be selfish about that. Robert is not very good with friends – he doesn't keep up any friendships. I rather think that Christopher is his only real friend, you know.'

Isabel gazed up at the ceiling. *How bleak to have Christopher Dove as your only friend.* Lettuce, she thought, is not what I thought he was. I have been unkind. I have been wrong. He may be insufferably pompous, but within him there's the damaged, frightened little boy trapped in an institution of bullies and oppression, wanting only the love of his mother, who was far away, in some place where Shell people went, a voice on the telephone in occasional, snatched conversations – that same frightened, uncertain little boy who was there within so many men. She thought of a politician she knew who had a reputation for bombast and bullying. That little boy was within him. Or the greedy tycoon who had tried to put a rival out of business through sheer canon power; that same boy's voice could be heard there too. No, it's Dove who's the one to watch; he's the Svengali, he's the Rasputin.

13

From the green Swedish car they looked out over a loch to their left, a long, narrow stretch of water overshadowed by the hills that rose sharply on either side. Jamie was at the wheel; they shared the driving, hour and hour about, neither of them liking to drive for long periods. In the back, strapped into his detachable car seat, Charlie had dozed off, still clasping his toy stuffed fox.

'This Seagull guy,' said Jamie. 'Who exactly is he again?'

'Starling,' corrected Isabel. 'He's called Neil Starling, and he's a friend of Peter Stevenson's. Peter was in touch with him.'

Jamie guided the car carefully round a tight bend. The road was following the edge of the loch closely, and the sharply rising hillside on the other side left little room for manoeuvre. 'Yes, you told me that,' he said. 'But what about him? What do you know about him?'

Isabel explained that she knew very little beyond what Peter had told her. When she had contacted him, after Peter's phone call, he had sounded warm and friendly, and had said that he would be delighted to see her. 'I'm going nowhere,' he assured her. 'Any day will suit me.'

They had made the arrangement, and Isabel had telephoned the small hotel he said would be a convenient place for them to stay. They were equally welcoming. Charlie would be no problem: 'We have high chairs, and our carpets, I assure you, can put up with anything,' said the woman who took the booking. 'Three-year-olds hold no dread for us.'

Jamie slowed down for another awkward bend. 'Do you really think we'll find anything out?' he asked. 'I mean, honestly?'

She looked out over the passing loch. 'No, I don't think we will. But if we can tell Kirsten that we've tried, then I'll feel much better.'

He took his eyes off the road for a few seconds. He glanced at her in fondness. 'I'm glad that you're the way you are. I don't think I'd like to be married to a selfish person.'

She blushed. She did not think of herself as at all exceptional. 'I'm every bit as selfish as the next person,' she muttered.

'No, you're much more altruistic than ... than anybody I know.'

'Thank you, but that's not really true.'

'No, it is. You're just ... really kind, I suppose.' He thought for a moment. 'Anyway, you know how I've said in the past that you should be much more careful about getting involved in other people's problems?'

She did not need to be reminded; he had begun to say it in the early stages of their relationship – when they were still just friends – and he had continued. 'I've heard you say that.'

'Well, I've changed my mind a bit. I still think you shouldn't jump in too quickly, but now I think that if that's what you do, well, it's what you do.'

She reached out and touched him gently on the forearm. She wanted to kiss him, to thank him for this little speech, but the winding road discouraged it. 'I'll give you a kiss later on,' she said.

He smiled. 'A lingering one?'

'As lingering as you wish.'

There was a noise from the back seat. And then a small voice: 'Hills.'

Isabel turned round to look at Charlie. 'Yes, hills, my darling. Hills. The Highlands.'

Jamie looked up at the driving mirror to see Charlie.

'Daddy driving,' said Charlie.

'Yes,' said Isabel. 'Daddy is driving now. Mummy will drive a bit later on.'

There was silence. Then the small voice said, 'No. Daddy drive.'

Isabel made a face. 'Oh dear. Where's that come from?'

Jamie grinned. 'Nothing to do with me,' he said. And then, over his shoulder to Charlie: 'Mummy drives very well, Charlie. Mummies are good drivers.'

'No,' insisted Charlie. 'Daddy drive.'

Isabel caught Jamie's eye. 'It starts very young,' she whispered. 'Do you think he's picked this up from somebody at nursery?'

'Possibly. I think it's probably best not to make too big a thing of it or he'll use it. Best to ignore.'

Isabel agreed. 'Look at the sheep,' she exclaimed in an attempt to distract. 'So happy in their fields.'

'We'll eat them later,' said Charlie, without malice. 'For dinner.'

It was, thought Isabel, an entirely understandable observation on the world. People did eat sheep – they could not hide such things from him – and with the honesty of childhood he

186

remarked on the fact; whereas we, she thought, don't care to mention it too directly. The blind eye develops as one gets older, she said to herself.

'We eat vegetables too, Charlie,' said Jamie.

'Poor vegetables,' said Charlie.

'They don't mind,' said Jamie.

'Mr Potato doesn't want to be eaten,' protested Charlie.

Isabel suppressed a laugh. Charlie had a book about Mr Potato, a grumpy, potatoesque figure who had constant problems with the other vegetables around him; and yet was, in his own earthy way, something of a hero. Of course Mr Potato would mind being boiled or mashed; of course he would.

'Nobody will eat Mr Potato, darling,' she reassured him. 'He's quite safe.'

The road they followed climbed up into the first large hills of the Highlands proper. Once through the pass at Glen Ogle, it crossed a wide sweep of country to Rannoch, a high, desolate moor dotted with small lochs, like silver patches, breaking up a landscape of heather and peat bog. Now the hills became mountains – high and brooding, bare of trees, scarred with lines of tumbling scree and white waterfall. Jamie pointed out Buchaille Etive Mhor, a sentinel mountain that guarded the mouth of Glen Etive. 'I climbed that,' he said. 'I went up with my father's cousin, one winter. She was a member of the Scottish Ladies' Mountaineering Club. I didn't realise how dangerous it was until I came down again and looked up to see where we had been. Then I knew.'

And if you had fallen . . . Isabel looked up at the forbidding face of the mountain. A veil of mist concealed the summit, even on this otherwise clear day; the distant brow of rock, almost sheer, glistened from the water that drained off the mountain in rivulets. Now she thought of it differently; it was not simply Buchaille Etive Mhor, it was the mountain that Jamie had climbed with his father's cousin. Everywhere that Jamie went was, in her mind, touched by his presence, as is often the case with lovers. The places our lovers have been to are no longer ordinary – the association, she felt, conferred on them a particular status, as a benediction does upon a holy place. We are fond of places because we are fond of people.

The road descended, dropping down towards the coast at Ballachulish. Charlie had been becoming restless, but the sight of boats bobbing on their moorings improved his mood. And then, when they took the small car ferry that crossed Loch Linnhe, his excitement seemed to know no bounds, and he gave sporadic, heartfelt squeals of delight.

Their hotel was a good hour's drive further along the Ardnamurchan peninsula, at the edge of a small village of whitewashed stone cottages. These cottages were dotted about, seemingly at random, without circumscribing gardens and fences. Sheep grazed at random, free to roam – on the verges of the single-track road, on the lower slopes of the hill behind the village, around the back doors of the houses.

'Before the land grab,' remarked Isabel.

Jamie was concentrating on finding the hotel. 'What?'

'The land grab. This was what life was like before the land was taken away from people. There were no fences. There were no walls. Just freedom.'

He thought he saw the hotel. 'Over there. That must be it.'

She glanced at the larger building at the far end of the village. It would have been the Manse, she thought – the house once occupied by the Church of Scotland minister – and it had now become a hotel. 'Yes, that must be it. Everything has been taken away – over the years.'

'I'm not with you.'

'Everything,' she said. 'The Gaelic culture suppressed. The language. The songs. The way of life.'

'But things change everywhere. The Industrial Revolution ... You can't uninvent technology.'

That was not her point. 'The problem was that people got in the way. You couldn't have a society of small farmers who lived according to a culture of sharing. That didn't fit.'

'Well ...'

She continued, 'So the people had to go, didn't they? Off to Canada and America.' She pointed ahead. 'I think that's the turning up there.'

'Where they were a bit better off, weren't they? Not that I'm justifying the clearances, but how many people in Canada, for instance, can look back with relief that their people made it over there? Or made it to America?'

He slowed down; a red post office van was approaching them on the road ahead; sheep were scattering.

It was not a conversation that was going to get anywhere. Jamie was concentrating on the driving, and she was dwelling on the past.

He turned the car into a short driveway lined with flowering gorse bushes. The scent of the gorse was powerful, and combined with something else – an iodine smell of seaweed. 'I love this,' he said. 'I love this sort of place.'

'Yes.'

'Let's come and live here,' he said. 'Let's leave Edinburgh and live somewhere like this. We'd be away from everything. No traffic. No noise. Nothing. Just these hills and the sea over there and the sheep all about us.'

Isabel laughed. 'What would we do?'

They had reached the hotel and Jamie turned off the engine.

There was quiet. In spite of his earlier excitement Charlie had dropped off to sleep again, lulled by the movement and the warm air.

'Does one have to do anything? What do the people who live here do? We could do that.' He paused, and she wondered whether he was serious. 'I could give music lessons. And you could run the *Review* from here. The internet has liberated everyone from having to be in a particular place. Cyberspace is a big country. You can do just about anything anywhere.'

'Have they got the right cables out here?'

He pointed to a wooden telephone post and the wires leading to the side of the building. 'That's all you need,' he said.

She smiled at him 'We could think about it.'

'I know I'm being unrealistic.'

She said that she thought he was being romantic.

'That's much the same thing,' he replied.

They had arrived at three in the afternoon, the journey from Edinburgh having taken them almost five hours. Neil Starling had told them that he would be at home some time after four. 'Just turn up at my place,' he said. 'We're very casual over here. If we're not in, just make yourselves comfortable in the kitchen. We don't lock our doors.'

The owner of the hotel gave them directions. She knew Neil, she said – everybody did. And she confirmed what Peter had said: 'He knows an awful lot, that man – an awful lot about ... well, everything, I suppose.'

A line of poetry came to Isabel. *That one small head could carry all he knew* ... It was Oliver Goldsmith's village schoolmaster. Another line came back to her: *Amazed the gazing rustics rang'd around* ... That was what amazed them – the fact that one head could contain so much. But heads did. There was Professor

Hawking, whose head, she imagined, contained the sum total of what we knew about physics; and Mozart, whose brain contained that extraordinary, seemingly limitless body of music.

'What were you thinking about?' Jamie asked, as they went out into the hotel car park. 'Back there, when she was talking about Neil Starling?'

'Why do you ask?'

'Because I can always tell. You get this odd expression, as if you're there, but not quite there.'

She shrugged. 'I was thinking of a poem by Oliver Goldsmith.'

Jamie shook his head in disbelief. 'How can you think about that when somebody's talking to you about something completely different?'

'I just do,' said Isabel. 'Don't you?'

'No, I usually think about what they're saying to me.'

They put Charlie back in his car seat. 'I don't want to go home,' he said.

'We're not going home,' explained Isabel. 'We're going to see a man. And then, when we've seen the man, we can go and look at the sea. Would you like that?'

He would, he said, but would like it now.

She planted a kiss on his cheek. 'Soon, my darling. Soon.'

'Will we see whales?' he asked.

Isabel did not want to raise his hopes too high. 'Maybe.'

She thought of what Jamie had said. She knew that she had a tendency to allow her mind to wander, but surely that was what made the world interesting: one thought led to another, one memory triggered another. How dull it would be, she thought, not to be reminded of the inter-connectedness of everything; how dull for the present not to evoke the past; for *here* not to imply *there*.

Neil Starling's house was a couple of miles away, separated from its nearest neighbour by a small clump of neglected Scots pines. It looked as if it had been a farmhouse, as there was a cluster of outbuildings behind it, one of which looked like a line of animal stalls. In front of the house, on a stretch of what might once have been a lawn, a boat sat on a trailer, its name painted in red on the bow: *The Gordon*. There was an attempt at a flower garden, but this had an untended look to it; it was a working house and yard.

Neil appeared at the door as they arrived. He was a tall man, somewhere in his fifties, thought Isabel, dark-haired and with a rather prominent aquiline nose. He looked fit, with the complexion of one who lived much of his life out of doors.

He greeted them warmly and they followed him inside, where they met his wife, Andrea. Isabel noticed that she, like Neil, was tall, and there was a similar aquiline nose. *We marry people who look like us*, she thought. She glanced at Jamie. *Was he her?*

Over tea in the kitchen, while Andrea and Jamie entertained Charlie with a jigsaw puzzle, Isabel told Neil about Harry. Peter had given him a rough idea of what their visit was about, but now he sat rapt while she filled in the details.

When she had finished speaking, Neil sat back in his chair. 'What an extraordinary story,' he said.

'Yes, it is. Of course, this little boy is probably imagining everything, but he's being so specific. That's what makes me feel unwilling to dismiss it out of hand.'

He agreed. 'I think we need to be open-minded.'

'Yes.'

He frowned. 'Let me get this straight: you want me to identify a likely house?'

'If you can. Or at least I'd like you to say that there isn't one here, if that, as I suspect, is what you feel.'

192

He rose from his chair and crossed to the window. He stared at the pine trees, and then turned round. 'The lighthouse is the key, I suppose. The boy claims that the house was near by? He said that, did he?'

'Yes. He said that they lived close to the lighthouse.'

'And could see islands? A big island behind a small one?'

'Something like that.'

'And a burn? He said that the burn was close to the house?'

'Just behind it, I think.'

He turned to face the window again. From the floor behind them, Charlie gave a cry of triumph. He had found a piece of jigsaw puzzle that fitted exactly. Isabel waited.

'There are a few houses,' Neil said suddenly. 'One in particular, I think. Yes, there is one that could match that description. But . . . ' He broke off, frowning.

She wondered what the qualification would be.

'There are other lighthouses. There are other islands.'

She told him that she knew that. 'But we have to start somewhere.'

'True enough, I suppose.'

He sat down at the table again. 'You said that the name of the people was Campbell?'

'Yes. I know, of course, that it's a common name round here.'

'It is. There are lots of Campbells and any number of Camerons.' He paused. 'The house that came to mind, by the way, has been in the same hands for a long time. It belongs to a family called McAndrew. Hugh McAndrew was a fisherman – he owned a couple of trawlers up in Mallaig and did rather well from them. He's in his eighties now, and I think he lives somewhere up near Shieldaig. The house has been lived in for quite some time by his son, Willy. He's a welder, and works over in Fort William during the week. His wife lives there with the children – they're high-school age, I think; there's a high school over at Strontian – they're there, I think. One of them is very good at something or other – you see his photograph in the *Oban Times*. Running, I seem to remember. Or rugby. Something.'

He stopped, and made a gesture of helplessness with his hands. 'Not much use, I'm afraid.'

'Any other houses?'

He thought for a moment. 'Not down there. The lighthouse is quite isolated, you see. That's why I thought of that place. Otherwise it would be pretty much needle-in-a-haystack stuff.'

Isabel struggled with her disappointment. She had been prepared for this, but somehow she had hoped that it might have turned out differently. 'Do you think I could see the place?'

'I see no reason why not. Would you want to meet them?'

'I wasn't thinking of that. I was mainly interested in the house. But I see no harm.' But then she thought again. 'No, I don't think I should meet them. There's no point. They're not the people. And the whole thing is absurd, anyway.'

He was impassive. 'So you just want to go and look at the house from the outside?'

'That would be enough. Yes.'

He smiled. 'People are hospitable round here,' he said. 'And I think you should meet them, you know.'

She gave a shrug. 'If you think it's a good idea.'

He did. 'Look, why don't I come with you? I can phone Willy McAndrew's wife and ask her to show us round. I'm sure she'll be happy to give us a cup of tea.'

Isabel hesitated. 'If you . . . '

'I don't mind at all,' he said. 'I have all the time in the world now.'

'You're fortunate,' she said.

He nodded. 'But lots of people have all the time in the world, and yet don't know it. They fill their time – that's the problem; they clutter their lives. Then they discover they have none. But they once did, even if they did not know it.'

'Yes,' said Isabel, and in the car, on the way back to the hotel, she said to Jamie: 'He's right about time.'

Jamie was not so certain. 'A bit. He's a bit right.'

Isabel wondered aloud: 'Can you be a bit right about something?'

A voice from the back of the car came up with an answer. 'No.'

Grinning, Isabel turned round to look at Charlie in his car seat. 'No,' he repeated.

'So you can't be right and wrong at the same time, Charlie?' she asked.

Charlie looked at her solemnly, and then shook his head. 'Yes,' he said.

Jamie laughed. 'Are you a little philosopher now, Charlie?' he asked over his shoulder.

'Ice cream,' said Charlie. 'Please may I have some ice cream. I want ice cream.'

'Don't we all?' asked Jamie. 'That's a bit of philosophy right there. We all want ice cream in this life. That's what we want. And that tells us an awful lot about human nature and the way we feel – which is what philosophy is all about, I would have thought.'

'Vanilla, please!' shouted Charlie from the back.

'And that,' Jamie continued, 'is where aesthetics comes into it. Taste. Preference.' He slowed the car down to avoid a small family of sheep that had wandered off the verge. 'Don't you think it would be a good thing if there were a book called *Philosophy for Babies*?'

'But of course,' said Isabel. 'Of course. I'd buy a copy. Everybody with a baby would.'

'It would have very simple stories for parents to read to their baby. Minimal text, of course: *Kindness is nice. Don't throw toys at other babies.* That sort of thing.'

Isabel warmed to the theme. 'Actually, it would have to be *Don't throw toys out of your pram.* That's the big issue with babies.'

'Would they understand?'

'They understand more than we imagine,' said Isabel.

'Look! Sheep!' shouted Charlie from the back of the car.

Jamie encouraged him. 'Yes, lots of sheep.'

'Ham,' said Charlie.

'No, pigs give us ham,' said Jamie. 'Sheep give us mutton.'

'Involuntarily,' muttered Isabel.

'Let's maintain a few illusions,' whispered Jamie in response. 'Along with Santa, and the Tooth Fairy, of course.'

Isabel smiled. 'What do you think the Tooth Fairy looks like?' she asked.

'I think of him as ... '

'Him?' she interrupted. 'I thought the Tooth Fairy was female. I've always thought of her wearing a tutu, sprinkling fairy dust and so on.'

Jamie shook his head. 'Oh, I pictured him as a him. I just did. He's a rather theatrical type, I thought.'

Isabel smiled. 'You shouldn't say things like that.'

He was surprised. 'Like what?' And then it dawned on him. 'No, I didn't mean it that way. I really didn't.' He shook his head again, apologetically now. 'I never thought of the Tooth Fairy as being gay. I really didn't.'

'He might be,' said Isabel.

Jamie conceded that. He grinned. 'Of course he might. I

don't think it's an issue, that's all.' He paused. 'More to the point: why does he collect all those children's teeth?'

'When I was a little girl, I was told that he built castles out of them.'

'Bizarre,' said Jamie. 'Perhaps he's just one of those people who can't resist filling their houses up with stuff – all sorts of stuff. Hoarding.' The idea appealed to him. 'That's it. He's a hoarder.'

Isabel considered that for a moment. They were approaching the hotel, and the afternoon sun had painted its rooftop, its white harling, its chimneystacks, with red. 'I've got news for you,' she whispered to Jamie, glancing over her shoulder to make sure that Charlie could not hear, but resorting, nonetheless, to their language of confidentiality, useful as long as Charlie never learned French. '*La fée des dents* – or *le fé des dents* – *n'existe pas.*'

Jamie pretended hurt. '*Il n'existe pas? Vraiment?*'

'*Vraiment.*'

Later that night as they lay in bed in the hotel, the curtains opened to admit the light that was still there at eleven, though faint, Jamie turned to Isabel and said drowsily, 'You told me earlier – when we were coming back here – you told me that the Tooth Fairy doesn't exist ... And I said *really?* or *vraiment?* And you replied with a nod of your head. So what else doesn't exist? Little green apples? Purity of heart?'

He was unclothed, as was she; the night was warm, and not even the top sheet, kicked down to the end of the bed, was needed. She reached out to lay a hand on his hip; his skin was smooth, and she thought, *You have no blemish, of any sort.* And you're pure of heart; of course you are – I could never love anybody who was rotten in his heart, as some are; who hate others or wish them ill; who are jealous and mean; who are unkind. Yet people – plenty of people – love people like that; in spite of all the evidence of their flaws, they love them. They love those whom they really should not love; are drawn to these objects of their affection, perhaps, like those unfortunate insects attracted to insect traps or the mantis that believes in a future with a female mantis and then discovers that he is the next meal.

'Purity of heart *does* exist,' said Isabel, her voice low, though there was nobody for them to disturb; Charlie was in the room next door, reached by a connecting, but now closed door, and the two other rooms off the corridor were unoccupied. But it did not seem right to talk at all loudly in this semi-darkness, in this air that smelled of the sea and the gorse in the fields; air that had come here from far away, from the Outer Hebrides, from the Atlantic, from Canada itself.

She continued, 'Mind you, I'm trying to think of anybody I know who's pure of heart.'

'There are people without guile,' said Jamie. 'They do exist, I think. But I'm not sure if being without guile is the same thing as purity of heart.' He stopped, and she wondered for a moment whether he was drifting off to sleep; sometimes their conversations in bed ended that way – a dialogue slowly became a monologue, and then silence reigned. But he had more to say. 'They could be a bit dull, couldn't they?'

He turned, and his back was to her. She took her hand away, to let him move, and then she placed it gently against the small of his back; it was an act of possession, she thought, this touching. He rolled over again, now lying on his back; his head turned slightly towards her. She saw that his eyes were open.

'You think the pure of heart are dull?' She did not want to reach that conclusion, but she realised he had a point. He was thinking of the same person as she was thinking of, she suspected, a completely worthy acquaintance who thought the best of everybody she encountered and never had a bad word to say about anything. Yet Chesterton had said, she remembered, that tolerance went with having no convictions. Was that true, or just a bit true? 'Maybe. Yes, maybe you're right. They can end up having nothing to say, I suppose.'

'Or just plain boring,' said Jamie. He smiled. 'I'm reading something at the moment . . . '

'That makes you smile?'

'Yes,' Jamie continued. 'It's that history of late-medieval Scotland that Hector MacQueen wrote. He gave me a copy when we played that game of cricket over at Broomhall, at Lord Elgin's. There's something in it about a fourteenth-century character called Hugh the Dull.'

She giggled. 'Hugh the Dull? Wonderful – such an expressive epithet by comparison with all those predictable "So-and-so The Great".' More odd descriptions came to her. 'Wasn't there a Charles the Fat, who was the Holy Roman Emperor at some point – not to be confused with Charles the Bald, another Carolingian?'

Jamie had heard of neither. 'Hugh the Dull was a member of the Douglas family. The rest of them were rather more colourful than he was. His brother was known as the Black Douglas and the Black Douglas's son was called Archibald the Grim. Hugh, by contrast, did not cut much of a figure – hence the name. History doesn't record his deeds because apparently they were too dull.'

'I love the thought of Archibald the Grim . . . '

He reached out to place a hand against her cheek. 'So do I.'

'And Archibald the Grim must have been so dismissive of his father's brother, his uncle. Can't you hear him saying, "Uncle Hugh is just so dull, so very, very dull"?'

He moved towards her and kissed her gently on the mouth. She closed her eyes. She could hear her heart beating within her.

'You know something,' he whispered. 'I'm feeling uneasy. I'm scared.'

For a while she said nothing. How could Jamie be scared – here, of all places?

She was solicitous. 'My darling, you can't be. You can't.'

'Not that sort of scared,' he said. 'It's just that I feel uneasy, I suppose. I don't know why, but I do.'

14

Neil had telephoned the McAndrews and made the
arrangements.

'Willy's wife Fiona told me they'll both be in,' he said as they
set off the next morning. 'He was out when I phoned, but she
said that he's on holiday this week. He might be going fishing,
though, depending on the weather.'

'Like his father?' said Isabel. 'You said that he had a trawler.'

Neil pointed through the car window towards the expanse of
blue that was the sea. 'Some of them still go out there from
time to time. They don't do it for a living, but they have prawn
creels that they keep going. The old ways cling on.'

The road they were following dipped down towards the sea.
Isabel looked out at what seemed like an unruffled field of blue;
towards the horizon the reflected sunlight made the surface a
stretch of spilled quicksilver. A fishing boat, tiny at this distance,
ploughed its way across this field, its wake a white trail behind
it. *These plains are for ever where cold creatures are hunted* . . . It was
Auden's description of the sea in his 'Journey to Iceland'. These
were the same plains, she thought – the place where the fish

were hunted, now, even in their diminished numbers, as they had been by the people who first lived in these same small white houses along the coast.

She caught Jamie's eye, and he smiled at her, as if to reassure her. He had mentioned his feeling of foreboding last night, and she had tried to reassure him. Now, though, she was herself feeling something of the same thing. There was something strange in this quest. It was, in one sense, ridiculous, almost risible – the pursuit of an imaginative child's dream – but in another she felt as if she were touching on something dark and dangerous. Reincarnation was about rebirth, but it was also about death. The child must die before he can become somebody else.

She remembered the phrase her father had used: *best left alone*. He said that about so many things, but particularly about the private affairs of others. He did not like gossip, and if Isabel should mention the misdeeds of another he would reply firmly, 'Best left alone, I think.' Her father had been a good judge of people, but he was charitable too, and the things that were best left alone were those that could hurt others.

She could say to Neil that she had changed her mind and that she did not want to see the house after all. Best left alone. Jamie would be surprised, but he would back her up; he always did.

She opened her mouth to say something, but it was Neil who spoke. 'You can just see it from here,' he said. 'You see those two houses down there – the white ones? The one on the left is what I had in mind. The one on the right is of much more recent construction – it was only built three years ago.'

She felt committed now. 'It's a magnificent setting.'

'Yes, in the summer,' said Neil. 'I'm not so sure that I'd like to spend the winter there. It's exposed to the north-east and if the wind comes from that direction one knows all about it.'

He gave instructions to Jamie, who was driving. Isabel, who was seated in the back with Charlie, pointed to the house, now only a few hundred yards away. 'We're going to see some people,' she said.

'Will there be toys?' asked Charlie.

'Possibly,' replied Isabel. 'These people have got big children – really big. But they may still have some of their toys. We can ask.'

Fiona McAndrew came out of the house to meet them. She was casually dressed, in blue denim jeans and a white linen top. Her shoes, green working clogs, were badly scuffed. She greeted Neil warmly and the two of them exchanged a few words about some local issue – a matter of road repairs, Isabel noted – and then she led them into the house. Isabel felt in her pocket for the slip of paper she had brought with her. Kirsten had given it to her: a rough map of the layout of the rooms of the house, as explained to her by Harry. She could not bring it out – one could not walk into somebody's house and immediately produce a floor plan – but she remembered what it showed. There was a small hall and then the living room. That was what was here; but then many houses have entrance halls and living rooms off them. Kirsten had said that he had given a description of a fireplace made of white stone. She hardly dared look as she entered the living room, but when she saw it she gave a start. Jamie noticed. 'You all right?' he whispered.

She felt curiously empty. 'Yes.' She pointed to the fireplace briefly, and then turned to Fiona, who had addressed her.

'My husband isn't here,' she said. 'Sorry about that. He had to go into Fort William today because there was a crisis at his work. He'll probably be there all day, although he's meant to be on holiday. They don't care, do they?'

Isabel assumed that it was the employers rather than the employees, or husbands in general, who did not care. 'No,' she said, her voice shaky from the shock of what she had seen. 'They don't.'

Fiona picked up her anxiety, and frowned. 'Are you okay?'

Isabel shook her head. She was not.

Jamie looked concerned. 'What's wrong? Are you feeling ill?'

She suddenly wanted to cry. She felt ridiculous; there was no call for tears. 'I'm so sorry.'

'You must sit down,' said Fiona. 'I'll get a glass of water. It's this heat, maybe. I felt a bit odd yesterday – we're not used to it.'

Isabel shook her head. 'Thanks, but it's nothing like that. It's just that I'm feeling a bit shocked.' She paused, trying to pull herself together. 'Did Neil tell you what this is all about?'

Fiona turned to Neil. 'You said something about a boy who stayed here some time ago. That was it, wasn't it?'

Isabel took it upon herself to answer. 'It was. But it's a rather more complicated story. I'd like to tell you myself, if I may.'

Jamie offered to take Charlie outside. 'He's going on about ducks,' he explained to Fiona. 'He said that he saw some ducks.'

She laughed. 'They'd like a visit, I think. They're round the back. You'll see a black bin we use for their feed. You can let him give them something, if you like.'

There was a pot of still warm tea on a tray near the hearth, and Fiona poured a cup for Isabel. Then she sat down and listened, along with Neil, to Isabel's explanation. Halfway through, a door opened and a teenage boy came in. He was introduced as Matthew.

'You're the runner, aren't you?' said Neil.

'High jump,' corrected Matthew.

'He's going to compete for Scotland next month,' said Fiona, proudly.

'Mum! We don't know yet whether I'm going to be picked. We don't.'

'You will be,' she said. 'It's as good as done.'

Isabel was struck by Matthew's ginger hair. She noticed his skin, which was so pale as to be almost translucent; it was a colouring that one often found in the north-western part of Scotland – Viking colouring.

'I have to go,' said Matthew. 'Jimmy's coming to pick me up.' He left, giving Isabel and Neil an open, friendly smile.

'He's a great lad,' said Neil as the door closed behind the boy.

Fiona thanked him, then urged Isabel on. 'But I've got to hear the end of this story. Please carry on.'

She finished, and there was a silence. She had ended the story with a reference to the fireplace, which had brought forward an exclamation of astonishment from Fiona. 'But we put that in,' she said. 'Two months ago. There was one of those gas heaters there before – but we got fed up with changing the cylinders. We decided to go for wood – there's any amount of that round here.'

Neil raised an eyebrow. 'Two months ago? Well, that settles that.'

Isabel felt almost relieved. 'I suppose so,' she said.

'Maybe he saw a photograph,' said Neil. 'Has this house been in any published photographs?'

Fiona thought for a moment. Then she smiled. 'Yes,' she said. 'It was in the *Scotsman*. In the magazine section. Very recently, as a matter of fact. There was an article on living near the Argyll coast, and they had a photograph – two photographs, in fact – of our house. I kept it.'

Isabel felt a sudden rush of relief. This was the answer. There was always a rational explanation to these things. The hovering UFO was simply an unusually dense cloud; the yeti was a moving shadow on the snow; the near-death experience was simply the dreaming of the oxygen-starved brain; she wished she could conclude otherwise, but she could not: there were no inexplicable phenomena; there was nothing that could not be measured or understood scientifically.

'Photos of what? This room?'

Fiona rose to her feet. 'I'll show you,' she said. 'It's in the cupboard.'

She left the room, and Neil gave a nervous laugh. 'Funny, isn't it? Not reincarnation at all.'

'I must admit I'm relieved,' said Isabel. 'I like a simple, realistic explanation. I like science and rationality to be vindicated.'

They sat in silence until Fiona returned; Neil, she had noticed, was not one to speak when he had nothing to say.

Fiona handed Isabel a protective plastic envelope containing a folded magazine. Isabel took the magazine out and examined the cover: *The Remote Life*, it proclaimed, *Five cottages on the edge*. She turned the pages to the article itself. There were the two photographs that Fiona had mentioned: one was of the view from the bedroom window, the other was of the living room. The fireplace was shown: *Snug, in spite of the gales*, ran the caption. And at the beginning of the article was the name of the journalist who had written it: George Campbell.

It took Isabel a moment or two to make the connection, but when she did she gave an involuntary cry of discovery. 'Campbell,' she said. 'The journalist's name was Campbell.'

Fiona shrugged. 'He came to speak to us. He came with his photographer. They were from Glasgow, I think – or somewhere near there. Airdrie, Motherwell – I get them all mixed up.'

'Campbell!' repeated Isabel, and this time the others saw what she was driving at.

'I see,' said Neil quietly.

Isabel said that she assumed that Harry could read. He was six, by which time a bright child at a good school – and South Morningside Primary was certainly that – would be a reasonable reader; certainly confident enough to read the sentence under one of the photographs: *From the window the view is of the Ardnamurchan Lighthouse in the distance and beyond that the islands of Muck, Eigg and Rum.* 'He must have seen this lying around somewhere,' she went on. 'Heaven knows where, but he would have seen this and filed it away somewhere in his memory. Later it must have come out as an impression of something he had himself done. That happens, I've been told.' It happened to her: she remembered lines of Auden at odd moments, unprompted; she was unaware that the memories were there, but they had been laid down, to surface uninvited when something triggered them. And sometimes – not very often, but occasionally – she would think that the line was hers, and that she had said it, had been the author of an aphorism or an insight.

Neil asked whether it was likely that a six-year-old would read the papers, but she felt that it was quite possible that he had just picked up that page somewhere and had somehow taken it in. 'That's not too fanciful,' she said. 'It could easily happen. Children drink things in – especially boys. They love facts and figures. They read all sorts of things: the backs of cornflake packets, instruction leaflets, the most unlikely books.' She remembered something. 'When I was seven I actually read some Bertrand Russell. I picked him up and struggled through ten pages or so. I was very proud of myself.'

'But you're a philosopher, aren't you?' said Neil, smiling. Yet he accepted her point, even though he had been half hoping for a different outcome; as had Fiona, who seemed disappointed.

'It's a pity,' she said. 'I rather like the idea of coming back. It's quite a story, isn't it? That wee boy – it would have been nice to have thought that he had been here before.'

'Well, it looks as if we've found a plausible explanation,' said Isabel. 'I'm sorry that it hasn't proved more . . . more interesting.'

'The world is prosaic,' said Neil. He realised that Fiona had not understood him, and he blushed. 'It's very ordinary.'

'Even when it appears not to be,' said Isabel. People thought that evil would be exceptional, but it was . . . what? Banal, pronounced Hannah Arendt, and she had seen it close-up in the trial of Adolf Eichmann. And she thought, too, of the torturer's horse in Auden's '*Musée des Beaux Arts*' scratching itself against a tree while suffering takes place elsewhere. Neil was right: the world was a disappointingly ordinary place.

She noticed that Neil was staring out of the window, searching the sky. 'There's a pair of Goldies up there,' he said. 'Do you mind if I go outside and take a look at them?'

Fiona explained to Isabel. 'Golden eagles,' she said. 'We have a breeding pair not far away. Neil is very active in the ornithological club we have here. Not me. I'm afraid birds don't interest me at all.'

'They lead their lives,' said Isabel.

Fiona said nothing.

'We've imposed on you long enough,' Isabel ventured. 'Perhaps we should . . . '

'You haven't imposed,' said Fiona. 'I've enjoyed meeting you.'

There was something in her voice that made the remark more than a mere pleasantry. Loneliness, thought Isabel.

Fiona noticed a movement outside the window. 'There's your husband,' she said, pointing. 'And your wee boy.'

Isabel stood up to look. Charlie, pursued by Jamie across a strip of grass, was shrieking with delight.

'He calls it rugby,' said Isabel. 'Jamie chases him in circles but

208

never catches him. 'He's understood that much about the rules of rugby.'

'I don't like my boys playing rugby,' said Fiona. 'There was a boy up in Fort William who was pretty badly injured from a tackle. He walked again, but for a time they thought he'd end up in a wheelchair.'

Isabel winced. 'There are so many dangers. You give a hostage to fortune when you have children, don't you?'

Fiona nodded. 'Yes. Yes, you do.' She paused, still watching the scene outside on the grass. 'He's beautiful.'

'Thank you. I suppose as his mother . . . '

'I meant your man.'

Isabel was momentarily taken aback. 'Oh, Jamie. Well . . . '

'You're very lucky.'

'To be married to him?'

Fiona smiled. 'Yes. If it were me, I'd never be able to keep my hands off him.'

Isabel struggled. It was an extraordinary thing to say to somebody you had just met. You did not signal sexual interest in another person's partner – even if you felt it.

She searched for a response. 'You have a husband.'

Fiona smiled. 'Aye, I have my own man. And he's a good man, right enough. I'm happy enough with all that.'

All that meant sex, Isabel assumed. She waited. She did not want to lead the conversation any further down that road, but there was a certain fascination for her to hear what this woman thought.

'We met each other when we were fourteen,' Fiona said. 'Willy and I were at school together in Strontian. We started going out – if you could call it that – at sixteen. We were married at seventeen. That was just over twenty years ago.'

'Oh.'

'He's the only man I've ever been with,' Fiona continued.

Isabel looked down at the floor. The carpet was cheap and badly worn in places. She looked up; she had to offer some exchange of intimacy. 'I was married before,' she said. 'I married an Irishman. It didn't last.'

Fiona seemed interested. 'He went off with somebody else?'

'More or less. It was that, and other things.'

'They do. They go. Irishmen, Scotsmen, Englishmen – you name it. They go.'

Isabel felt that she had to defend men. 'Not all of them.'

'No, not all of them. My man hasn't. I thought at one time he might be because he was coming back really late from work over in Fort William. Then he went off to a job in Aberdeen and I thought that this was just an excuse, but then, you know what?'

'What?'

'I discovered he had been working overtime. Saving up for a new car for me. Aye, that's what he'd been doing and I'd been thinking the other thing.'

Isabel smiled. 'Sometimes we need to be reminded of trust,' she said. 'We all suspect, I suppose.'

'Yes, we do,' agreed Fiona.

'Maybe because it's dread,' Isabel continued. 'We hear of how it's happened to other people and we worry it's going to happen to us.'

Fiona looked out of the window again. Her eyes followed Jamie. 'You must worry with him,' she said. 'If you have a gorgeous man like that, you must worry that there are women looking at him all the time, undressing him with their eyes.'

Just as you're doing right now, thought Isabel. She looked at her watch. 'We told the hotel we'd be back for lunch,' she said. 'And we have to drop Neil off at his place.'

'Of course.'

'Would you mind if I took a photograph of the house against its backdrop? The sea and the islands – the lighthouse?'

'Go ahead,' said Fiona. And then she said, 'Look, he's picking the wee boy up. I love that. I love it when you see a strong man holding a child. It's so lovely. It makes me ... '

'My camera,' said Isabel busily. 'I must get it from the car.'

In the car on the way back Neil said, 'That boy.'

'What boy? Harry?' asked Isabel.

'No, their son, Matthew. The young man we met briefly.'

'Yes. What about him?'

'You saw his hair?'

From behind the wheel Jamie interjected, 'I did. Viking.'

'Exactly,' exclaimed Neil. 'Exactly the type. What makes it interesting is that the parents – Fiona and Willy – are local. If your grandparents came from here – as theirs did – then the odds are that they've been here, generation after generation, for heaven knows how long. They could easily have been here since the ninth century, when the Vikings arrived.'

'On the basis of hair colour?'

Neil defended himself. 'Not just that. You get to recognise the type. They're tall. They have that hair. There's just something about them, and you think *Viking*.'

He sensed that she was sceptical. 'I don't convince you, I see.'

'Who was here before them?' asked Jamie. 'Who did the Vikings have to rape and murder?'

'Picts,' said Neil. 'This was Pictish territory, although it was very much on the border with the Dál Riata, a bit further south. That was made up of bits of Ireland and southern Scotland.'

Isabel had not thought about the Picts for a long time. What was the name of that teacher who went on about them? She remembered: Miss MacReadie. She pictured her in the classroom telling the class of fourteen-year-old girls, 'We know very little about the Picts, girls, very little.' It had sounded as if she were issuing a warning: *Don't go out with a Pictish boy, girls: we know very little about them!*

'Weren't the Picts a bit mysterious?' She almost said, 'We know very little about them.'

'We know a bit more about them these days,' said Neil.

Ah! Miss MacReadie, I'm happy to tell you something. You may have retired to St Andrews or Melrose or somewhere like that; you may even be dead, but I have something I must tell you: we now know more about the Picts!

Neil continued, 'They've discovered some very important sites. There was a big Pictish monastery up in Moray. Before this, we thought the centre of Pictland was in Perthshire – not any more. It was further north, and then they swept down, pushing out various other people. Angles, Britons in Strathclyde, and so on.'

'Then the Vikings came?' asked Jamie.

'Yes.'

Isabel made an observation. 'Human history seems to me to be one long story of people sweeping down – or up, I suppose – replacing other people in the process. A struggle for somewhere to live. A struggle for resources.'

'Yes,' said Neil. 'Even today. It's exactly the same thing, although we don't always see it that way. Look at the Middle East: arguments over land, and who has it. Think of the Kurds. Look at every territorial dispute you care to mention. Northern Ireland, for instance.'

'Religion in that case,' Jamie ventured.

'Not just. Religion was the badge of identity, but it wasn't

212

really about whether you went to Mass or to a tub-thumping Protestant chapel. It was a result of the movement of people. The Protestant planters – many of them Scots – replaced the native Irish, remember? Movement of people again.'

Isabel mentioned Russia and the Ukraine.

'Movement of peoples,' said Neil. 'Cultural conflict, *Lebensraum* and so on: all intertwined.'

'So what do we do – if we want peace?' asked Jamie. 'Build fences? Berlin walls?'

Neil shook his head. 'People build borders and issue passports, but do they seriously think that can control human tides? They can't – they just can't.'

'It's down to numbers?' asked Jamie.

'Yes,' said Neil. 'Pressure of numbers.'

'But people don't like to talk about it?' Jamie pressed.

Isabel knew why. 'Because we recognise the humanity of the others – the ones who want to come in. Nobody likes to be hard-hearted. Nobody likes to defend what they've got against all-comers. We want to live in peace with others; we don't fancy being constantly on guard, pushing people away.'

'So you think we're going the way of the Picts?' asked Jamie.

Neil smiled. 'Perhaps.'

Isabel looked back towards the sea, now behind them. It was a rough coast, a coast of high cliffs and pounding waves; nature defended it. But it was, when all was said and done, one of the coasts of a country that was a lifeboat, and that lifeboat was under siege by people who wanted to be taken on board. She thought of the southern shores of Italy and the boats that came from the south, crammed with the desperate of North Africa striving to get into Europe. The vessels capsized under their human cargo; there were people in the water, their dream coming to a watery end. How could one turn one's face against all of that? What sort of person would one have to be to sail past?

They were approaching Neil's house.

'Thank you for sorting this out for us,' she said. 'You must have wondered what on earth it was all about.'

'I understood why you wanted to do it. Of course I did.'

Isabel smiled. 'And it was all a wild-goose chase.'

'You could call it that.'

They arrived at Neil's gate. 'It was worth doing,' said Jamie. 'I suppose it showed us something about how there's an explanation for everything – even the things that look most odd.'

Neil agreed. Then he added, 'But what if we hadn't found that *Scotsman* article? Would we have ended up believing in reincarnation of some sort?'

'Not on the basis of one case,' said Isabel.

'And yet the existence of one black swan disproves the proposition that all swans are white.'

'It does,' said Isabel. 'Provided you know for sure that the swan is black.'

'Oh, I see,' said Jamie. 'The swan might have been covered in soot. It might have been sitting on somebody's chimney. Or . . .'

'But there are black swans,' said Neil. 'They're native to Western Australia. But there are a tiny number of escaped ornamental black swans in Britain. Under fifty, probably. They're very lonely.'

Charlie had been silent on the journey, engrossed in some private game with his stuffed toy fox. But now he looked up. 'Swans are white,' he said.

That night, Jamie said to Isabel, 'I don't know what it is, but that place gave me the creeps. And that woman . . . I didn't like the way she looked at me.'

Isabel hesitated, but then said, 'I'm not at all surprised.'

'Why? Why aren't you surprised?'

Isabel shrugged. She was disinclined to repeat her conversation with Fiona. 'The way she spoke. It's difficult to put one's finger on it. She assumed inappropriate intimacy, I think. You shouldn't talk to people you don't really know about sex.'

Jamie's eyes widened. 'Is that what she did?'

'More or less.'

'Creepy,' said Jamie.

'Yes, a bit.'

'And sad,' Jamie added. 'There she is, cooped up in that remote place with that lighthouse and the sea and . . . that son who looks as if he's about to jump into a Viking longboat and go off for a bit of pillaging.'

'Poor woman.'

'But at least we sorted out the business about Harry.' He paused, and looked enquiringly at Isabel. 'We have sorted that out, I take it?'

'Yes,' said Isabel. 'Sorted out.'

'You're definitely going to let go of it?'

'Yes,' she said. 'Definitely.'

15

They returned to Edinburgh the following day. The hot weather, brought about by a zone of high pressure that had settled over Scotland, gave way to cooler air from the south-west. Isobars tightened and the sky, clear for days on end, was now laced with fast-moving cirrus cloud. Falling ice crystals, thought Isabel, looking up at the delicate, dizzyingly high wisps of cloud; the first shy announcements of a change in the weather.

Jamie had gone with Charlie to the Zoo again and Grace had taken the day off to visit an elderly aunt in Stirling, leaving Isabel alone in the house. There was work to be done, of course, but Isabel felt disinclined to do it. The short trip to Ardnamurchan, though involving only two nights away, had unsettled her. Living in a city, one might forget the hinterland, and this had reminded her of a Scotland she wanted to pay more attention to. In particular, she wanted Charlie to be brought up to know the country he lived in, a country that was so much more than its cities. Returning from the quiet of Ardnamurchan, the city seemed restless; there were too many people making too many journeys by car. Ardnamurchan had seemed empty; Edinburgh, with the opening of the Festival not far off, seemed far too full.

She had been unsettled, too, by the trip to the McAndrews' house. She was not quite sure what she had expected to find there – nothing, really, and so it was not a question of having experienced an anti-climax. There had been a note of sadness to the whole affair, right from her first meeting with Kirsten, and the Ardnamurchan trip had seemed to crystallise that. She realised, of course, that she would have to visit Kirsten and tell her what she had found out, and she was unsure how the news would be received.

She had made an arrangement to meet Kirsten for lunch at Glass and Thompson's in Dundas Street, and she would tell her there. Before that, she decided that she would call in on Guy Peploe in the Scottish Gallery, a few doors down the hill. Guy was mounting a small Scots Colourist exhibition and had promised to show her some of the pictures before they were hung. After lunch, she would buy something for herself. She was not sure exactly what it would be, but the prospect improved her mood, lifting the slight sadness she had been feeling. Of course she knew that retail therapy was about as useful as a sugar rush, and about as long-lasting; but the anticipation, at least, had some effect.

She decided to walk into town, rather than to catch a bus. The cooler temperature seemed perfect; it was not so low as to chill, but low enough to make it pleasant to stroll down the Mound and through the crowds thronging Princes Street. In normal circumstances, Princes Street in the high summer induced a feeling of being trapped, but it did not do that now, and even as she was almost barged into by a group of self-engrossed teenage girls on a shopping trip, she could not bother to feel irritated. None of us as a teenager, she thought, really believes in the existence of others – not really; at that age we were as close to perfect solipsism as we ever came.

Guy Peploe, who ran the Scottish Gallery, met her at the door. She was slightly early, but Guy had finished what he was doing and was ready to show her the paintings, stacked against the wall in the lower gallery, ready for hanging in the main gallery above.

'You mentioned you'd been over in Argyll,' he said as they went downstairs. 'Business or pleasure?'

She found it difficult to answer in those terms: it had not been business in a sense that anybody would normally recognise, and yet it had not been for pleasure. Perhaps I should say I was interfering, she thought.

He noticed her smile. 'Did I say something amusing?'

She shook her head. 'I was thinking. Some of the things I do are clearly business – things to do with the *Review*. But then there are other things I do that are rather difficult to classify. You could call them *interferences*. That's what made me smile.'

Guy laughed. 'I don't think you interfere. I get the impression that you help people. That's not the same thing, surely.'

'Well, I think I'll use the term *interference*. I was over there on an interference.'

'And?'

'I found what I was looking for.'

She did not want to think about it just yet. Lunchtime was not much more than an hour away and she would have to speak to Kirsten then. She hoped the other woman would be relieved to hear that a rational explanation had been found, but she was not sure of that. What would Kirsten do? She could try to explain to her son that his memory had played a trick on him; she might even show him the *Scotsman* article. But that would probably make no difference – a child's imagination, and the convictions it spawned, would surely be beyond the reach of rational deflation. And as Jamie had pointed out, there was something ineffably sad about this whole affair; an unhappy little boy would be made no happier by anything that his mother chose to tell him.

Guy led the way down to the lower gallery. 'Here we are,' he said. 'Fifteen Colourist paintings. Seven borrowed; eight for sale – some of them real gems.'

'Peploes?' she asked. Guy was the grandson of the great painter and had recently written a book on his work.

'Three,' said Guy. 'But they're all on loan.' He paused. 'A lovely Fergusson – if your walls are feeling bare.' He reached down to extract a painting from the stack. 'This is a later post-war Fergusson, and as you will see . . . '

'Fecundity,' said Isabel.

'Precisely.'

'And a certain erotic element,' she added.

Guy inclined his head. 'Both of those. But isn't it rather lovely?'

Isabel stared at the picture of the woman painted against a lush background of greenery. The curves of the woman's body were suggestive, as were the twisted forms of the plants. 'I couldn't live with that,' she said. 'It's magnificent, but you almost feel that the painting's going to insinuate its way out of its frame.'

Guy laughed. 'That's a good way of putting it.'

Fecundity. She thought: *Will I have another child?* She had tried not to think about it, but the Fergusson painting had touched something within her. *Am I that woman?*

'And this,' said Guy. 'What do you think of this.'

She recognised the style. 'Cadell?'

'Yes. But clearly not one of his women in hats.'

She leaned forward to examine the painting more closely. It was a picture of a male bather sitting on a rock; the face, though, was indistinct.

'That's probably a picture of Charles Oliver,' said Guy. 'Bunty Cadell had a friend whom he had met during the First World War. He took him on as a companion and man-servant. He used to give elaborate dinner parties when he was living in Ainslie Place and Charles would act as butler. But he would also act as his sales agent and would sell pictures for him.'

'Close friends?'

'I assume so,' said Guy. 'But the people at the dinner parties would have understood.'

Another painting caught her eye. 'And that?'

'Hunter. But not one of his best. That painting has been looking for a home for rather too long, I think. We show it for the owner, who wants to sell it, but the problem is that Hunter ruined it. He never knew where to stop. It's important for an artist to know when a painting is finished. I'm not sure that Hunter always got that right.'

'Whereas James Cowie stopped rather early,' said Isabel. 'Some of his paintings were deliberately unfinished. He just stopped in a corner, and rather faded away. I have one like that.'

They spent half an hour looking at the other paintings. Then Guy said, 'Is something troubling you? You seem a bit distracted.'

Isabel sighed. 'Yes. Frankly, Guy, everything's troubling me. I've got myself mixed up in a rather sad little matter and I don't feel comfortable about it. And then . . . '

He waited.

'And then Cat has got herself in tow with another man, and that always worries me. He lives near here, by the way.'

'Oh yes?'

'In Drummond Place. He's called Mick. I've met him and . . . '

Guy stopped. 'Tall? Dark hair? A bit like your Jamie?'

Isabel gave an exclamation of surprise. 'Exactly. Jamie's double, in fact.' She paused. 'You know him?'

'Yes, of course,' said Guy. 'He's very interested in art.'

'He recognised my Thomson.'

'Well, there you are. He's extremely nice.'

She said nothing for a moment, and Guy continued, 'Is it serious?'

'I think so. But, then, you can never tell with Cat. In general, she has awful taste in men and has had the most appalling boyfriends. She always gets rid of them; she can't seem to stick to one man. Now there's this one. I also thought he was nice, by the way.'

'Well, he is. So where's the problem?'

'Because he's too nice for her,' said Isabel. 'And I wonder whether I should tactfully make sure he knows what he's getting into.' She frowned. 'No, did I really say that?' As she spoke, she thought too about Lettuce. Lettuce was about to get a job in Edinburgh. She may have reassessed her attitude to him, but she was still deeply suspicious of Christopher Dove. Should she warn somebody in the University about the possible manipulation of Lettuce by Dove? But if she did that, and Lettuce's appointment did not go ahead, then she would be causing grave disappointment to Clementine Lettuce, for whom she harboured no ill feeling.

There was a note of concern now in Guy's voice. 'Listen,' he said. 'I don't think you should. You don't have to go round warning others about the people they're getting involved with.'

'Don't you?'

He seemed certain of his answer. 'No. It's not your business. People have to make their own mistakes.'

'So we're not our brother's keeper?'

'Sometimes, but not in a case like this.'

She gazed at the Fergusson picture of the woman. 'Does art make us feel better? Is that its role, do you think?'

'One of them,' said Guy. 'It can give us answers. It can promote happiness.'

'Happiness? Is that what we want?'

Guy looked surprised. 'I thought that's what you philosophers believed in. Aren't you meant to help us know how to be happy?'

'I don't know,' said Isabel. 'Perhaps that's what philosophy is meant to do. To show us that we don't really know.' She looked at her watch. 'Sorry, I have to go. And I'm sorry, too, that I burdened you with my doubts. Your paintings, by the way, have made me feel a bit better.'

'Then they've worked,' said Guy.

'But I still don't know what to do about Cat,' said Isabel.

'Then do nothing.'

She smiled weakly. 'Maybe.'

'Not maybe,' said Guy, more firmly this time. 'Definitely. Keep out of it.'

'Best left alone,' muttered Isabel.

'Precisely,' said Guy.

She realised that his advice was sound; doing nothing was the right thing to do. She began to thank him. 'You're right, you know, I have a tendency to . . .'

She was interrupted by the ringing of her mobile phone. She glanced at it. She could ignore the call – another instance of doing nothing – but something prompted her to answer.

'Isabel Dalhousie?' The voice seemed familiar, but she was not sure why. 'Neil Starling. Is this a good time?'

Guy signalled that he would leave her to take the call in peace, and he left the room. She moved over to the window.

'As good as any. Thank you, by the way, for all your help the other day. I've written you a note.'

'Well, that's what I'm phoning you about,' Neil said. 'A development.'

She caught her breath. 'Yes?'

'Fiona McAndrew phoned me. She said that her husband had reminded her of something. She was apologetic for not having remembered it. A Campbell family did stay in that house, apparently.'

Isabel closed her eyes. 'Oh, I see.' She waited for him to continue.

'You're still there?'

'Yes,' she said. 'Please carry on.'

'They rented out the house from time to time. They did it for a couple of months each summer – to holidaymakers – to raise a bit of money. They would go and stay with her parents at Ardgour. One year the house was rented by a family called Campbell – it was about six or seven years ago. They had two young sons, as she recalled.'

Isabel's heart turned. She knew that she had been looking for something precisely like this, but now that it had turned up, this information was far from welcome. This disturbed the neat, rational solution she thought she had found. So there had been a Campbell family, and this meant that what Harry said was confirmed. A coincidence? Of course it was; it had to be, it simply had to be.

'She had an address for them,' Neil continued. 'She wasn't sure if they'd still be there, but they had an address on the lease

223

agreement – fortunately, they kept all of those. She gave it to me. Would you like it? It's in Edinburgh – or just outside. Near Roslin.'

There was a note of satisfaction in his voice – a suggestion of excitement.

'This is quite extraordinary, isn't it?' he said. 'I hadn't imagined we would find anything like this, and yet there it is. Amazing, I think.'

Her response was flat. 'Yes, I suppose it is.'

He picked up her tone. 'I'm sorry . . . I hope I've done the right thing in getting in touch again.'

She realised that she must have sounded churlish; he was doing her a favour, and her response must have sounded almost rude. 'Please forgive me,' she said. 'I'm just a little bit shocked by this.'

'Oh, I can understand that. I felt very odd too. I suppose it's how you feel when you come across something inexplicable like this. It's disturbing, isn't it?'

'Yes it is. But I'm very grateful to you and, yes, I'd like their address. A long shot perhaps, but yes.'

She reached into her bag for a pencil. There was a leaflet on a table by the wall, and she used this to note down the address he gave her. She thanked him, promising to keep him informed about what happened.

'My curiosity is well and truly aroused,' he said. 'If you could let me know what happens I'd be interested.'

'Of course.'

They rang off and she replaced the phone in her pocket. She looked at her watch. She would be a few minutes late for her meeting with Kirsten, and now that meeting would have to be quite different and, she suspected, rather more difficult.

*

Kirsten was already there when she arrived at Glass and Thompson's. Seated at one of the tables towards the back of the bistro, she was engaged in conversation with Russell, the proprietor, who was leaning nonchalantly against one of the chairs, a cloth in his hand, emphasising a point with his free hand. He smiled as he saw Isabel.

'I'm telling your friend how to use Stilton in soup,' he began. 'She was being very unadventurous. You can put *anything* in soup, I said.'

Isabel smiled. Russell was known for his ability to make conversation on any subject, with anyone. 'I take it that there's Stilton soup on the menu.'

'Order the soup and find out,' said Russell. 'It's our mystery menu day. We bring you something and then you identify it. It's a challenge.' He laughed. 'Not really, but an idea, don't you think?'

He left them with the real menu while he went to fetch the sparkling water that Isabel had ordered.

'I'm late,' she said. 'I took a phone call.'

Kirsten hesitated. 'About ... '

Isabel nodded. 'Yes, it was.' She paused. 'How's Harry doing?'

Kirtsen's reply was perfunctory. 'He's fine. Fine. The call ... '

Isabel plucked up her courage, and remembered something that her moral philosophy tutor had said in that very first year at university: *There are very few circumstances − very few − when paternalism is justified. You should not keep the truth from people.* She had forgotten virtually everything else that he had said to her, but she had remembered that, probably because at that stage in her life she still thought that it was all right to keep things from people. But he was right. Poor bumbling Dr Fordewell, with his dreadful dress sense − he wore a moth-eaten cardigan and brown corduroy trousers − had been right about that, just as he was right about so many other things. She tried to remember the book he had written that had been published during that first year, and how impressed she had been. Here was somebody who had written a book on philosophy – an actual book! She had viewed him with awe, ignoring the cardigan, which, in the circumstances, seemed so utterly appropriate; anybody could look smart, but only a moral philosopher who had written a *book* could wear a cardigan like that with pride.

You should not keep the truth from people.

'The call was from a man called Neil Starling. He helped us find the house that Harry's been talking about.'

Kirsten drew in her breath. 'You've looked for the house?'

Isabel nodded. 'Yes, I decided to do what I could to ... to verify, I suppose, Harry's story.'

Kirsten was staring at her.

'You did ask me,' said Isabel. 'You did ask me to help.'

'Of course, of course. I'm sorry, it's just that I didn't know that you had actually done something so quickly.'

'Well, we found a house that matched the description, and we went up there. I had an introduction to this Neil Starling, who was very helpful.'

Kirsten was listening intently. 'And?'

Isabel explained about the article. 'To begin with, I thought we had stumbled over the solution. There was an article in the press that mentioned the house. There was a picture of it.'

Kirsten looked puzzled. 'But how ...'

'I thought that Harry must have seen it. You know how children pick up things.'

Kirsten looked unconvinced. 'Do you really think so? I've not seen him reading the papers.'

'The author of the article was called Campbell.'

This had its effect on Kirsten. 'Oh,' she said, sounding deflated.

'But I no longer think that,' Isabel went on. 'Since then I've found out that there actually was a family called Campbell who stayed there – for a short time – a few years ago. They had two sons, apparently.'

It had been easier than she anticipated to deliver the news. Now she watched Kirsten's reaction.

At first the other woman seemed not to react, but sat quite still, her eyes fixed on Isabel but betraying no emotion. Then, quite suddenly, she crumpled. 'So it's true,' she said quietly.

'Well, we don't know, do we? All we know is that there is a house that looks like the place Harry's been talking about. Then we know that a Campbell family spent some time there. But Campbell, as you know, is a very common name in Scotland – probably one of the most common names there is.'

Kirsten agreed. 'I know hundreds. Half my family are Campbells.'

'So how can we explain this?' Isabel continued. 'Coincidence, I'd say. An astonishing coincidence, yes, but then coincidences are, by their very nature, astonishing.'

Kirsten seemed to pay little attention to this explanation. She pulled herself together, and asked briskly, 'So? What now? What do we do now?'

'I've been given an address for these people,' explained Isabel. 'They live just outside Edinburgh, or they did some years ago – the address may not be a current one. If it is, I intend to go to see them.'

'Do you want me to come?'

Isabel did not. 'Not at this point, if you don't mind. I don't know what their reaction is likely to be. They might resent the intrusion. So I'll do it.'

Russell returned with the water and took their order, and it was then that Isabel realised what Kirsten had said.

'You said something about Campbells. You said that half your family . . .'

'Yes, half my family are Campbells. My mother was a Campbell and my grandmother on my father's side. They were all from Argyll – real Campbell territory.'

Isabel shook her head in disbelief. 'Well, that rather changes things.'

'Why?'

'Your little boy knows all this? He knows that there are Campbells on your side?'

Kirsten shrugged. 'Yes, he would know that, I suppose. He was quite close to my mother. She lived in Linlithgow and so she was able to see quite a bit of him. She babysat a lot when he was younger. In fact, she did that until about six months ago. She died.'

'Six months ago?'

'Yes, a little over. Maybe seven.'

'And you say that Harry was close to her. Did he stay with her in Linlithgow?'

'Often.'

For a few moments, Isabel felt something akin to irritation. How could Kirsten have failed to make the connection? And yet, even as she felt this, she reminded herself that this was a woman who had been upset by something that had frightened her, and that she was by herself and had been unable to talk to anybody about it. She should not be cross; she should not be impatient.

'I think I can see what's happened,' Isabel said, keeping her voice even. 'It's obvious now.'

Kirsten frowned. 'Because of the Campbells on my mother's side?'

'Did she – your mother that is – have a photograph album? Did she talk to him about the family?'

'Yes, I think she did. She certainly had photos – lots of them.'

'Of Argyll?'

'Yes. She had an old biscuit tin full of ancient black-and-white photos of her as a little girl.'

'Where would that have been?'

'They lived near Oban. Seil Island.'

Isabel looked up at the ceiling. The situation had now become embarrassing.

'I'm a bit surprised,' she began.

'By what?'

She hesitated. She could say that she was surprised by Kirsten's failure to see something that was now so glaringly obvious. But she did not. 'Can one see a lighthouse from Seil Island, I wonder?'

Kirsten started to answer. She was not sure . . . She trailed off. 'Oh, I see.'

'Yes,' said Isabel, smiling. 'I think this solves the whole thing, don't you think? Harry's grieving for his grandmother. He's made up a life for himself as a way of handling that grief.'

Kirsten started to smile. 'I've been stupid. I should have thought . . . '

Isabel reached across to put her hand on the other woman's wrist. 'You haven't been stupid. It's extremely easy to miss things under your nose. I do it all the time. Everybody does.'

'You're being very kind.'

'I'm just relieved we know where all this comes from.'

Russell returned to take their order. 'Stilton soup?' he asked.

'In the circumstances,' said Isabel, 'yes.'

'For two?' asked Russell.

'Yes,' said Kirsten.

16

She told Jamie that evening. He listened, bemused. He was not surprised, he said, that the real explanation should be so much more credible than that of a child seeing a photograph in a newspaper. 'It's obvious, isn't it?' he said. 'Completely obvious.'

'After the event, maybe,' said Isabel. 'Hindsight bias.'

He looked at her enquiringly. 'The wisdom of hindsight?'

'Yes. When we know an outcome, we tend to say that it was foreseeable or highly likely to occur. We look at a course of events with the knowledge that we now have, but didn't have then.'

'So it's as if we say we knew all along when . . . '

'When we didn't,' she supplied. 'We now know that such and such a thing was likely to result and we *think* that we would have known that at the time when that result hadn't yet occurred. But in practice, we wouldn't have known it. We just wouldn't.'

'So in this case . . . '

'In this case,' she said, 'you're effectively saying that you would have enquired about whether there were Campbells in the family or whether there was any relative who might have been talking to him about life in Argyll in the past – a relative who lived near a lighthouse, for example. It seems so obvious now, but it wasn't then.'

Jamie shrugged. 'Well, all right. Leaving aside hindsight issues, it does seem pretty obvious, doesn't it?'

'Yes, it does. And I must admit, I'm happy that we found a totally feasible explanation.'

'So that's it?'

She hesitated for a few moments before she replied. 'I suppose so. There is the additional factor of that Campbell family who stayed in the house one summer, but frankly I don't think there's any point in looking into that. The whole idea must have come from the grandmother. It must have.'

Jamie thought so too. 'The only point in putting those other Campbells in the picture,' he said, 'would be if one were still to believe in the possibility of reincarnation.'

'Which I don't,' said Isabel. She interrogated herself: I don't, do I? Of course I don't. I believe in things that are proved; I believe in things that withstand laboratory examination, that can be reproduced under the eye of science; I believe in things that are here and now, are tangible, observable, measurable; Ockham's razor should be wielded on the rest.

Jamie shook his head emphatically. 'And neither do I.' He paused. 'So no further enquiries?'

'None.'

'Good.'

But a few hours after this conversation, Isabel picked up the telephone in her study and dialled the number of her friend Charlie Maclean, who lived near Roslin. 'It's idle curiosity, Charlie, but I wonder if you could find out about some people who I think live near Roslin. They're called Campbell and they live in a house called Wester Brae Farmhouse. Or I think they might.'

Charlie was used to Isabel's odd requests. 'Find out what?' he asked.

'Just about them in general: who they are, what they do, and so on. Any local gossip.'

'There's always plenty of that,' said Charlie. 'Most of it false, malicious, and fundamentally unbelievable – except sometimes.' He laughed. 'Sometimes it's right on the nail . . . not that I pass it on, you understand.'

'Of course not.'

'Mind you, I've got a shocker of a story to tell you. Remind me some time.'

'I shall.'

They returned to her request. Charlie said that he knew somebody who lived in Roslin – in the village itself – and who knew everyone. He would ask her, he said, and let Isabel know as soon as possible.

'You couldn't get in touch right now, could you?'

'I suppose so. Is this urgent?'

She could not say that it was, but he picked up her eagerness to hear, and he agreed to get in touch with his friend immediately after Isabel got off the line.

She rang off and went to sit in her study. She opened the book that she had been reading, *The Habits of Happiness*. She was planning to devote a future issue of the *Review* to the topic of happiness, and she would ask the author of this book to contribute. She liked his style – and his approach. Perhaps he would write a sequel, *The Novel Habits of Happiness*, and come up with some new insights. Happiness was not as simple a proposition as it was sometimes believed to be: there were even those who believed that the pursuit of happiness was a bad thing, restricting the growth of knowledge and awareness, encouraging us to withdraw into an anodyne world of intellect-numbing benevolence. Proust had warned about this, she recalled, when he had said that happiness might be beneficial for the body but it was grief that developed the powers of the mind.

She started to read, making the occasional note as she worked her way through the book. After twenty minutes or so, the telephone rang, bringing her back from the world of happiness and its implications.

It was Charlie. 'Success,' he announced. 'My friend knows them quite well. You said Wester Brae Farmhouse, didn't you?'

'Yes,' said Isabel.

'I know the house myself, as it happens,' Charlie continued. 'I drive past it quite often. It's set back a bit from the road. Nice place.'

She waited for him to continue.

'He's something to do with an engineering firm,' Charlie went on. 'And there were other bits and pieces of information – I've made a note here. Let me see.'

She took a deep breath.

'He's called Alan,' Charlie said. 'She's Olivia. He was on the local council for a couple of years – a Liberal Democrat, apparently – and she was on the school board. They were very much involved in the Roslin Chapel restoration project, and still are involved down there in some capacity.'

'Children?' asked Isabel.

'Two,' said Charlie. 'A boy and a girl. The boy is at the high school in Penicuik; the girl goes to a school somewhere in town. Apparently there was a third child, a boy, who died six or seven years ago. Apparently he had a completely unsuspected heart condition. It can happen, I'm told. Apparently she's never really recovered – and that's understandable enough. That sort of loss . . . '

Isabel caught her breath. Yes. That must be the worst loss one could suffer, the very worst; six or seven years ago.

'Isabel?' Charlie asked. 'You still there?'

'Yes.'

'You went quiet.'

She made an effort to concentrate. 'I'm sorry. It was your telling me about the boy they lost – I thought about . . . '

'The nightmare all parents dread,' said Charlie. 'Yes, of course.' He became businesslike. 'Do you want me to try to find out anything more? I could always ask.'

She told him that this was enough, and they ended their conversation. She stood up and stared out into the garden. A movement outside had attracted her attention, and she stepped closer to the window. Brother Fox had emerged from the undergrowth of a rhododendron and was standing in the middle of a small square of lawn, the sun on his back, his fur seeming to glow red with the light. Isabel stood quite still, as she did not want him to see her; she did not want to disturb him in this private moment. But he, of course, had sensed her with that extra sense, that subtle radar, that animals have and that we can only imagine; he sensed her and looked round sharply, so that they were staring directly at one another through the glass of the windowpane.

What would you do? she whispered.

Brother Fox held her gaze.

But you have no dilemmas, she said. *None. You are pure instinct.*

Suddenly, he turned and padded off, his long, brush tail flicking as he moved. Isabel saw a lower branch of the rhododendron sway as he brushed past it, and then become still again. She turned and looked at her bookshelves; the cumulated wisdom of moral philosophy was shelved there in front of her, in book after book, but none of these books contained anything on how naked and unsupported were the decisions of real life. It would be simplicity itself to pick up the phone and tell Kirsten that something new had turned up. But what exactly was it? Another possible explanation, another strange coincidence? And then it occurred to her that the woman who had lost her son might be interested to hear that there was a little boy who spoke as if he had been there, with them. Would that provide some comfort for her in the desolation from which she was thought never to have recovered?

She made up her mind. Charlie was having his rest and Jamie was in charge. She would explain herself to Jamie later; if she told him now what she proposed to do he would raise objections and they might even have one of their very rare rows. She had to tell Kirsten about this because ... She thought of a number of reasons why she should do this, but in the forefront of her mind was the simple precept: *you should not keep the truth from people.* It was a cornerstone of the anti-paternalist argument, a position on which a strict Kantian would go to the wall if needs be.

She told Jamie that she was going to Morningside and would be back in an hour or so. That was strictly true – she was going to Morningside, where Kirsten had her flat, but she knew that Jamie would interpret things differently and would think that she was going to the supermarket. That was the way she put it when she went shopping – going to Morningside. The thought crossed her mind: *I'm keeping the truth from him because I'm allowing him to misunderstand me.* But it was too late, and sometimes, she told herself, there were conflicting duties that had to be weighed against each other. *Hard choices.* There was a book of that title on her bedside table by an author whom she admired;

her own choices were so insignificant by comparison, but that did not make them any easier to make. All of us had hard choices, she thought; the greatest of us and the least of us, and we had to feel our way through them and accept that there would sometimes be regrets.

She went to the garage and opened the door. Unlocking the green Swedish car, she got into the driving seat and put the key in the ignition. She turned it. There was silence. She turned the key again. A light flickered on the dashboard, a brief sign of electrical life, and then that went out.

It was dark in the garage, as there were no windows and the only light came from the open door, which was itself quite shaded by an unruly clematis that had established itself against the wall and in the guttering. There was an odd smell, too; the smell of petrol from the leaky lawnmower that Jamie used to cut the lawn; the smell of mould from an old canvas tarpaulin that her father had refused to throw away and that had remained for years, half-unfolded, at the back of the garage. There was an earthy smell from a bag of compost that she had bought for use on the flowerbeds and that she had opened but not used very much.

She leaned back in the driver's seat. Jamie had suggested that she should sell the car and get a newer, more practical vehicle; he had even sent for a leaflet setting out the merits of a new hybrid petrol-electric car that promised great economy and a good conscience. She had declined, even if it had been difficult to argue against the case for a greener means of transport. She loved her Swedish car and now they were no longer making them because the factory had proved uneconomic. Other cars were very different; they were not Swedish; they all looked identical, being born in the same wind tunnel; they lacked character, which the green Swedish car had in great measure, even if it sometimes would not start. Somewhere in the works there was a short that drained the power from the battery when the car was not in use. Her mechanic had looked into it and had scratched his head. 'Electrical issues are a dark art,' he had said enigmatically, and then had said, 'I can get you a new car, you know, where this sort of thing just wouldn't happen.'

She was not sure how long she sat in the car, but she thought it was rather more than half an hour. Then she got out, opened the battery compartment, and connected the terminals to the charger that was habitually left ready for use in the garage. Lights on the charger glowed red; power, and motion, would be restored, but not for some hours. And by now she had made a fresh decision.

'That was quick,' said Jamie.

'I didn't go anywhere,' said Isabel.

'Sometimes that's best,' said Jamie, watching her. 'Sometimes nowhere is the best place to go.'

She looked at him fondly. He was lying on the sofa, in his stockinged feet, reading a magazine. *I don't want you ever to be any different from how you are now*, she thought. *But you will be, won't you?*

'Thinking of?' he asked, over the top of his magazine.

'Unrepeatable thoughts,' she said.

He smiled. 'Shameless.'

She thought: *Do you know how beautiful you are?*

He said: 'I think that you're rather unsettled. Am I right?'

She sat down on the arm of the sofa. He reached out and laid a hand on her knee – the gesture of a friend rather than a lover.

'Yes,' she said. 'I am. This whole thing with that little boy and his mother and . . . and . . . '

He waited. But she needed encouragement before she would continue.

'Cat?' he asked.

'Yes, I worry about her. I know I shouldn't, but I do.'

He sighed. 'Cat's going to be fine. I saw her yesterday, you know. She said that she's going to come to see you. She said she had an announcement to make.'

Isabel had suspected that this might happen. 'That'll be about Mick.'

He nodded. 'Accept it. Cross fingers for a good outcome. I think she's changed, by the way. I think she's settling down at long last.'

'At long, long last.' She paused. 'I'm worried on his behalf. Perhaps I should have spoken to him.'

'Don't,' warned Jamie. 'Don't even think about it.' He dropped the magazine on the floor. 'And what else is on your mind?'

'Professor Lettuce,' said Isabel. 'There's a danger he's going to get a job here in Edinburgh, and he's planning something with Dove. And yet I feel rather sorry for Lettuce now.'

'Not your problem,' said Jamie. 'Can't you see it, Isabel? The whole world is not your problem. We think that it is – I know that plenty of people feel they have to shoulder the burdens of the whole planet, but we can't, can we?'

He searched her eyes for understanding and agreement.

'You do see it, don't you?' he continued.

She looked away. 'Yes, I do. I see it.'

'Lettuce's appointment is not something you should do anything about. Even Christopher Dove is none of your business. You may have to accept them.'

'Yes, yes.'

He took his hand off her knee and glanced at his watch. 'I'm going to cook tonight.'

'Again?'

'Yes. I want you to do nothing. And to do nothing without worrying about doing nothing . . . '

That was a Friday; over the weekend that followed, Isabel caught up with her work for the *Review*. The first of the papers for the anniversary issue had now arrived; she suspected that more than one of them had been retrieved from a drawer and dusted down for the purpose, but that was understandable, and she did not mind. Amongst them, though, was Professor Trembling's paper, 'The Ethical World of my Mother', fifteen closely typed pages when printed out. Isabel sat down with this on Saturday afternoon while Jamie played cricket – or a version of it – with Charlie in the garden, substituting a tennis ball for the hard red missile that the real game used.

She began to read. Geoffrey Trembling's mother, he explained, had been brought up in the Midwest, but had moved to California when her father had died, her own mother having died when she was still quite young. She had found a job at the naval base in San Diego, as a civilian secretary, and had married a petty officer she met there. That was Geoffrey's father. He drank, and when he was posted to Florida, Geoffrey and his mother stayed in San Diego. She had given up her job at the naval base and now found work as a clerk in a government seismology office. She was determined that her son should go to college, and she had taken in part-time typing work to help finance this. She transcribed medical reports from dictated tapes, often typing late into the night. 'She never complained about work,' he wrote. 'She just did it. People like her did that.'

Isabel read on, and as she did so, she found herself drawn into the rather ordinary world of this secretary and her son. The father defaulted on alimony payments, was dismissed from the service, and disappeared. The Navy did its best to help find him, but failed. His wife became ill and had to have a hysterectomy. For years they suffered from an abusive, intimidating neighbour. A cousin won a competition that gave her two tickets to Paris. She gave the tickets to them, and so Geoffrey had his first trip abroad at the age of sixteen. He won a scholarship to Berkeley. His mother wept with pride, he said, when they received the letter.

Her ethical world was laid out for the reader. It was founded, her son said, on intuition. She knew what was right because she felt it. He asked her about this and she explained that she thought her intuition had something to do with pain. She intuitively understood whether an act would cause pain to another. If it did, then she avoided it. He had asked her why one should avoid causing pain in others, and she said that was because of love. We loved them and did not want to cause them pain. She asked what could be simpler than that? 'You have your books and your theories, Geoffrey,' she had said to him, 'but I don't need those because my nose tells me when there's something wrong.'

And then he wrote, 'Obviously the professional philosopher will find much of this pretty low-level stuff. The avoidance of pain in others hardly comes from any profound insight; nor will the expression of love for others seem in any way radical. But what interests me in all this is the good that lies behind my mother's attitude. She is an ordinary woman, not a person of great education or sophistication. Her life has never amounted to much – it has been a matter of work, of struggling to make something of a hopeless marriage; it has been a matter of helping at church functions, lending a hand with looking after various people who could not look after themselves; it has been one of doting on me, her only child, and taking pride in anything that I did; it has been one of trying to run a house and meet payments on the car and wiping away the tears of others when they encountered disappointments and sadness and loss. And all the time she has done this without question, she has done it because there was something within her, deep within her that amounted, I think, to a notion of the good. It was like a source of warmth within her, something indescribable, something that has shone on her very ordinary, unexceptional life, but has made it a good one. It is the power of good, glimpsed through the agency of intuition; it is there, and she sees it because she has opened herself to goodness, as one opens a door to allow a friend to come in. That is what it is. That is what I have seen in my mother, and it has given my life more sense of direction, more meaning, and ultimately more joy than anything else I have ever seen. I am not ashamed to say that; I am not ashamed.'

Isabel finished reading. She laid the paper down on her desk. She would publish every word of it. She would change nothing. She remembered how she had shown his letter to Jamie, and of their amusement and their talk of mother's boys; Professor Trembling had said he was not ashamed, but I am, she thought; I am.

Now she moved on to the special issue on happiness. She had written to a number of people to solicit contributions and they had, for the most part, responded positively. One, though, had declined on the grounds that he was committed to a book he was writing and could not find the time to write an article 'even for you, my dear Isabel' and had then followed this with an emoticon of a happy face. Another had said that he had been flattered to have been asked, but that he was, quite frankly, too depressed to write about happiness. 'What's the point?' he had asked.

On the Thursday of that week Kirsten phoned to ask Isabel to meet her. Isabel suggested La Barantine in Bruntsfield, and was waiting there for Kirsten when she saw the other woman crossing the road. She waved, and Kirsten waved back. There was a cheerfulness in her demeanour as she entered the café.

'You look happy,' said Isabel.

Kirsten smiled. 'Do I? Well, that must be because I am.'

'Ah.'

'Yes, I'm happy. You could say I'm very happy. Jimmy's back.'

'Your husband?'

'Yes, he's leaving the Army. He's going into partnership with another Army piper. They're going to do weddings, dinners, that sort of thing – any time anybody needs a piper.'

'He'll do well,' said Isabel.

'He thinks so.'

'And he's pleased to be back with you?'

'He's relieved. And so am I.'

The young woman from behind the counter came to take their order, and then went off into the kitchen at the back.

'And Harry? He's pleased to have his dad back?'

Kirsten beamed. 'You bet! Pleased as punch.'

'Well, that's good. I know it sounds trite, but a boy needs a father. If at all possible, of course.'

Kirsten nodded. 'Of course. But the wonderful thing is this: he's stopped. That business about the house and the Campbells and so on – stopped completely. I asked him about it, and he simply said, "I've forgotten now." And that's it. Everything has improved – his school work, his state of mind.'

'He's happy?'

'As a ... as a ...' Kirsten looked at Isabel for help.

'You can pick your expression,' said Isabel, smiling. 'As a dog with a bone, or two bones perhaps. As happy as a sandboy is another one.'

'What's a sandboy?'

'They were boys who sold sand in Victorian times,' said Isabel. 'They were thought to be happy. Either that or it's an insect that hopped around on the sand. These things can be vague.'

Their coffee arrived.

'May I ask you one thing?' said Kirsten. 'Do you really think it all came from what my mother had told him? From her photographs?'

Isabel lifted her cup to her lips and took a sip of coffee. This gave her time – time to remember Dr Fordewell in his cardigan and his injunction about never hiding the truth. But then she thought: *I don't know what the truth is, at least not in this particular set of circumstances.*

She chose her words carefully. 'If I had found out something else,' she said slowly, 'would you want me to tell you? I mean, would you want me to tell you now that everything seems to have worked out so well?'

Kirsten gazed at her intently. She began to say something, but stopped. Then she began again. 'I don't think so ... '

'Are you sure?'

Kirsten became more decisive. 'Yes, I'm sure. I don't see what the point would be, do you?'

'I don't see any point at all,' agreed Isabel.

For a few moments nothing more was said, and then Kirsten broke the silence. 'I'm very grateful to you, you know. You've helped me so much.'

'It's kind of you to say that. But I don't think I really did very much. The problem seems to have sorted itself out – which is what often happens, I think.'

'Maybe. But you were kind to me. You were.'

Isabel lowered her eyes. 'Thank you for saying that.' And she thought: *hard choices are sometimes less hard than we think.*

*

On Friday afternoon, she saw Edward Mendelson walking across the Meadows. She had Charlie with her, asleep in his pushchair, his stuffed fox clasped to his chest. She and Edward spoke in hushed tones so as not to waken him.

'I have news for you,' said Edward. 'Professor Lettuce has been announced as the next Director of the Institute.'

Edward imparted this information in the tone of one unveiling a piece of bad news: a major dip in company profits, the outbreak of a distant war, the failure of a promising line of scientific research.

Isabel received this with equanimity. 'I thought it likely,' she said. 'I met his wife, you see. She spoke to me about it.'

Edward looked surprised. 'You're not too alarmed?'

'No. I imagine he'll be very pleased. And he has his good points, I think.'

'Well, I'm much relieved that you seem to be reasonably sanguine about it. And there's news on the Christopher Dove front.'

This was the signal for Isabel to look more worried.

'He was turned down, apparently,' said Edward. 'I heard from one of the other people in the Institute. Dove had applied for a post in the University – a teaching post, unlike Lettuce's new position. And he failed to get it. They've appointed somebody from Cambridge.' He gave the name, and Isabel realised that it was that of a regular contributor to the *Review*.

'I'm pleased to hear that,' she said. 'I was worried about Dove.'

'So, there's no need to worry,' said Edward.

Isabel laughed. 'Apart from all the usual reasons,' she said.

'Well, we know all about those,' said Edward. 'And, generally speaking, we keep them in perspective.'

'If we can.'

Charlie began to stir. A breeze had arisen and was beginning to move the tops of the trees that lined the lateral walk across the grass.

A line came to Isabel. '*The winds must come from somewhere when they blow . . .*'

Edward gave a smile of recognition and supplied the next line: '*There must be reasons why the leaves decay . . .*'

Isabel looked at him. 'I find that poem utterly haunting,' she said. 'And it has two of the most beautiful lines that Auden wrote.'

'Let me guess,' said Edward. 'I imagine that this is what you have in mind: *If we should weep when clowns put on their show . . .*'

She finished for him: '*If we should stumble when musicians play . . .*' She looked up at the tops of the trees, still moving, the leaves little black dots waving against the sky. 'I think I know what he meant about weeping when the clowns came on. We know that we should laugh, just as we know that we should be able to dance when the musicians play. But we can't, because we're weak and the world is beyond our control. Things will happen whatever human attempts we may make to alter the course of events.'

Edward nodded. 'You can look at it that way,' he said.

She cooked for Jamie that evening. She had a new book, published by a chef who had just been awarded his first Michelin star. She chose one of the simpler recipes, but even that, it seemed, required two hours of preparation time. Once Charlie had been put to bed, Jamie came down to help her. She gave him carrots to chop.

'There was a boy at school with me who had the tip of his finger missing,' he said. 'He told us that he had lost it when he was chopping carrots. He thought his finger was a carrot.'

245

Isabel winced.

'But he had a vivid imagination,' Jamie continued. 'We didn't believe him.'

'Still, he had lost a bit of his finger,' Isabel pointed out. 'He must have cut it off somewhere.'

'He became a dentist,' said Jamie.

Isabel, grating cheese, raised an eyebrow. 'His patients must have seen the missing joint. They might have thought that some-body had bitten it off in the middle of some dental procedure.'

'That must happen,' said Jamie. 'It must be an occupational hazard.'

The sauce was taking shape, and Isabel, half an eye on the recipe book and half on a simmering saucepan, needed to concentrate.

When the meal was eventually served, Jamie pronounced it well worth the hours of preparation. He did the washing-up while Isabel checked up on Charlie, and then they went into the music room. He played the piano while she sat and listened. He sang the song she asked him to sing. Then he closed the lid of the piano and stretched.

'Fatigue,' he said.

They went upstairs.

Isabel had something to tell him, and she thought that now was the moment. She would need confirmation, and she would go to the doctor's surgery the following morning; she had already arranged the appointment.

She waited for him; he often took a shower at night, just before going to bed. She heard the shower, and when she closed her eyes she thought how like the sound of tropical rain it seemed – a good, long, soaking downpour.

He spoke as he towelled himself dry. 'Let's try this evening to increase our little family.'

She watched him. She would tell him, but not just now; she would wait, and tell him later, just before they went to sleep, although she knew that the news would keep them both in wakefulness. But it would be good news on which to close one's eyes.

'Isabel,' he said from the other side of the room. 'Yes?'

She nodded, and she waited while he came to her, caught in the gentle light of the late summer evening when Edinburgh never really got dark; caught in that light he came to her, like an angel.

Alexander McCall Smith is the author of over eighty books on a wide array of subjects, including the award-winning The No.1 Ladies' Detective Agency series. He is also the author of the Isabel Dalhousie novels and the world's longest-running serial novel, 44 Scotland Street. His books have been translated into forty-six languages. Alexander McCall Smith is Professor Emeritus of Medical Law at the University of Edinburgh and holds honorary doctorates from thirteen universities.